PRAISE FOR CAROLINE MITCHELL

'Be warned: Mitchell keeps digging deeper even after the main mystery is solved for more and more nasty revelations.'

—*Kirkus Reviews*

'Mitchell's . . . macabre stand-alone thriller tantalizes with a diabolical closed-room mystery slowly sloughing its secrets . . . With cagey plot twists, nuanced characters, and a pleasant young romance thrown into the mix, Mitchell's thriller warms the heart as it tingles the senses.'

—*Library Journal*

'A creepy read that ramps up the chill factor all the way to the end.'

Tariq Ashkanani

'For me, this book had everything – an excellent police procedural with tension, pace and a compelling storyline. With the added psychological element, there was nothing more I could have asked for.'

—Angela Marsons

'Fast-paced, twisty, and chilled me to the bone . . . I loved every minute of it!'

—Robert Bryndza

'The writer's conflicted heroine and twisted villain are superb characters.'

—*Sunday Express* magazine

'Heart  desperate to read more.'
—The Book Review Café

'The very definition of a page-turner.'

—John Marrs

'The tension built up and up . . . I devoured every page.'

—Mel Sherratt

'With her police officer experience, Caroline Mitchell is a thriller writer who knows how to deliver on plot, character, and, most importantly, emotion in any book she writes. I can't wait to read more.'

—*My Weekly* magazine

THE
SURVIVORS

ALSO BY
CAROLINE MITCHELL

Time to Die

The Silent Twin

Detective Ruby Preston Series

Love You to Death

Sleep Tight

Murder Game

Slayton Thrillers

The Midnight Man

The Night Whispers

The Bone House

THE
SURVIVORS

CAROLINE
MITCHELL

THOMAS & MERCER

This is a work of fiction. Names, characters, organizations, places, events, and incidents are either products of the author's imagination or are used fictitiously. Any resemblance to actual persons, living or dead, or actual events is purely coincidental.

Text copyright © 2024 by Caroline Mitchell
All rights reserved.

No part of this book may be reproduced, or stored in a retrieval system, or transmitted in any form or by any means, electronic, mechanical, photocopying, recording, or otherwise, without express written permission of the publisher.

Published by Thomas & Mercer, Seattle

www.apub.com

Amazon, the Amazon logo, and Thomas & Mercer are trademarks of Amazon.com, Inc., or its affiliates.

ISBN-13: 9781662524592
eISBN: 9781662524585

Cover design by The Brewster Project
Image credits: © Mr.Banyat Manakijlap / Getty; © PaoloBruschi © S_Hoss
© Resul Muslu / Shutterstock

Printed in the United States of America

To Ivy with love.

PROLOGUE

Private Facebook Group: The Insider's Guide to Ireland

Doolin, a quaint village along the rugged coastline of Ireland's County Clare, is nestled in a landscape of charm and intrigue. It is fondly known as the gateway to the supernatural world due to its proximity to the lunar-like rocky landscape of the Burren National Park. The mythical Aran Islands are a gift to city-weary travellers. The roar of the ocean waves forms a constant backdrop, interrupted only by the cries of gulls riding the salty sea breeze.

Doolin is a panorama of dramatic contrasts. To the west, the Atlantic Ocean crashes against the towering, mist-cloaked Cliffs of Moher. The village itself is a hodgepodge of whitewashed and colourful cottages, each one holding stories in its weather-beaten facade. The aroma of turf fires curls from the old stone chimneys, mingling with the tantalising smell of freshly baked soda bread and simmering Irish stew.

As dusk falls, the lilting melodies of traditional Irish music drift from local public houses. The lively tunes of the fiddle and tin whistle merge with the rhythmic drum of the bodhrán and the soft murmurs of 'Sláinte' as pints of Guinness are raised.

But there is a dark side to Doolin, one spoken of in hushed whispers when the locals get together and stories are told. Upon the crest of Misery Hill, a solitary cottage stands stark against the bleak Irish skies. The home of Maura Claffey instils both reverence and unease among the villagers.

Its whitewashed walls are faded, its thatched roof hunched low against the harsh Atlantic winds. The windows are deep-set eye sockets in stonework, and stare out blankly across the landscape – a chilling reminder of its occupant's ever-vigilant gaze.

Few dare to tangle with 57-year-old Maura, for her reputation is as chilling as the winds that batter Misery Hill. She's a figure shrouded in whispered rumours and hurried glances, as much a part of Doolin's landscape as the Cliffs of Moher.

On Misery Hill her cottage is a beacon of solitude, as haunting and enigmatic as the woman who calls it home.

Posted by: Anonymous.

CHAPTER 1

MAURA

Little chips of white paint disappear into my nails as I grip the window ledge. The autumn chill seeps through the old glass pane, but I barely feel its touch. Halloween isn't for another four weeks, but a certain amount of creepiness hangs in the air. I can't keep my eyes off the long, winding road that descends from my cottage on Misery Hill. I lick my hand and smooth down my hair. The strands are coarse and stubborn, so unlike my sister's. But then when I compare myself to my twin, I see her as she was, over twenty years ago.

I didn't move from this spot for six hours after she left, waiting for her to come home.

Daisy, they called her – beautiful, bright and sunny Daisy. Mammy hadn't known that she was expecting twins at the time, and told everyone that I was 'a shock'. I was just plain old Maura, an afterthought named after my grandmother. Not the nice one from Cork, who had sweets in her pockets and told bedtime stories that sent you to sleep with a smile. No, I was named after my mother's mother – the miserable cow with the fleshy jowls who would tan your backside if you so much as looked at her the wrong way. But not the bold Daisy. She wasn't beaten. How would she be? Her wrongdoings were blamed on me. Yet I still spent my childhood following her around like a lost lamb in this very cottage. This place holds so many memories. Good or bad, they are all I have left. At least, until today.

The mist has closed in, as it often does this high up. My cottage affords me an eagle-eye view of the village of Doolin, and all the bastards who live there. I hope Fionnuala, my new house guest, will take care driving by the cliff edge. It's claimed its fair share of victims. I should know.

I inhale a deep breath: in through my nose and out through my mouth, like I'm blowing through a straw. It doesn't make me feel any better. That fancy therapist in Dublin hadn't a clue what he was on about. I couldn't claim my disability allowance without seeing him. Not all illnesses are of the body. Some are unseen, hiding in the dark, quiet corners of the mind.

'Come on, Maura,' I mutter to myself. 'Fionnuala is family. You'll be grand.'

The back of my legs ache, but I've taken root nevertheless, and my eyes never leave the lonely stretch of road. I've been waiting for this moment for years, dreaming of the day when I could finally reconnect with family. And now that it's here, my poor stomach is twisted in knots.

'Hello, dear,' I practise, my voice cracking with nerves. I cough to clear my throat and start again. 'Lovely to see you. And is this my little grand-niece? She's a dote. A dote . . . she's a dote.' I wince at how unnatural it sounds, the words stiff and foreign on my tongue. If a babby is ugly – as they often are – I'll usually say so. But not today. Today I'll lie, even if the babby has a face that would drive rats from a shed.

'Maybe tea first.' I tap my fingers against the window ledge in a rhythmic pattern that helps calm me down. 'Yes, tea.' I check my watch. It's a big round thing that used to belong to my father. There's an inscription on the back: *Nannie & Bertie, 3 January 1964*. The date of their wedding. Mammy had a matching women's watch, but the strap was too big for her skinny wrist, and she lost it in the bog turning turf. I've got my grandmother's sturdy frame. That would never happen to me.

I make my way to the kitchen, my thoughts like a runaway train. Will Fionnuala find me odd? Will she think I'm unfit to be around the babby? The china teacups clatter against the delicate saucers as I lay them down. They used to belong to Granny Maura, permanently on show on her sideboard. She'd roar at anyone who tried to touch them. A smile rests on my face. She can't stop me now.

I've made some ham sandwiches with thick slabs of soda bread that I bought from the village shop. Geraldine – one of the few people in Doolin that I tolerate – said you can't go wrong with some ham sandwiches and a bit of apple tart for afters. Six euros for an apple tart. Six! My niece will make do with some buttered digestive biscuits, dear enough at nearly two euros a pack.

I check my watch again and the knot in my stomach twists even tighter. The kettle is whistling on the range; I pull the sleeve of my woollen jumper over my hand and put the kettle to one side. I like the way my cottage is laid out. The front door brings you straight into the sitting room, with no need for fancy porches or hallways. You are straight in, from the cold to the heat that the inglenook fireplace provides. To the left is the kitchen – the heart of the home. If I did entertain, that is where I would take my guests. To the right are the bedrooms and bathroom. The loft houses the belongings of those who have gone before me: Granny Maura's clothes, Father's collection of tools and automobile magazines, and

Mother's old records and clothes. I don't go up there much. I like everything on the same floor. The walls are thick stone, the doors heavy on their hinges, and the rooms are big enough.

I square my shoulders, as I often do when I'm faced with social interaction. It feels like I'm going into battle as I try to remember the right things to say and do. I hope she doesn't try to hug me, but if she does, I must remember not to pull away. Geraldine said it's rude, but I said it depends on who's doing the hugging. I asked her if old Seamus with the rotten teeth and piss-soaked trousers tried to hug her, would she pull away then? She laughed, although I couldn't see what was funny about me asking a simple question.

Now I'm back at the window next to the door, my breath fogging the pane.

'Family,' I whisper, the word bringing both comfort and terror in equal measure.

My mind drifts back to the last time a baby entered my home. It feels like centuries ago. The second bedroom, once filled with laughter and coos, now lies dormant, untouched by the passage of time. An old crib sits in the corner, its once vibrant colours faded from years of disuse. I wonder if Fionnuala would like any of the baby clothes I'd stored away in the loft. Visitors are a rarity on Misery Hill, apart from the people driving past to the beauty spot. It's also where people go to canoodle. They think I don't see them driving up there for their illicit meetings, but I know who they are. My jaw hardens as long-buried memories come to the forefront of my mind. The arrival of my niece and her baby has stirred up all sorts of emotions.

I tear my eyes away from the window to glance around my cottage one more time. My three-bedroom thatched house is dark because of the small windows, shrouded in an everlasting gloom. You get used to it after a while, and the wide open fire chases away the shadows of an evening. But my heart feels heavy with worry. I bustle about, lighting two more lamps, as if the ESB were giving away electricity for free. Just for today, until she gets used to the gloom. I'm not made of money. The glow of the lamps brings with it a small measure of comfort, making the space feel a little less foreboding. But I can't shake the feeling that it's not enough.

I should have picked some fresh flowers to brighten the place up. When I was young, I'd bring home bunches of red clovers, cheerful ox-eye daisies and some pineapple weeds to enhance the scent. Mammy would say how lovely they were, while Granny Maura would snort that I'd brought home a pile of useless roadside weeds. People like flowers though, don't they?

'Yes, flowers,' I say as I twist my hands together, trying to stop myself from raking my nails down my arms. Fecking therapist. I went to him for months and he still couldn't make me stop. Making me talk about my childhood and dragging all that stuff up with my sister.

I keep my eyes fixed on the road, anticipating the imminent arrival of my family. Growing up, family has always felt like strangers who share my blood but not my life. The sudden appearance of headlights on the winding road catches my attention, my heart quickening its pace. That's not Fionnuala. They're going the wrong way. I watch them head down the serpentine path away from Misery Hill. What were they doing up here at this hour of the day? Another set of car headlights emerges from the darkness, their beams cutting through the night like knives as they approach the hill. My grip tightens on a lock of my greying hair, nearly pulling it out by the roots. I continue to twist it, the familiar habit providing some small relief amidst the rising tide of panic. I watch, paralysed with fear, as the two vehicles speed closer, surely on a collision course. 'Slow down!' I demand, terrified for the family I have yet to meet – the fragile connections that might be severed before they have a chance to form.

And then, just as suddenly as they had appeared, the cars are out of sight, swallowed by the mist beyond. The night is still once more, leaving me standing here, rubbing the back of my neck. It's too late for me to stop whatever happens next. With a rising sense of dread, I realise that fate will take its course on Misery Hill.

CHAPTER 2

Then

Maura

'Jesus, Mary and Joseph! If I've told you once, I've told you a thousand times. Tidy up after yourself and don't be bringing plates into your room!'

I knew without asking that Mammy was not shouting at Our Lord Almighty and the blessed Mary and Joseph, but me. She stood in the doorway of our bedroom, hands on her thin hips. She was wearing a blue dress that tapered at the waist and was far too young for a woman her age.

'It's not my mess!' I rounded on her, flapping my hands in the air. 'It's Daisy's!' But as always, I was wasting my breath as I tried to defend myself.

'Now, now, pet.' My father's Cork accent rose as he intervened from the hall. 'Don't raise your voice to your mother. It doesn't matter who left it there, one of you should have cleaned up.' I knew what he was thinking as he eyed the plates: Daisy was in bed with a cold. She would never have eaten that much food on her own.

My thoughts grew dark as I gathered up the offending crockery. No point in arguing. No point at all. All I asked for was to have the place to myself once a week so I could read in peace. It was why I went to the inconvenience of attending our small church on a Saturday evening, rather than a Sunday morning with the rest of the Claffey clan. I wasn't interested in the local car boot sale, which they religiously attended after prayers, not when I could have three blissful hours of peace on my own. But not that day. That particular Sunday, Daisy had decided that she had taken ill. But it was as plain as the freckled nose on her face that there was nothing wrong with her.

'We're going to be late!' Granny Maura cawed from the front door. Years of smoking a pipe had left her voice thick and rasping. It was a thing back in her day apparently, although I've never seen another woman smoke one since. It was why her teeth were tar yellow, and her breath stale. Sometimes, after she died, I caught the stench of tobacco lingering in the air. It frightened me to think that she was still about, watching me with those beady eyes from beyond the grave. Especially after everything I'd done. How ironic that I was named after the person I'd hated most in the world. But on that Sunday in 1984, Culture Club were playing low on the radio in the kitchen while the cottage smelled of Daddy's Kiwi shoe polish and Mammy's hairspray. She always went to great efforts for church, and Daddy whistled as she pulled on her new coat. 'I married an Irish rose,' he chuckled, which was met with great disdain from Granny Maura, who he'd learned to ignore.

By the time I'd finished carrying the plates to the sink, Daisy was out of bed, pulling on her favourite polka dot jumper and ra-ra skirt. Daddy had barely started the engine of our old Toyota Corolla.

'You're not to say anything, do ya hear me?' She gave me the eye before taking the hairbrush from the drawer.

Now, I wasn't particularly loyal to my sister, but we had an agreement, Daisy and me. She kept me in chocolate bars and *Jackie* magazines and I kept my silence about her slipping out to meet some boy. We may have been identical twins, but Daisy was much brighter than me, and I don't just mean her intellect. Everything about her shone. Her eyes sparkled from the moment she awoke, and in the summer her brown hair was highlighted blonde from the sun. She could always think of something funny to say. Despite my chocolate addiction, we both weighed around the same and were a reasonable size twelve at the time. 'What are you doing?' I watched as she gathered her thick brown hair up in a ponytail.

'Put the kettle on. We're having a visitor.'

I sighed. A 'visitor' could only mean one thing. Daisy had lots of girlfriends from secondary school but she never invited them home. 'Who is it now?' I said, because my sister had every fellah in the island traipsing after her, while I had never been kissed. Almost. Someone almost kissed me once at the disco in Doolin town hall two years before that when I was fifteen. It was dark and he mistook me for Daisy, but then I screamed and ran away because his breath smelled of Tayto cheese-and-onion crisps and I didn't like his crooked teeth.

Daisy responded with one of her little patient sighs that I'd come to hate. 'Don't be weird, okay? Why don't you go into your room and read your book?'

'I wanted to read next to the fire.' I glowered at her, overcome by a sour feeling of resentment. This was my routine and here she was, changing it without a care in the world for me.

'Grand. That's settled then.'

What was settled? I followed her into the bathroom as she brought her make-up bag in.

'God, this light. Why can't we live in a house with proper windows?' she muttered to her reflection.

The temptation to bump her elbow as she applied her mascara was strong. 'What's settled?' I spoke my thoughts aloud this time. 'What did you mean?'

'You can read your book by the fire, and Jimmy and I will take the bedroom.'

'Jimmy?' I asked, because I must have heard her wrong. Not him. 'Jimmy Walsh?'

She blinked at her reflection a couple of times before glancing back at me. 'Yes, Jimmy Walsh. Sure what other Jimmy would it be?' She applied a slick of lip-gloss, oblivious to my devastation. My dismay materialised as a heat rash, which rose from my chest to my throat. Jimmy Walsh was the only man I'd ever loved. He was years older than us, a newly qualified doctor, in fact. The most eligible bachelor in Doolin to be sure. Now he was coming to *my* house. To drink *my* tea and sit in *my* bedroom doing God knows what with *her*.

'But he's mine,' I said, in a small, quiet voice.

Daisy turned to me incredulously and bleated a soft laugh. 'Yours?' She rested a hand on my arm. 'Oh, Maura. You never said. Have you got a little crush?'

My cheeks burned as I finally found movement in my legs and took two steps back. 'It . . . it's nothing,' I blurted, struggling to find my breath. The kettle was whistling on the stove, sounding like an impending train.

I will never forget the humiliation of that day. I hid in the kitchen as Jimmy made an appearance, but listened at the bedroom door as the pair of them chatted and laughed. It was scandalous. Why couldn't that be me? I began pulling on my split ends. She didn't love him. Not like I did. She didn't care how I felt. I swiped at the tears that dripped from my jawline. Their chatting turned into soft murmurs and then, finally, silence. The bitch.

CHAPTER 3

Finn

My grip on the steering wheel tightens, my knuckles turning white as I navigate each dangerous curve of the road. The time flashes four o'clock on my car dashboard. I can't believe how quickly that darkness has closed in. The guard-rails loom ahead of me as I negotiate the bend. They're not exactly on the cliff edge, but near enough that it freaks me out. I wish I hadn't waited this long to visit Ireland for the first time. The October weather seeps the colour from the mountainous landscape as it casts it in a slate grey hue. Cold, salty air seeps through the crevices of my old car and chills my skin.

My eyes dart to the rear-view mirror where Saoirse sleeps in her car seat. Bless her. So much has happened in the five weeks since she was born. A mix of excitement and nerves churns inside me at the prospect of meeting Aunt Maura. I'm not just meeting my aunt; I will be greeted by a carbon copy of my mum. I know it's wrong . . . No . . . not just wrong but *unhealthy* to try to heal the pain of my loss by replacing her. But how many people get the opportunity to see their loved ones one more time? I swallow as grief ambushes me, latching on to my throat and causing it to constrict. Is it possible to escape the pain of bereavement? Is that why I'm really here? *It's not her*, I remind myself. *It's Maura. But just one hug* . . . I sigh, hoping this is a good idea.

Mum and Maura hadn't spoken in decades, and I'd like to know why. Maura couldn't make it to the funeral. Apparently, she's a bit of a recluse. But her letter gave me comfort. She apologised for not being confident enough to travel overseas to say goodbye, but she hoped that I could come and see her soon. In a world ruled by technology, it felt odd to put pen to paper and respond by post. I relayed my sadness that Mum didn't live long enough to meet baby Saoirse in the flesh. I don't have any other family. I need to treasure what's left.

Saoirse's cries suddenly pierce through the silence, sharp and relentless, as mist coils around my old Fiat Punto. I thought the drive on to the ferry from England was daunting enough, but now my anxiety levels rise further while I tighten my grip on the steering wheel. My sweaty palms stick to the leather and the car swerves ever so slightly as I struggle to maintain control.

'Shh, shh, it's okay,' I mutter, my voice wavering as her wails grow louder. Her crying is adding to the mounting pressure and my doubts threaten to consume me. A small part of me whispers a silent prayer of thanks for her existence in the world. Any normal twenty-seven-year-old in my situation would worry about being a single mother. Having Mum nearby was the driving factor in my decision to keep my unexpected baby. She is the by-product of a drunken one-night stand and her father wasn't interested. What do I know about parenting? But now Mum's gone, I'm feeling adrift in the world. Saoirse is my anchor. My reason to take each day one at a time.

'Shhhh, sweetie, we're nearly there.' I can't focus because I hate to see her so upset. She's spat out her dummy, her little hands clawing the air in distress. The pacifier hangs from a pink ribbon, which is attached to her coat. But now the road seems to grow narrower with each turn. Mist hangs low, cloaking the precipice, and anxiety ferments in my gut. A small milestone looms ahead, then a battered luminous sign warning of another hazardous turn. The haunting sight of various bouquets of dead and plastic flowers tied to the low guard-rails suggest that people have died here. In the back seat, Saoirse fidgets, her cries growing louder and more desperate.

'Okay, okay, let me get around this bend, and I'll find it for you,' I promise. I'm used to motorways and streetlights. This darkened pot-holed road is like nothing I've driven before. I clench my jaw, navigating another hairpin turn that never seems to end. I wipe my clammy palms on my jeans, trying to steady my nerves. Maura warned me about this road, but I never imagined that it would be as bad as this. At least there's no other traffic about. I ease my foot off the accelerator. I'm getting nowhere like this. Saoirse's cries tug on every instinct. Perhaps she's picked up on my reticence, but she's clearly in distress. 'It's okay,' I say, 'here . . .'

I reach back for my daughter's dummy while keeping one hand on the wheel.

CHAPTER 4

KATHRYN

My car speaker booms with my father's impatient voice. I don't know who gave him my number but I'm too scared of him to hang up.

'Kathryn, I don't care what you've got going on over there. You come back to Dublin right now.' It's an order, not a request.

Danny Toíbín is not a man you say no to.

I swallow hard. I may be thirty-six but right now, I feel like a child.

'Dad, I can't just drop everything and—'

'Enough!' he shouts, cutting me off.

Sweat dampens my armpits, despite the chill outside. It was meant to be a quick photo shoot for my YouTube travel channel, but a blanket of mist came down fast, taking me by surprise. As always, my daughter slept in the back of my car as I took my land-scape shots. She's an angel, truly she is. She hardly ever cries. I even have to wake her for feeds.

My BMW hugs the sharp turns of the country road as I try to keep my focus. Once I'm clear of this God-awful hillside I should be back to my flat in Galway in just over an hour. A bath, a bottle of wine and a baby feed is due. David's letter sits unopened on the table in the hall. As soon as I saw the handwriting, I knew that it was from him. He's found me, and a part of me – the selfish part – is glad to hear from him again. I don't need to open it to know what it says. He loves me. He needs to see me. We can put the past behind us and start again. He doesn't know about his baby. It's better this way. I'm bad news, me and my family. David deserves better. My family have caused him enough harm.

A sigh leaves my lips. I'm going to have to move home again. My pulse accelerates as my father's warnings ring clear. I can't go back to Dublin. Not now. If he's this angry about my relationship with David Kenny, what will he do when he finds out about the baby? The Kennys and Toíbíns have hated each other for as long as I can remember. You wouldn't think that my father was once school friends with Brendan Kenny. Now they're rivals in every sense of the word. He'll kill me if he finds out.

'Please, Dad,' I plead, my voice trembling. 'I need some time on my own.'

'Time? What's all this bollocks? You're a Toíbín. You belong at home.' His anger reverberates through the speaker, making me flinch. 'Your mother's out of her wits!'

I doubt that very much. The only thing Mother cares about is the latest designer trend. My grip tightens on the wheel as I fight back tears, my vision blurring even more. I press my foot down harder on the accelerator, my only means of escape from this onslaught.

'Kathryn, are ya listening?' he snaps, invoking a whole host of bad memories as I flinch in response.

'Of course I'm listening, Dad, but I'm driving. I'll call you back.'

I briefly glance back at Kiera, who is fast asleep in her car seat. With her thick black hair, she's a Kenny through and through. But she's only a month old. Maybe it will change to blonde when it's grown. She's so content, unaware of the storm brewing in her mother's life.

'Damn it, Kathryn!' Dad's anger flares, filling the car with tension so thick I can practically taste it. 'Why can't you be more like your brothers? You always make life difficult . . . Fecking David Kenny . . . of all people.' He grumbles angrily beneath his breath. From my earliest memories, Dad was an imposing figure, standing a towering six feet tall. His battle-scarred face now tells a story of a youth spent in the boxing ring. Each imperfection is testament to fights fought and won, a map of resilience etched into his skin. His hair has started to retreat in an inevitable surrender, leaving a broad, balding expanse that only adds to his formidable presence. He is broad and robust, despite the lean muscle of his younger years giving way to a comfortable fullness. The passing of time may have softened his frame, but his power is undeniable. My dad is an unshakeable force. His dark moods are thunder. You just have to sit them out.

I negotiate the winding roads to the backdrop of his rants. I've heard it all before. Six months have passed. I had hoped that Dad would have calmed down by now. He got his revenge on the father of my child. David won't be touching me again, not from the confines of his wheelchair.

At last, Dad stops shouting. The silence that follows is deafening. How can I protect my daughter from the inevitable fallout once her identity is revealed? The weight of my secret threatens to crush me. I'm going too fast, but speed delivers a sense of control.

A sudden sharp turn looms ahead. My mind, dulled by anxiety, registers the danger a fraction too late. The tyres screech in protest, but the momentum of my car is unstoppable.

'Shit!' I cry out, seeing the oncoming car headlights too late.

The crash of metal against metal is deafening as our cars collide. The force of the impact sends a violent jolt through my body, ripping a scream from my throat. Glass shatters, scattering like confetti in my hair.

Kiera!

She's all I can think of when my car veers off the road. Airbags punch my body as we tumble down the embankment towards the cliff edge. The world outside becomes a dizzying blur of green and brown, each impact punctuated by the sickening sounds of crunching metal and snapping twigs.

I am thrown around in my seat, my body like a rag doll. My bones are broken, but I have no sensation of pain, no feeling in my limbs at all. The steering wheel feels like a foreign object, the air in my chest collapsing inwards as the airbags press against me with force.

Finally, after what seems an eternity, the car comes to a shuddering halt. It lies battered and broken, upside down. The sound of the sea pounding against the cliff edge is a steady backdrop to my pain.

Smoke curls from the wreckage. My view of the world is distorted. We've come off the road and are hanging precariously on the side of the cliff. One more tumble, and we will be in the sea.

'Kiera?' I croak.

My blood feels like ice water as my body turns cold. I'm fighting against pain and disorientation, straining to hear any signs of life from my precious child.

I try to crane my neck to look in the car seat behind me, but black blobs are floating in my vision and my body feels paralysed. My world has tilted and, for a brief moment, I am suspended in time. The air becomes thick with smoke and the acrid scent of burning rubber. With every breath, I feel as though I'm inhaling fire itself.

I fight against the blackness, but my body is limp as it shuts down. There is movement outside my periphery. I reach back to touch my baby as darkness closes in.

CHAPTER 5

FINN

The world swims into view as harsh fluorescent lights stab my sensitive pupils. My head is throbbing, each pulse accompanied by a sickening wave of nausea. I grip the stiff white sheets, trying to make sense of my surroundings.

It feels like I've been trampled by a herd of cows. I inhale a sterile scent, and take in the distant hum of machinery in the background. With trembling fingertips, I touch my inner elbow where an IV needle has pierced my arm.

A memory enters my consciousness: a vivid recollection of a cacophony of shattering glass and crumpling metal. I've been in an accident. Fragments of the ordeal return – the winding road, the blinding headlights bearing down on me, the terrifying crunch of two vehicles colliding with force. A face swims before me. Someone I know, yet different.

'Mum?' I ask, knowing it couldn't possibly be true but clinging to hope just the same.

The woman before me has an uncanny resemblance to my mother – but she is heavier, with unbrushed grey hair. Her skin is weather worn, her face make-up free. Deep frown lines furrow her face. She is a monochrome image of the person I want her to be.

She smiles, a sad wistfulness touching her eyes. 'No, a *leanbh*. I'm Maura, your aunt.'

Of course. She's my mother's twin sister. Aunt Maura. The person I was on my way to see. The pieces of my family puzzle are slowly falling into place. A surge of emotion fills my chest as tears well up in my eyes. 'Saoirse. Where's my baby? Please. Tell me she's safe.' I try to rise but my head throbs a warning, forcing me back down.

Aunt Maura's touch offers gentle reassurance as she rests a warm hand on my arm. 'Your little one is safe and healthy. I've been looking after her while you've been recovering. You gave me quite the fright, so you did.'

The weight that lifts off my chest is palpable. 'Thank you.' My voice is a whisper, gratitude mingled with relief. I allow myself to bask in my new-found connection. She is a harsher version of my mother, but it feels good to have her here.

Satisfied, I fall back into the soothing oblivion of sleep.

The creak of a chair gets my attention, drawing me into the realm of the waking world. Aunt Maura is sat beside me, reading a book.

'Where is she?' I manage to say, grateful that the throbbing in my head has subsided. I don't know how long I've been under but the clock on the sterile hospital wall reads ten to three.

'Geraldine, my neighbour has her.' She earmarks the page then closes her book as she reads my troubled expression. 'She has nine grandchildren. Saoirse's in good hands.'

A thought so dreadful enters my mind that it makes me feel nauseous to say the words aloud. 'Are you sure?' I try to shuffle into an upright position but every muscle in my body is stiff. 'You're not just saying that she's alive?' Tears prick my eyes and I blink them back.

'Now why would I do such an awful thing?' She reaches down and picks up an old leather handbag from the ground. She undoes the wide clasps and slips her hand inside. 'Geraldine showed me how to take a photo of her on your phone so you could see what you've been missing.' She gives me a small smile. 'I guessed the password was your date of birth.'

I don't care about the intrusion. I just want to see my little girl. Maura places the phone in my outstretched hand. It's a challenge to hold it and access the photos. My fumbling hands feel weak. How long have I been out? I gasp as I draw a blurry image up on to the screen. A short, stout woman in a flowery pink cardigan cradles a baby close to her chest. 'That's not . . .' I look at Maura earnestly. 'That's not Saoirse, is it?' She looks different, but then the image isn't clear.

Maura chuckles. The smile looks odd on her face, as if it's not used to being there. 'Sure who else would it be? You've been drifting in and out of consciousness for the last four weeks.' She gazes at the photo. 'Look at her, the image of you. That car seat of yours did a grand job of keeping her safe.'

I'm grateful to my old banger of a car for getting us through the accident in one piece – but four weeks? Have I really been out of it that long? How has Saoirse coped without me? Maura's voice breaks into my troubled thoughts.

'I'll bring her in when you're strong enough to see her. Maybe tomorrow.' Maura tilts her head to one side. 'And you haven't even asked if you're okay. A good mother, sure enough.' As Aunt Maura's voice relays what the doctors have told her, the tension in my muscles begins to loosen. My body has taken a battering and I'll be slow on my feet for a few weeks, but I should be out of hospital soon. My eyelids are growing heavy as sleep tugs on my periphery. Aunt

Maura sits watching me, her fingers drumming softly against the seat armrest. As my focus softens, I pretend that she's my mum.

The next time I awaken, the world comes into sharper focus, and I see that Maura has gone. A nurse is at the other side of my bed. She has cropped blonde hair and a tattoo of a lotus flower on her wrist. It rings the bell of a memory and I have a feeling that I've spoken to her before. But my consciousness has been clouded by medication up until now. I don't like feeling so out of it. I can't believe that it's November already. I keep missing chunks of time. Where's Saoirse? I want to see my little girl.

'Your aunt said she brought her in to see you earlier but you were out of it, I'm afraid. How are you feeling today?' She hands me a glass of water and speaks like she's asked me this question many times before.

'Fuzzy,' I manage to say, angry with myself for not being there for my child. 'When can I leave?'

'Soon. We're reducing your morphine so you'll feel more with it, although you'll have to cope with the pain.' She talks about physio treatment getting me back on my feet.

My memory of the accident has sharpened and I need to know what happened that day. 'The other car . . . What happened to the driver?' The nurse appears hesitant as she drifts by my bedside, glass of water in hand. She directs the straw to my lips. The liquid is lukewarm but water has never tasted so good.

She smiles softly, but there is a hint of sadness in her eyes. 'The other driver is in intensive care. It's as much as I can tell you.' She places the glass on my bedside table and turns to fix my sheets. 'Get some rest. That's what your body needs now.' Her steps are quick as she leaves the room, and I sense that something's not quite right. She's not the only one who's being evasive. Maura's acting strangely too. I haven't seen my daughter since I crashed in Misery Hill. Where is my baby now?

25

CHAPTER 6

MAURA

As I push the bouncy pram through Doolin, I take comfort from the feel of my thick tweed skirt swishing against my black wool tights. It's my grandmother's skirt, which I rescued from the loft. The tights are my own, bought from Primark in Dublin at only two euros a pack. Every penny is a prisoner and my benefits only stretch so far. There is no sense in wasting money when there are perfectly good clothes lying about. Not that Granny Maura would be thrilled about this situation, given that Finn is unwed. Once upon a time in Ireland, such a thing brought great embarrassment. I won't be shamed by anyone. My charge is a beautiful babby, and she has brought light into my world. Head high, I push the old pram in the direction of the convenience shop. The once vibrant blue paint is now chipped and faded, and it creaks with each rotation of its spoked wheels. But it's preferable to the modern jalopy that Finn had in the boot of her car. That nearly took the thumb off me, as I tried to stand it upright. I gave it a few kicks for good measure and it seems there's no chance of it working now. I glance inside the pram at the wee babby, who is bundled up and protected from the cold. A warm feeling swells up inside of me. It's been so long since I felt it that it takes me by surprise. Love. This is love. This is what the great Irish poets such as Yeats and Joyce wrote about. But now it's all rap songs and *do ya do ya want me baby, bang me up against the wall*. To think that the local kids blare out such rubbish without an ounce of shame.

Doolin was a charming little town once, with its thatched-roof cottages and lush countryside. The air smelled of peat fires and freshly baked soda bread. But now it's greasy fish and chips and tourists beeping their car horns. They drive around in their swanky electric cars which have stickers about climate change on the windows, then they leave their Coke cans and food wrappers blowing in the wind. I push away the thoughts that normally get me riled up. I have no time to waste; I'm on a mission. Get in and out of Doolin as fast as I can.

'Evening, Maura,' calls out old Sam from his cottage door. He is bathed in an orange glow as the sun goes down. He rests a hand above his forehead, squinting at the sight of me with a pram. I nod curtly, not slowing my pace. He's a widower. This place is full of them. If you as much as give them a half a smile they'll be turning up at your door with a bunch of half-dead carnations and a bar of Cadburys Wholenut chocolate to seal the deal.

The locals exchange wary glances as I pass by. Eyes linger on the pram, but I pay them no mind. I'm used to their wariness and it suits me just fine. This way, I won't be caught up in any wasteful chit-chat.

'Ah howeya, Maura,' Patrick, Geraldine's husband, declares. 'Is that Finn's baby?' He follows me with his eyes as I enter his store.

'No, I found her in a box outside my door,' I snap, grabbing the necessary supplies for the babby. Patrick always states the obvious, and it gets on my nerves. He's a stout little man; at barely five foot four, he comes up to my shoulder. I don't know what

Geraldine sees in him. I remember asking her once, when we were young and drinking cider in the car park at the back of the village church. She smiled and said something about a small jockey having a big whip. She giggled like it was the funniest thing in the world. I've still no clue what she was on about, because he's never kept horses, or whipped any as far as I'm aware.

I push the pram around the small supermarket, my eyes narrowing as I survey the shelves. The babby is sleeping, little bubbles of drool rising from the corner of her rosebud lips. I have everything mapped out in my head – nappies, formula and some wet wipes for the child. I ignore the Christmas decorations and the unwelcome Christmas tunes warbling from the radio on the counter. I find such commercialism offensive. I'll decorate the cottage with fresh holly, push cloves into oranges to make nice-smelling hedgehogs and hang them near the fire. I'll make fresh wreaths, bake Christmas cake and light a candle for the front window on Christmas Eve. What I won't do is buy one gaudy bauble from this shop.

'Need a hand?' Patrick leaves his post from behind the till and ambles in our direction.

'Keep your hands to yourself,' I retort, quickening my pace. 'I can manage.'

'Sure enough,' he chuckles, digging around the baggy pocket of his old brown corduroys. 'How about a luck penny for the baby instead?'

Now that's more like it. I still my movements, allowing him to slip ten euros beneath her blanket. It's an old tradition and a welcome one, given how much these things cost. I clench my jaw and give him a grateful nod, and I stop myself from telling him that it's too late for luck now.

I get to the till, and Patrick jumps in ahead of me, ready to ring up my purchases. I don't ask after Geraldine. If she was about

28

she'd already be here, begging me for a 'hold of the baby' and given all she's done for me I'd have no choice but to give in. I've known her and Patrick all my life. We sat next to each other in school and she's hounded me ever since. In truth, she had a girl crush on my sister, but Daisy wouldn't give her the time of day so I was the next best thing. To be fair, Geraldine came into her own after Finn's accident, bringing nappies and formula and looking after the babby when I needed to sort things out. My blood turns cold as I relive the minutes straight after the car crash.

'Maura? Earth to Maura.' Patrick laughs at his own stupid joke. 'Off with the fairies again, I see.'

The smile drops from his face as I narrow my eyes in a glare. 'Actually, no, I wasn't with the fairies. I was thinking about the crash. Those cars, all twisted and crushed. The smoke, and the blood. Finding my niece like that and nobody around to help.' Then not knowing if any of them were dead or alive.' I snatch my bag of shopping from the counter. That shuts him up. Two young lads are dawdling behind me and I barge through them with my pram.

My cheeks burn as they burst into laughter. Usually I'd tear a strip off them both, but today I feel exposed and vulnerable. It must be the little one. I grit my teeth and push on, the pram rolling unsteadily over the footpath.

An elderly woman leans on her walking stick as she lowers herself on to a nearby bench. I can't remember her name but I've seen her around the place. She's one of these blow-ins, who moved here a few years ago. She may be smiling but I know what she's thinking: that any child in my company is an unfortunate one. I know what they say about me. I've heard it all before. They think I'm some kind of morbid scavenger, just because I'm able to get to the accidents before them. They should be nicer to me. They might find themselves on the wrong side of that cliff one day. 'Nice day for a walk, isn't it, Maura?' she calls out. 'Who have you got in the pram?'

'Mind your own business,' I shout, quickening my pace. Her smile falters, and for a second I feel bad. This is why I hate coming into this little town. How am I meant to know who's laughing at me and who's not?

Judgemental gossips, all of them, I think bitterly, scanning the townsfolk who seem to watch my every move. I don't need their pity or fake kindness. I can take care of this child all by myself. I've not always been on my own. I nursed my mother and my father before they passed to the other side. Of course, Daisy was nowhere to be seen by then. She wasn't there for the bed baths, or the incontinence pads I had to change. And when Mammy's mind went . . . well, death was a kindness by then.

My resentment grows with each step as I take the shortcut back to the cottage. The little one is still fast asleep. At least with babies, they're a blank slate. I imagine the locals whispering behind my back. The thought of their assumptions makes me feel wretched, and I long to put them all in their place. Sometimes I stand on the top of Misery Hill and imagine watching Doolin burn. I stare into the pram and breathe in through my mouth . . . then out like through a straw. Three breaths later and the ugly thoughts are gone. Well, fancy that. It worked this time. Maybe the breathing works better when I have someone else to focus on. I'll have to make more of an effort. If Finn is going to live with me then she'll want to go into town.

As I reach the outskirts of Doolin, I breathe a sigh of relief. Cold prickles of mist dampen my sweaty brow as I head home. Misery Hill has its own weather system. It might be a nice day in Doolin, but mist and fog closes in fast this high up the hill. I'm always the first to get snow, and black ice has taken many a car off the road . . . that, and other things. The sun dips below the horizon, casting a sepia hue over Doolin. I push the old pram up the final part of the hill, my eyes fixed on the path. I realise that my tongue is sticking out the side of my mouth and I hear my mother's voice in my head. 'Why do you do that, Maura? It's ugly when you stick out your tongue. People will think you're slow.'

Sure enough they did. I heard one of the teachers comment on it when I was in primary school. I ran everywhere after that, until I realised what they were getting at.

'Almost there,' I whisper aloud, my breath ragged from the exertion. I'm going to have to get fitter if I'm going to be pushing this pram up and down the hill. I don't use the car if I can help it. I've seen what happens when they come off the road.

A flock of noisy seagulls squawk overhead, drawing my attention for just a moment. Winter cloaks the cliffs and my thoughts roam to the backdrop of the Atlantic's restless churn. I inhale the briny scent of the sea, picking up the earthy aroma of damp heather and gorse. In the grey light of the shortening days I stand separate from the rest of the world.

The baby begins to grizzle. It's darker than it was, and I realise that I've been standing here for some time. I don't like it when I fade out of reality. Not when there's a baby in my care. I peep into the pram.

'Whist now, my love. We'll soon have you inside.'

I push the pram towards the house and I don't look back.

CHAPTER 7

Then

Maura

I knew it wouldn't last. The minute my sister went to Limerick, that was the end of her and Jimmy Walsh. It's ironic, given that he inspired her to become a nurse in the first place. Of course, she couldn't break it off with him like a normal person. Daisy didn't like confrontation, we all knew that. Instead, she told him they'd make it work. That she would be home every weekend. Three weeks. That was how long it took before she was 'too busy' to come home. She'd set herself up in a nice little flat from the money Mam and Dad had saved up. Had they known about Jimmy Walsh, they might not have been as keen to throw their money away on her.

Nobody asked if I wanted to go to college. It was a running joke in our family that Daisy had been 'blessed with all the brains'. No, I had to be content with working in the kennels of the local dog pound where Daddy worked.

Poor Jimmy. He was in bits after he found out that Daisy hooked up with someone else. But Jimmy wouldn't be single for long. Not with his looks. He was beautiful. His floppy brown hair, full lips and his skin . . . so clear. God, just the thought of him made me melt.

Still, it gave me hope when Daisy called it a day. If he loved her, he could love me – at least, that was what I thought at the time. But it was hard. If I found it easy to talk to boys, then I would have opened up to Jimmy when I was sixteen. That was when he first caught my attention, and only because he was kind to a hedgehog that the boys were poking with sticks on the playing fields.

Jimmy was a good ten years older than the lads in the playing field, and big enough that they backed away when he tore a strip off them. I watched in awe as he pulled off his V-neck jumper and wrapped it around the terrified hedgehog before picking it up. Sure the thing was probably riddled with fleas and lice, but Jimmy didn't care. He seemed to have a way with animals and people alike. I was walking one of the dogs that Daddy had brought home from the pound, a skinny collie named Jake. Jimmy steadily plodded past me, whispering words of comfort to the creature in his arms. Silently, I followed him way down to the end of the lane where he checked the creature over before depositing it in a safe space. He smiled at me then, and oh my God, did I fall hard for him that day. I've watched him ever since. Every now and again, I walked towards him, biting my bottom lip and hurting myself, because I lacked the courage to stop and talk. And there was Daisy, who only had to click her fingers and he was at her beck and call.

I hated her for having him, then discarding him like he was nothing. Hated myself for missing her after she left. Limerick offered her more than Doolin ever could. But what about me? Nobody offered to put me through university. Daddy said that I wasn't to resent Daisy for getting the college fund, because they had it all worked out. My twin would get qualified and start her fancy new life in Limerick, whereas I would stay in Doolin and be given Granny Maura's cottage. Everyone, including Daisy, was happy with this agreement except for me. Ownership of the cottage on Misery Hill came with a hefty price. I would be expected to skivvy after them in their old age. Like I didn't want a life of my own. But as it turned out, Maura died quite suddenly. She was getting doddery in her old age. She overdosed on medication. At least, that was what her death certificate said.

CHAPTER 8

KATHRYN

'Kathy, wake up.' The order comes from far away at first. 'There. Did ya see? Her eyelashes fluttered. What did I tell you?'

It is the voice of my father, and I retreat into myself. I'm not sure where I am, but I don't want to wake up to him. I lie, unmoving, feeling the heat of my father's stare.

'Danny, I'm parched. You wouldn't get us a cup of tea, would you?'

That bird-like voice is my mother's. Coaxing, gentle. But only in his presence. The women in Danny Toíbín's household know their place when he's about.

'You want to drink that muck out of the machine?' my father grumbles. 'I'll get you one from across the road. You'd think what I've paid for this place that I'd have a fecking butler serving us.'

Sharp footsteps follow as he leaves the room. A broad, heavy man with expensive Italian leather shoes tapping against a tiled floor.

I blink, because now everything is coming back to me. Through my woozy haze, I recall waking up before. I'm in hospital. But I've not been able to arrange my thoughts cohesively until now.

A thin, icy voice cuts through the silence. I open my eyes to find that I was right. My mother is sitting next to my bed, her arms crossed tightly over her augmented chest. She's Botox smooth but there's a darkness beneath her eyes that hasn't been there before. She's fifty-six pretending to be thirty, and twenty years older than me.

'Wha-what happened?' I stammer. My throat feels like I've been swallowing dry sand.

'Does it matter?' Mother's tone is bitter. 'You've always been nothing but trouble, Kathryn. Your father has been hell to live with since the accident. And you, lying here without a care in the world. A baby? How could you do that to us?'

My mother's words feel like a slap to the face. I'm used to her disapproval, but now it's all coming back. The baby. An accident. Dad's voice, triggering me through the car speakers. Driving too fast. I glance at the IV dripping fluids into my arm, the blip on the heart monitor moving in sync with my racing pulse.

'Where's Kiera?' I manage to say, fear tightening my chest. Because I only have a short while before my father comes back. I remember calling my baby's name just moments before . . . before what? I know there was an accident but what happened next?

'We've been to hell and back because of you. And me a . . . a . . . grandmother!' Mam blurts the word like an accusation, refusing to meet my gaze. 'Your father nearly had a heart attack when he found out about the baby . . .' She's talking too fast, and there's a shake in her voice. She reaches for her designer purse and slips her hand inside. I've seen the container of tablets before. It seems her addiction to Valium is still going strong. 'He had to be rushed to hospital with chest pains . . .' Her eyes are bulging now. 'Can you imagine if that got out?'

'Please . . .' I whisper, tears welling in my eyes. 'Kiera. Where is she?'

'Calm down,' she snaps. 'I'll tell you. But this changes nothing between us, Kathryn. You've made your bed, and now you have to lie in it.'

I struggle to sit up as pain presses down on my chest, making it difficult to breathe. If my daughter survived the accident, my father's another matter. He put Kiera's dad in a wheelchair. What if he hurt Kiera too?

Mam takes a deep breath, directing her gaze to the sterile hospital floor. 'I can't believe that you kept your baby a secret from me. Have you any idea how it felt, finding out like that?'

I can hear the pain in her voice, but she won't meet my eyes and that's what's scaring me the most.

'Please.' My knuckles turn white as I grip the sheets. 'Just tell me where she is.'

For a moment, her gaze flicks between me and the door. Finally, she swallows hard, her shoulders slumping in resignation. 'She's gone, Kathryn. She didn't survive the accident. They said . . .' She clears her throat. 'They said it was quick.'

A low, deep howl fills the room as the weight of my loss crashes down on me. I can't breathe. I can't think. I can't live in a world without her.

'Quit your wailing. I can hear you halfway down the hall!' My father is at my side, his face beetroot red as he grips a takeaway cup in his hand. But he can't intimidate me when I have nothing left to lose.

Not my Kiera. She can't be gone.

I cannot vocalise what I need to say. I turn my face into the pillow and scream.

'Make them leave!' I manage to cry, and I raise my head from the pillow to see a nurse entering the room. She looks at me in dismay, her thin lips parted. A doctor isn't far behind her and they suggest that it's better if I'm given time to absorb the news.

So it's true. My little girl is dead.

I can't bear to look at my parents. This is all their fault. I would never have run away if it weren't for them.

'Fine,' Mother replies coldly, gripping her bag as she turns towards the door. But my father stares at me, nostrils flaring as he slams down the tea on to the table over my bed. Brown liquid seeps over the sides and drips on to my sheets. He shakes the tea from his hand and points a finger at me. The doctors can only do so much, because even they are afraid of him. It's always been this way. Nobody messes with a Toíbín. They know exactly who he is.

'Did you really think you could hide this from me?' my father hisses, his voice low and venomous. 'You thought you could have that bastard's child, and pretend like nothing happened?'

I can't speak. My throat is constricted by grief. I just want to be left alone.

'Well, now you've paid for it,' he continues in his verbal assault.

'Danny.' My mother touches his arm. Her voice is steady while she tries to keep some dignity amidst my pain. 'Why don't we come back later? She's only just found out. She needs time to grieve.'

'She doesn't deserve any sympathy.' My father pushes away her hand. He leans in so close to me that his breath tickles my face. 'This is all you deserve.'

His words are just a whisper but they cut me to the bone.

'Get out,' I whimper, my voice carrying the weight of my heartbreak. I can't take any more of his cruelty.

'Fine,' my father sneers. 'But you should know – the doctors said there was barely anything left of your precious baby. She was thrown from the car. A pitiful sight, she was.'

'Mr Toíbín.' The doctor is young, but he manages to come between us. 'Please.'

After delivering his final barb, my father turns on his heel and strides out of the room. My mother totters after him. She throws me a regretful glance before walking out the door. I'm on my own. I have nothing to live for. I'm never seeing my baby again.

CHAPTER 9

FINN

It's hard to get used to the cottage, where my frugal Aunt Maura barely turns the radiators on. The place carries an air of eerie time-lessness, with its collection of knick-knacks and worn furniture. Every piece tells a story, from the faded floral armchair next to the fire, to the creaking shelves burdened with books of all kinds. They contain Mills & Boon romances, cookbooks from the seventies and even old manuals about DIY. The dressers are lined with an array of trinkets, from keepsakes celebrating the Pope's visit to Ireland in 1979 to cheap plastic statues of the Virgin Mary purchased decades ago in Lourdes. But Maura doesn't seem all that religious. The holy water font next to the front door is dry, and the bulb in the small light in front of the picture of Jesus needs replacing. These items are surely inherited. Then there are the cute little felt hedgehogs that sit inside the nooks and crannies – on shelves, between books, and even on picture frames. Judging from the recent hedgehog-themed calendar, I'm guessing these are all hers. The place is a testament to Maura's lifestyle: practicality over comfort amongst a cluttered collection of memories and possessions. I sit by the cavernous inglenook fireplace, its flames casting more shadows than light. I'm grateful for a few minutes alone as Maura potters about in the kitchen. Not that you ever feel truly alone in her house on Misery Hill.

I glance at the framed photos of my grandparents and great-grandparents hanging from the uneven walls. The people in the faded photos are smiling – all except for one. Granny Maura, from what I've been told. This woman sits on an armchair, pipe in hand. She's wearing a tweed skirt, thick black tights and sensible flat leather shoes. But it's her eyes, dark and sinister, that seem to peer into my soul. I can't pass that picture without it making me shudder inside.

But it's more than the image of my great-grandmother chilling my bones. I travelled to Ireland with good intentions, but now I'm plagued with the guilt of almost killing my little girl. It's been six weeks and two days since my accident. Huh. I feel like I'm at an AA meeting. But as I sit in the living room in Aunt Maura's cottage, I'm just trying to take stock. I can't believe that it's the middle of November. I don't know where the time has gone.

Maura has been kind, looking after Saoirse for so long, but it's time for me to take over the role as mother now. Ever since the accident I've felt so disconnected from the world. I thought I'd feel better once I got out of the hospital, but my life has been turned upside down. I don't know what I would have done without Maura. Saoirse could have ended up in foster care. Sure, I've had concerns. I mean, what would a fifty-seven-year-old single woman know about rearing a baby? Maura's not like Mum. She's the complete opposite, in fact. But she's tried so hard to accommodate us both.

I glance around the humble space, so different to my warm house in Lincoln, which I'm renting out as an Airbnb. My bestie, Taylor, has been amazing. His hairdressing business is expanding, but he still found the time to sort my place out for me. I didn't think I'd miss working for him as much as I do. It's not about the hair. Styling isn't the most thrilling of jobs, and standing all day hurts the backs of my legs. No, it's about the people. The *real* joy comes from the stories that unfold: the confessions and shared laughs. Each client brings their world into the salon and for the duration of their appointment, I'm granted a snapshot of their lives. It's why I always take extra care with them. *Did,* I correct myself. I'm not a hairdresser now. The absence of the blast of the hairdryers and the hum of conversations only adds to my growing loneliness. Maybe one day I'll run my own salon, but that seems like a pipe dream now.

I can't leave Maura when she's done so much, and she's so good with Saoirse, much better than I could be now I'm hobbling around. I'm lucky to be alive. I pick at my fingernails as the moments before my accident return to haunt me. I'll never forgive myself for taking my eyes off the road that night.

It must have affected Saoirse, as she hasn't sucked a dummy since. It's almost as if she associates it with something bad. She could have died, and all because I couldn't bear to listen to her cry for another minute more. I halt my spiralling thoughts and take a few deep breaths. Maura has taught me the benefit of breathing exercises. She was quite upfront about her therapist, despite her calling him a 'charlatan'. She never said why she attended therapy. I suppose it's not easy when you live on your own in such an isolated spot.

Maura's thatched cottage is so dark and Misery Hill seems to be permanently cloaked in mist. But there are times of the day when it's breathtaking, like during sunrise when you can see the village of Doolin below. It's strange how this lone cottage is perched on the side of this hill. It feels more like a mountain to me. Maura has an air of superiority as she stands at her window, looking down on the town a kilometre below the hill. Misery Hill has had its share of bad fortune. Are we staying in a cursed place?

CHAPTER 10

FINN

The springs in the old wrought-iron bed creak as I shift my weight. At least the mattress is soft and comfortable, and I open the latch on the little window, welcoming the crisp blast of morning sea air. The sounds of the seagulls as they coast the skies make me long for freedom of my own. Last night, the rhythmic waves of the sea were a soothing backdrop. The aroma of peat, rich and sweet, permeates Maura's home on all but the most pleasant of days. I've only been here a short while, but I can see the appeal of country life, for a little longer anyway. There's no Wi-Fi in Maura's cottage but at least I have my phone. There's an old-fashioned television in the corner of the living room that she rarely turns on. She's partial to the radio, and sometimes she'll sway her hips if her mood is good and the right song comes on.

There is movement in the old crib. I'm using it for now, because Maura was so proud of herself for having it all set up upon my return. It's a huge thing, duck-egg blue with painted pictures of angels at each end. I'm not sure how safe the paint is, but at eleven weeks old, Saoirse isn't able to climb and it's not as if we'll be staying for very long.

'Come on, lefty,' I mutter as I shift my weight on to my injured leg. I'm still walking with a limp, favouring my right side to minimise the pain that shoots through me like lightning each time I put pressure on it. My physical limitations make me feel trapped in my own body, but as I said to Angie, my physiotherapist, it could have been a whole lot worse. I don't like to think about the other woman whose baby didn't survive. I've no right to complain considering what she's going through. Has she had her baby's funeral? Is she still thinking about that night? Does she think about me? It's only natural for her to want to blame someone, given what she's lost. It's early days with the insurance claim but the consensus seems to be that the accident was down to hazardous weather. Neither one of us was to blame. I didn't tell them that my attention was taken from the road. It's hard enough to live with the guilt.

I fumble with the childproof cap of my medication. Maura has been a godsend, picking up my oxycodone from the chemist. It's weird though, as sometimes not all the tablets look the same. She said the chemist often mixes old and new stock together, but they all do the same thing. Soon the familiar fog will creep into my mind. I'm not thrilled that Maura enters my room when she thinks I'm asleep, but she seems like a lonely soul so I'll forgive her for now. The pill rattles out of the container, and I quickly swallow it with a gulp of water from the bottle next to my bed. I hear Maura shuffling outside the door, no doubt listening for signs of life. It's a strange kind of torture, living with someone who looks so like my mum.

'Mummy's coming, baby girl.' My voice is strained yet determined. As I hobble across the bedroom, I won't allow the throbbing ache in my leg to bring me down.

The clock on the whitewashed stone wall gloomily counts the seconds, its hands inching closer to 7 a.m.

I pick my daughter up, hoping for the millionth time that the accident hasn't caused any damage that the doctors have yet to find. I coo and smile, cradling her in my arms.

'Have you got a wet bum?' I whisper, gently laying Saoirse on the bed. I slip a plastic changing mat beneath her and get to work freshening her up. I have a lovely changing station at home, but the hand-stitched quilt on the bed is a family heirloom and reminds me of Mum. My vision blurs as the medication takes effect. The oxycodone is numbing the pain, but leaves me drowsy and disoriented – a state far from ideal for caring for my baby. Should the medication be this strong?

'Are you hungry, sweetie?' I ask, trying to focus on my daughter's face. But the room spins around me, making it difficult to focus on her needs. 'Woah. Just . . . just give me a second,' I say, as Saoirse begins to cry.

There's a gentle tap on the door and it's open before I have a chance to respond. Maura's been standing there, listening in. I dismiss the thought as I sit on the bed and catch my breath. This medication is knocking me for six.

'Here now, let me take her for a bit.' Maura's tone is gentle yet firm. Her tweed skirt swishes softly as she steps inside, her practical shoes clicking on the floor. 'There you are, my little lamb.' She scoops Saoirse into her strong arms. When her face lights up like that, she looks exactly like Mum. It makes me catch my breath. Maura's not one for hugs, but I have asked for one on occasion when I'm feeling low.

She tells me to use my crutches. 'Come. Your breakfast is on the table. You need a good meal inside you to build up your strength.'

I utter my thanks, pushing myself on to the crutches that I wish I could do without. I will find a way to overcome the pain, the drugs and the dependence – for myself and for my child.

Saoirse's cries quieten almost immediately, and a pang of envy mixed with gratitude washes over me. I enter the kitchen, catching sight of a humane mouse trap in the corner of the room. 'Don't you have a cat?' I turn to Maura, who is chatting to Saoirse in her arms. Most homes in rural Ireland contain a cat to keep away the mice.

But she seems reluctant to speak about it as she shakes her head.

'When I was in the hospital, you talked about the cats you once owned.'

'You were listening, were you?' She raises an eyebrow. 'I thought you were out of it most of the time.'

'I remember bits.' I smile, resting my crutches against the table. 'You talked about a dog named Shep, and then there were the kittens, and the hedgehogs that you took in.' I glance around the room, looking for feeding bowls or tins of cat food. There's no evidence of them here. 'Maybe you could get a kitten,' I continue, because company would be good for her.

'No.' The word is flat and decisive. 'No more pets. Not here. They don't stay. Not any more.'

Her mood has changed in an instant. I've obviously hit upon a sore subject. I nibble my bottom lip, filled with a need to make it up to her. 'Would you like me to style your hair?'

'My hair?' She runs a hand over her head, smoothing it down.

'I'm a stylist. I could give you a nice cut . . . or a colour, if you'd like.'

'No,' she says bluntly, and as my awkwardness grows, I wish that I'd never asked.

'Thanks, this smells good.' I settle down to eat the cooked Irish breakfast that is plated up on the table. 'I could have just had toast, you didn't have to do all this.' One thing about Maura – she's an exceptional cook.

'Ah, nonsense.' Maura rocks my baby gently in her arms. She takes a bottle from the fridge and sits it into the pan of recently boiled water to warm it through. 'Sure it's no trouble. I've been thinking, Finn . . .' Her face breaks into a hopeful smile. 'It's clear you're struggling. I want you to stay with me long term. Let me look after you both.'

I hesitate, my fingers tracing the edge of the blue patterned plate. I need help, but the thought of imposing on Maura weighs heavy on my mind. 'I don't know, Maura . . . I don't want to be a burden.'

'Family is never a burden,' Maura insists, her eyes locked on to my daughter's. 'And you and little Saoirse here are the only family I've got. Stay as long as you need. Six months, a year, whatever it takes for you to recover.'

The mention of family instils a sense of longing. I've felt so adrift since Mum's death.

'Please,' Maura presses, her voice softening. 'Daisy's death . . . it's hit me hard too. Let me do this for you both. She wouldn't want you to be on your own.'

The room feels suddenly smaller, the air heavy with the weight of Maura's offer. She's standing over me now, waiting for my answer. I close my eyes, taking a steadying breath.

'That's good of you, thanks. We'll stay a little longer. As long as you're sure.'

A warm smile spreads across Maura's face. 'You're home now.' She speaks on an inhale, in words directed at my baby. 'Home at last.'

As she turns her back on me, I wonder if this has been a mistake. Because if Mum wanted me to be close to Maura then why didn't she introduce me years ago?

'A couple of months,' I add. 'That should give me enough time to get back on my feet.'

46

'Grand. It'll be nice to have company over Christmas.' Maura tests the milk on her wrist to feed my baby. A lump forms in my throat. This isn't how it was meant to be. I should be celebrating Saoirse's first Christmas with Mum, not in the home of a stranger.

CHAPTER 11

FINN

I hobble into the local shop, my crutch thudding softly against the linoleum floor. The air inside carries the scent of fresh bread and aged Cheddar – a pleasant mix of Doolin's everyday life. I balance myself on my crutch, scanning the shelves for my groceries. Maura isn't thrilled about my solo excursion this afternoon, but I'm going stir crazy within her four walls. At least we've had a break from the rain today.

'Howeya, Finn. Great drying out, isn't it?'

It's Geraldine's usual greeting as she catches sight of me at the end of the aisle. Her face is bright with optimism, her fleshy cheeks a healthy shade of pink. She's Maura's only friend from what I know, and despite her being a lovely soul, my aunt barely tolerates her.

'It is.' I return the warmth of her smile. Any day without rain in Ireland is considered a candidate for 'great drying' for the clothes hanging on her line. Geraldine's brown hair shines with tiny streaks of silver as it hangs loose from a ponytail low on her back. Her laughter lines tell stories, and her eyes are always sparkling, like she's in on some private joke. Unlike Maura's muscular build,

Geraldine's frame is comfortably padded, most likely from the soda bread and cakes that she sells in her shop. I can see why she's popular. She has a gravitational pull that draws you in. Sadly, for most people in Doolin, Maura's magnetism is set to repel. While Maura dresses in drab tweed skirts, thick jumpers and outdated sensible shoes, Geraldine's outfits are a bright mishmash of colours that should look out of place but don't. She's like a walking stained-glass window, uplifting everyone she meets.

She and her husband make a lovely pair, and their playful teasing gives me hope that one day, I'll have a relationship like theirs. Ever since I got here I've been craving connection – this place is my mother's home, after all. Mum didn't like to talk about Doolin, and would always say that too much water had passed under the bridge to bring it up. But I hope to stitch together the pieces of my heritage while I'm here. I've spoken to Geraldine before, and thanked her profusely for helping out with Saoirse, but I haven't delved any deeper yet. Geraldine waved my gratitude away, because such selfless acts are second nature to her. Today she leaves me to my own devices as a queue has formed at the till. The shop is busy for a Sunday, and the line is slow while Geraldine chats to each customer in turn. I try to steady myself as my leg delivers another jarring sensation of pain.

'Can I help you with that?' A man's voice rises from behind me. I turn to face the stranger and he offers an outstretched hand. He has the build of someone who knows their way around a gym but isn't a slave to it. He's tall – at least six feet two. But it's his accent, melodic and humble, that makes me melt a little inside. I've never been what you'd call hugely independent, so a little kindness goes a long way when I'm feeling low.

'Really? Well, if you're sure.' I lean more fully on my crutch as my left leg is throbbing now. The walk down Misery Hill to Doolin was harder than I thought. Doolin is a close-knit community where even tourists are welcomed into the fold. But I'm not sure where Maura fits in. I sense her preference to remain separate and I wonder what made her that way.

'No bother,' the stranger replies, taking my basket. 'Happy to help. Are you on your holidays?'

'Sort of,' I admit. I'm surprised he hasn't figured out who I am by now. 'My mother grew up here. I'm researching my roots.'

'Ah, well, welcome to Doolin.' His infectious smile eases the heaviness in my heart.

'Thanks.' I gaze up at the pack of nappies that rests on the top shelf. 'You couldn't grab me that pack of Pampers, could you?'

He cheerily complies. I was going to buy tampons too, but I'll leave them for another day.

We approach the checkout counter, our small talk punctuated by the rhythmic clacking of my crutch against the shop floor. The line moves slowly as we wait our turn. It's nice to connect with someone so genuinely kind. I notice a wedding ring on his finger, and given I'm buying nappies, it's obvious he's not trying to pick me up.

'Shocking, isn't it?' The exclamation comes from one of two older women with their backs turned to us, their shopping baskets overflowing with the usual staples of milk, bread, cheese and eggs. They have leaned in close to one another while they exchange gossip of some kind. 'That *poor* Aiden,' the first woman sighs, shaking her head. 'Eight weeks she's been gone now. And *poor* little Joy, only four years of age, without a mammy.'

'It's chronic,' the thinner of the two women agrees, her eyes scanning the shelves. 'I know she's always been flighty, but how could she leave little Joy? Poor Aiden must be finding it hard.'

I glance at my helpful stranger and we exchange an awkward smile. I'm glad when we reach the checkout and pack our groceries into eco-friendly bags.

'Did you hear those two?' The shop bell tinkles overhead on the way out. The air is cool but refreshing, the sunlight casting long shadows on the pavement. I can't help but smile. 'I wouldn't want to be in "poor Aiden's" shoes right now.'

'You and me both,' the man agrees, his eyes dancing with amusement.

'Anyway, thanks for that.'

'Happy to help.' He takes a deep breath, and as he continues to hold my groceries, it seems he's not ready to let me go just yet. 'How long are you planning on staying in Doolin?'

'Maybe a couple of months.' I drag my hair off my face as it is caught in the breeze. 'I want to really get to know this place, you know? Mum's past feels like a puzzle that I'm meant to solve.' I've no idea where that came from, but it feels true to me.

'Sounds like a great adventure.' The man grins. 'You're sure to meet plenty of interesting characters along the way.'

'Like you?' I tease. I'm shamelessly flirting now, but it feels nice to speak to someone so engaging. Lately my life has been about physio, nappy changes and Maura grumbling about the price of everything.

'Maybe.' My new friend's cheeks turn rosy pink. 'Or maybe I'm just someone who stands in the shadows, ready to carry groceries for those in need.'

'Good luck finding your superhero name,' I chuckle, my heart swelling with appreciation. 'I'm Finn,' I continue. Even though she christened me, Mum always insisted on the shortened version of my name.

'A legendary name in these parts!' The man pauses, taking in my confused expression. 'Haven't you heard of the Children of Lir?'

I shake my head, engrossed by the soothing cadence of his voice.

'Fionnuala was put under a spell by her jealous stepmother Aoife, and was cursed to spend hundreds of years as a swan. She was banished to the lakes of Ireland with her brothers Fiachra, Conn and Aodh.' He speaks with the voice of a storyteller as he continues. 'After nine hundred years they were freed, when a marriage broke the curse. There's a song and everything. I told you. Legendary name.'

I'm surprised my mother never imparted any of this. I make a mental note to look it up. 'And do *you* have any legends to your name?'

'Quite a recent one, it seems. I'm Aiden – "*poor* Aiden", if you believe the gossip.'

A wave of embarrassment washes over me. The two women in the shop couldn't have seen us standing there. 'Oh . . . Foot, meet mouth.' I squirm beneath his gaze.

Aiden laughs at my obvious discomfort, kicking a small pebble with the tip of his shoe. 'It's not like it's a secret around here. My wife did leave me, after all.'

'Are you okay?' I lean on my crutch while I comfort this virtual stranger. Pain lurks behind his eyes as he attempts to shrug it off.

'Most days,' Aiden admits, his voice barely above a whisper. 'But on others . . . not so much.'

'Life has a funny way of testing us,' I agree, my grip tightening on my crutch.

'What happened to the leg . . . if you don't mind me asking?'

Now it's my turn for pause. 'Car accident.' I look upwards, towards Misery Hill. 'We came off the road up there. I'm staying with my aunt . . .' My gaze briefly turns to her cottage where it stands bleak and alone. I'm taken aback by the look on Aiden's face. 'What's wrong?'

'I . . . um . . .' He rests the bag of groceries on the wide pavement. 'Maura Claffey is your aunt?'

I tilt my head to one side. I know that Maura's a bit grumpy, but his reaction is unsettling me. 'Yes, she's my mum's twin.'

'So you're the girl that came off the road. God, I'd no idea. I'm fierce sorry. Here's me, lost in my own problems and you . . .'

'Yes?'

'Nothing.' His smile returns. 'You took me by surprise, that's all. I imagined Maura's niece to be different. You look nothing like her.'

'Well, my tweed skirt needs a good airing. I can slip it on for the next time we meet.'

Aiden responds with a smile. But something has shifted between us. I can feel it.

'Where's your car?' Aiden says finally, his voice steady once more. 'You'd better get your ice cream home before it turns into soup.'

Maura will faint when she discovers that I've paid five euros for a tub of Ben and Jerry's, but it's worth every cent.

'I walked here.' I look down at my leg. 'It'll be a while before I'm able to get behind a wheel again.' Not that I want to. The memory of the crash is too fresh to even contemplate it. 'Just shove it all in my backpack. I'll walk back up the hill.' But even while I'm saying it, I wonder if I should try to get a taxi instead.

'Follow me.' Aiden picks my groceries back up. 'My car is across the road.'

Within minutes, he's transferring the shopping into the boot of his BMW. I hate taking the road on the cliff edge, but my leg is screaming for rest. 'I promise I'm not a serial killer.' Aiden shuts the boot with a satisfying thud. We exchange smiles, both acutely aware of the connection that has formed in the short time we've spent together.

'Fair enough,' I respond.

His car is warm and luxurious. I appreciate the heated seats. As Aiden drives, I refuse to look out the car window, and chew my lower lip as I gaze down at my hands. RTÉ Radio 1 is playing, and the weatherman forecasts more rain.

A moment passes, heavy with shared vulnerability, and I search for the right words. 'You live in the village. What's Maura really like? And why does she hate Doolin so much?'

Aiden glances surreptitiously over, before returning his gaze to the road. 'You're best asking her that, Finn. I leave the gossiping to the likes of Mrs O'Donnell and her cronies.'

I'm guessing he's referring to the women in the shop. 'But there's something.' I risk a glance up at him, my pulse accelerating as I take in a glimpse of the road. 'Isn't there?'

'She's a character, sure enough.' I see his grip on the steering wheel tighten. 'Just . . .' He looks over at me, beeping the car horn to warn oncoming drivers before taking the bend with ease. 'Just don't be afraid to ask for help if you need it. Geraldine's always in the shop and if you'd rather not ask her, then . . .' He nods towards his mobile phone, which he has stored in a pocket in the centre aisle. 'Stick your number in there, I'll send you a text, and if there's anything you need, like a lift to the shops . . . or anything. Just call. Day or night.'

'You're worrying me now.' I pick up his phone and direct it towards his face to unlock the screen. I quickly type my number into his contacts list under 'Finn'. I'm hoping he's just being kind, rather than the alternative, which suggests that there's something worryingly wrong with my aunt.

'Here we are,' he says, as I try to calm my racing heart. I'm not sure I'll ever be okay with that road. He hops out of the car to get my shopping from the boot.

'Can you manage from here?' He hands me the bag while I get used to standing again.

'Of course.' But my heart skips a beat as I sense his wariness. 'Aiden,' I sigh. 'Is there anything I should know?'

There's a story behind his eyes and his lips part to speak. But one glance at the cottage is enough to rob him of his words. I follow his gaze towards the cottage window to see Maura staring at us both. Her eyes are narrowed in silent fury, her lips pressed together into a bloodless white line.

CHAPTER 12

MAURA

I stand at my front room window, gripping the ledge so tightly that my knuckles have blanched an ashy white. I stare out at Finn and Aiden, holding on to my composure by a thread. Saoirse is asleep in her cot, while Finn is chatting with Aiden as if they've known each other for years. A knot of jealousy twists in my stomach. I hate feeling like this. Life is less painful when you live alone.

Finn runs one hand through her wavy hair as she drags it back from her face. Why wouldn't Aiden talk to her, with her exotic English accent and big brown eyes? But every friendly gesture and shared laugh feels like a betrayal. I've worked so hard to bond with Finn, and now here she is, talking to him without a care or a thought for the person who's looked after her all this time. It's not as if nappies come cheap. Her smile fades as she catches sight of me. I've been caught out. I retreat from the window and pace the room, my stomach twisting tighter. The clouds have blotted the sun outside, and the room grows as dark as my thoughts. It's not fair. I've spent years alone, ostracised by my twin, waiting to reconnect with family. And now that Finn and the babby are finally here, young Aiden Walsh is working his way into our lives. He's better off without that brassy wife of his, but this was never on the cards.

'Maybe Finn just needs a friend,' I whisper to myself. But the words are bitter on my tongue. The idea of sharing Finn's affections is unbearable. This is meant to be *my* time. Finn belongs with me. I return to the window, and grind my back molars as Finn throws back her head and laughs. She's never done that with me. *He's after something more,* an internal voice warns. It makes me feel sick inside.

I can't stand it any more.

I'm aware of my rising temper, but am helpless to stop it. I'm beyond breathing exercises now. I turn on my heel and march into the bedroom where Saoirse is sleeping in her cot. A sharp pinch on the leg is all it takes for her to awake with a scream.

'There, there, don't make such a big fuss,' I say, as plump tears form on her bewildered little face. I lift her from her cot and bounce her on my shoulder as I leave the room. Forcing a rigid smile, I open the door of the cottage.

'Sorry to interrupt.' I force the pleasantries. 'But I can't settle her. She wants her mammy.'

'Oh, sure, sorry!' Finn's expression changes to one of dismay. 'I bumped into Aiden in town. He gave me a lift back.'

I feel like saying that it's obvious he gave her a lift as why else would he be here, standing like an eejit with his big jalopy of a car parked on my drive. I keep my mouth tightly shut, approaching Finn with Saoirse, who is kicking up quite a racket. The wind whips around us as the weather takes a turn for the worse. Living mountainside brings its own set of challenges. Being permanently exposed to the elements is just one.

Finn looks at me, her expression creased in pain. 'Oh, um . . . would you mind carrying her inside? My leg's killing me.'

Of course. I've made myself look a fool. Heat creeps from my chest to my neck as I realise that she can't manage her crutch and a crying baby. Letting her walk to Doolin was a bad idea. I'd hoped that it would teach her a lesson not to do so again. But it appears to have backfired on me because now she has a friend. I hear her thank Aiden after he offers to bring her shopping inside. Saoirse's cries turn into a whimper as she settles down.

'Have you time for a cup of tea?' Finn asks, making me bristle. 'Isn't that what you Irish live off?'

Aiden ducks as he enters the low doorway. 'It is indeed. The Irish have been known to spontaneously self-combust if they're not sufficiently hydrated on the hour.' He rests the groceries on the coffee table in the living room before glancing across at me. 'But I don't want to get in the way. Another time, maybe.'

'It's no bother,' I say, as Finn takes a seat. It stands to reason that if Finn has a friend, she's more likely to want to stick around. She's whitewash pale, and there's a sheen of sweat on her brow, despite the chilly day. 'Shush now, pet,' I whisper to Saoirse. I'm overcome by self-loathing, now the sting of my anger has faded. How could I hurt her like that? I kiss her warm forehead and whisper that I'm sorry. I don't know what I was thinking.

'Can I get you a pillow?' I say to Finn, who raises her arms for her daughter.

'Just my painkillers, thanks,' she replies, wincing as she shifts her weight.

'Here you go, love.' I force a smile when I hand them over, although I can't relax with Aiden in the house. I'm not used to male company in my cottage these days.

Aiden joins her on the sofa, admiring the little one while I put the shopping away. My mind races as I prepare the tea, torn between my need to protect Finn and my own possessiveness. I can't let them go, can't bear the thought of losing everything I have worked so hard to reclaim. But how can I keep her and little Saoirse by my side without driving them away? Then I remember why she came here in the first place – because she is grieving the loss of my sister. Perhaps there is room in her life for me after all.

I stare through my kitchen window at the wind tousling the unkempt grass out the back. Memories of past abandonment feel like a leaden weight. My gaze lingers on a particularly overgrown patch of grass near the fence. It shivers, as if chilled by an unseen presence. Misery Hill hides many secrets. Secrets that could tear my new-found family apart. If Finn ever found out . . .

My thoughts are interrupted by the sharp whistle of the kettle on the range. I take a sudden breath, grounding myself.

'Thank you, Mrs Claffey,' Aiden adds politely, as I hand him the tea. There're two slices of apple tart in the fridge but I'm keeping that for supper and I won't waste my last bit of food on a man.

'Call me Maura, dear.' I give him an icy stare, my voice dripping with false sweetness. I'm doing this for Finn.

Aiden smiles, shifting uncomfortably beneath my gaze. I catch the faintest scent of spicy aftershave and quickly draw away. After giving Finn her tea, I leave them alone. He can't get up to anything while the babby's on Finn's lap anyway. I drink my tea in the kitchen and will stay here until Aiden leaves. I can't remember the last time a man set foot in this place.

It won't happen again.

CHAPTER 13

KATHRYN

Sleep is a long way off as I stare at my bedroom ceiling. I'm fourteen all over again, dreaming of the days when I can escape my parents' grip. But now, I've nothing to escape to. I don't want to exist in anyone's world any more. My life has been snatched away. The days since my hospital discharge have passed in a haze, each one blending into the next. I don't want to be here, but neither am I well enough to look after myself.

My father made it quite clear: either stay in their care or I'm completely on my own. Just like before, he's orchestrated things so that I'm fully dependent on him. My bank cards, my passport – he has them all.

To an outsider it might look as if I'm being well cared for. Yvonne, my carer, is here for my every need. She sits in the corner of the room, her *Take A Break* in hand. Every now and again, she glowers at me through the thick lens of her glasses, her discontent magnified ten-fold. I wish she'd leave me alone. Her short bobbed brown hair only adds to her owlish appearance and does her no favours. She's got one of those bowl cuts, the sort you see in old school photos that make you inwardly cringe. She's surprisingly strong for her small frame, and can heft me around when she needs to. But then I've lost so much weight since . . . I can't bear to think about it. She licks her finger and turns the page.

Yvonne is a distant cousin – I'd never met her until she got this job. Dad needed someone to watch me, she's what he terms 'family' and newly qualified. She certainly knows her place, as when she's in my father's company she looks like she's about to faint. Every movement I make is monitored because she reports back to him.

I touch the side of my head for the thousandth time. The scar is revolting but healing, and the bruises on my body have faded from black to purple to yellow. I'm an ugly canvas of bad memories, my once healthy skin now disfigured and scarred. When they discharged me from hospital, I felt as though I was walking through a nightmare, my surroundings blurred in a fog of grief. But now, an ember of doubt refuses to be extinguished.

At last, the owlish Yvonne gets up from her chair. 'Is there anything you need before I go?'

'No, thanks, I'm going to get some sleep.' *Write that in your notebook,* I think, *and shove it up your—*

'Grand,' she replies. 'I'll be off then.'

It's only ten. My mind wanders to my mother, who will be propped up in bed reading one of her romance novels on her Kindle, smoking a cigarette. I haven't seen her all day. I slip my mobile phone from beneath my pillow and give her a call. She answers after just two rings.

'What's wrong?'

I sigh at her curt response. 'Nothing. At least, nothing new.' Silence falls between us. 'Mam, I need to see her.' My voice is croaky and I swallow to clear my throat. 'I need to see Kiera's grave.'

I'm devastated that I missed her funeral. They could have waited until I recovered. They didn't even tell me that it had been held until it was too late. I imagine Mam and Dad by the graveside, the Catholic priest uttering a few rushed prayers as Kiera's tiny white coffin is placed into the ground. This would have been a low-key affair.

Dad was looking over his shoulder for some time after he paid his thugs to have Kiera's father, David Kenny hospitalised. He deserved to be worried after what they did to him. David was just like me. He wanted no part of the family business. But now it seems that his family and mine have reached a truce. Dad turns a blind eye to the parts of Dublin that the Kennys have taken over, while continuing to develop his county lines using his furniture business as a front. David and I are pawns, nothing else. Neither family really cares about us. Now our final bond has broken, as our little girl lies in the cold, harsh ground. I have to say goodbye if I've any hope of getting over this.

A fragment of a dream returns to mind: David, standing by my bedside, holding my hand. But that's not possible, because he will never walk again. Tears well in my eyes and I blink them away.

'Do you know what time it is?' Mother sucks on her cigarette.

I don't know how she stands sleeping in a room polluted with smoke. Dad sleeps down the far end of the house now. It's better than the screaming rows.

'Please, Mam. You promised.' I keep saying 'Mam' as a reminder of what she's meant to be. Because she's never been a proper mother to me.

She responds with a deep sigh. 'Alright.'

For a moment, I brighten. I didn't want to face my daughter's grave alone.

'Yvonne will take you tomorrow.'

Then she's gone. Back to her trashy novel and the pull of her cigarette. She's always been distant. I was stupid to think that things would change.

◆ ◆ ◆

I sit in Yvonne's car as she parks up outside the graveyard. My fingers wrap around the small pink teddy bear that used to take up space in Kiera's cot. One last tangible link to my baby girl.

'Ready?' Yvonne asks, sighing from the inconvenience.

I don't expect compassion but a little empathy would be nice. I nod, determined to see my daughter's final resting place and maybe, just maybe, find answers to the questions plaguing my waking thoughts.

Yvonne unclips her seat belt. The sound of the material zipping back into its compartment makes me shudder. I hate cars since the accident. I hate every sight, smell and sound that they produce.

'I'll go on my own.' My grip on the teddy bear tightens. I'm in no mood for Yvonne as she twitches her beaky nose in discontent.

'I don't know . . .' she begins. But I'm ready for her.

'I need to say goodbye to my baby. It's not a spectator event.'

She has the decency to blush. 'I'll keep a distance. I won't get in your way.'

I stare at the footwell, my voice growing firm. 'Are you not listening? I need to do this on my own.' The mood shifts between us. Up until now, I've done everything she's asked without question.

'I suppose I can see you from here,' she relents. 'It's not as if you're going very far.' And there it is. Confirmation that her job is to keep an eye on me.

'Thanks,' I say softly. Once upon a time, the old me would have told her exactly where to go. I'm more like my father than I care to admit. It frightens me sometimes. But having Keira softened me.

It's hard for me to admit it now, but I didn't want her after she was born. By the time I realised that I was pregnant, it was too late to do anything about it. Kiera's existence was another complication

63

in my life. I was forced to give up drinking, and my cocaine-fuelled parties ended. Sobriety forced me into reflection, and I couldn't stand to be alone with my thoughts. It was hardly surprising that I struggled to love my daughter in the early days. The weight of my guilt is a tangible burden. I slide a hand into the pocket of my parka and touch the cold metal of my father's hip flask. He hasn't missed it yet. I need it more than he does anyway. I stand on the path, rows of graves ahead of me, feeling utterly alone in the world.

I neck back a mouthful of straight vodka, enjoying its warmth as it spreads to my stomach, providing momentary relief. My daughter's headstone looms before me, a silent sentinel under a heavy sky. My family have their own plots in a private part of this graveyard. Each gravestone has elaborate crosses and heavenly paraphernalia. As if it could grant any of the Toíbíns a place in heaven.

My breath catches in my chest when I catch sight of the oversized stone angel. She gazes at me with blank eyes as she stands above what can only be Kiera's grave. It is layered in flowers, some wilted, some fresh. I inhale a strengthening breath, catching the scent of damp earth and moss hanging in the air. I approach the grave, clutching the pink teddy like it's a lifeline. I curse myself for wanting my mother as tears brim in my eyes.

My fingers trace her name across the smooth granite, a stark reminder of a life taken too soon.

'Kiera,' I whisper her name, my voice breaking under the strength of my pain.

A torrent of memories overwhelm me as a cold breeze touches my skin. Suddenly, I'm back in the car, twisted metal creaking around me, pinned in place amidst the wreckage. Blood blurs my vision while I fight the pain, desperate for a sign of my baby girl. But they said she was thrown clear from my car the moment we came off the road.

Damp earth seeps through the knees of my jeans as I kneel, lost in the past. I can smell the gasoline mingling with the acrid scent of burnt rubber. Time has changed, leaving me suspended in a nightmare from which I cannot awake. I can barely catch my breath when I call out for my child.

The memory begins to fade, replaced by the cold reality of the graveyard. I hold the pink teddy bear in my trembling hands, its soft fur offering little comfort. I don't know why, but I feel that, somehow, I'm getting nearer to the truth. Rain begins to patter on the gravestone as I force myself to relive the painful memory once more.

Another flashback sweeps away the grey hues of my graveyard surroundings. I'm back in my car, the world outside a dizzying blur spinning out of control. Glass shatters in a cacophony of sharp, biting sounds.

'Kiera!' I scream, my voice strangled with fear and desperation as the car tumbles over once more.

The seat belt cuts into my shoulder, a reminder of my precarious position while I hang upside down. The car has finally stopped, and I've gone from an explosion of pain to nothingness. Is that what dying is like – a slow surrender to the darkness?

The sound that reaches my ears makes my heart lurch. It's so real, so ingrained in that hidden memory that I clutch the rain-damp teddy tighter to my chest. It's Kiera, and she's crying in the back of the car, her tiny voice barely audible above the creaks and groans.

The sensation of the cold rain on my face jolts me back to the present. I blink, my mind racing to process what I've remembered. The graveyard stretches out around me, tombstones casting eerie shadows as the morning sun edges behind a cloud.

Had I really heard Kiera crying?

But Dad said Kiera died when she was thrown clear from the car. Why would he lie about something like that? I think of my father and how much he hated Kiera's mere existence in the world. He couldn't accept a child with Toíbín and Kenny blood. Could he be tied up in this tragedy somehow? But he didn't know about Kiera. Not at the time of the accident. Yet . . . someone *was* at the scene, before the police and ambulance arrived. I drifted in and out of consciousness long enough to remember that. I squeeze my eyes shut, trying to draw out the memory like pus from a fetid boil. It won't come, not now, but it will. A choked sob leaves my lips as the realisation washes over me.

My baby didn't die in the crash. Kiera is alive. I don't know *how* it happened yet, but it's true. I'm laughing when Yvonne finds me, and I allow her to guide me back to the car.

'Let's get you home.' Her face is creased in sympathy and concern – a chink in her armour. She clicks my seat belt into place. 'Kathryn?' Yvonne leans over me, so close that I can smell the mints on her breath. 'Are you . . . Are you okay?'

Tears stream down my face and I deliver a nod. I'm laughing and sobbing and must look like I'm mad with grief. But Kiera's not under the frosty ground, she's above earth, with warm blood running through her veins. Only now do I allow myself to feel it. The conviction that my baby never died. She wasn't thrown from the car when it came off the cliff edge. She was taken. And somebody knows where she is.

CHAPTER 14

Then

Maura

There are times in my life that I will never forget. The first day that I was alone with Jimmy on Misery Hill counts in my top ten.

It was a chilly November, the anniversary of the day that one of Ireland's most respected poets, Patrick Kavanagh, died. His words often moved me. I thought about his poems as I waited for Jimmy, my nose red from the cold.

The hill was a silent sentinel overlooking the village of Doolin, providing a breathtaking view. The village below was a tapestry of colours, the ocean breeze so salty that I could taste it on my tongue. It played with tendrils of my hair, teasing them free from my loose braid. I remember the wild grass swaying back and forth, as if the wind couldn't make up its mind which way it wanted to go. I pushed my hands into the pockets of my thick cardigan, the wool a barrier to the nip in the air. The evening's chorus was already beginning as the distant lowing of the dairy farmers' cattle could be heard. This part of the hill was a secret haven back then, a rocky barrier from prying eyes, carved by nature's own hand. I climbed on to one of the rocks, being careful not to slip and fall. I saw Daisy do it once, and she'd looked like an enchanted creature as she'd stared out to sea. But all it did for me was make my eyes water, blow up my skirt and tangle my hair. The sight of Jimmy's approach was enough to make me climb back down and fix my unruly waves into their clips.

Back then, he walked – no, *plodded* – like a man with a weight on his shoulders. But the shadows beneath his eyes did little to erode his good looks. Something told me it was more than work keeping him from his sleep. How could my sister have had such a lasting effect on him? My heart gave a little jolt as his face lit up a little bit at the sight of me.

'For a second there you looked like your sister.' Pink-cheeked and out of breath, he approached.

My smile faded. 'Well, we are twins.' I was unable to keep the sharpness from my voice.

He tilted his head as he took me in. 'Is that her jumper?'

'Yes.' I sighed. I'd worn it in the hope that he'd find me as attractive as my sister.

'Did she give you a message?' He checked his watch. He was so handsome that he made me feel all wobbly inside. Nobody on this earth had the effect on me that Jimmy Walsh did.

'No.' She was having a grand old time in Limerick with all her new friends. The last flicker of hope left his face and I felt a sharp prick of remorse. I watched his jaw harden and I almost lost my resolve. I had rung the doctor's surgery and asked to speak to him direct. But the message I left had been cryptic as I asked to meet him after the surgery closed.

'Then why call me up here?'

'Because . . . be-because,' I stammered, picking out my nails. Sooner or later I had to force myself to look at him.

'Well, what is it then?'

I took a breath so deep that I almost lost myself in it. The sea was gentle that day despite the breeze. I stared, mesmerised by its white foamy fingers grasping at the rocks below. 'Jimmy, I know you miss Daisy. But you don't have to.'

'Why?' He perked up a bit. 'Has she said something?'

'I've just told you she didn't.' This was so hard, but I had to get it over with. '*We* can be together,' I said, finally turning towards him. His face creased in confusion.

'Sorry, what's that now?' But I could tell by his expression that he knew exactly what I meant. He was just buying time.

I forced the words from my mouth as a flush of embarrassment heated my cheeks. 'We can be girlfriend and boyfriend.' I didn't know what the etiquette for this sort of thing was. I had no idea how Daisy got so many boyfriends, and when I asked her about it at the time, she just laughed and said she'd never had to think about it as *they* came to *her*.

A small smile curled on to Jimmy's lips, one of amusement and disbelief. I hated him for that, but I loved him too. It's funny how the people I was the most passionate about made me feel such a tumult of emotions – a mixture of hate and love with no in-between. Such strong emotions scared me. Because when I was riding that seesaw, I was capable of anything. This wasn't turning out the way I'd hoped. I'd imagine him opening his arms wide, telling me that he had loved me all along, but he had always thought I was too shy or uninterested when it came to dating him. I dreamed about us having a house of our own. We would have three children. I had even picked their names. As my fantasy life disintegrated, Jimmy took a step back.

'Maura . . . I had no idea.'

'You don't have to miss Daisy, that's all I'm saying. Because you can be with me.' I continued to dig myself deeper, my heart ready to beat its way out of my chest. 'I'll never leave you.'

It was meant to be a promise, but as the words left my mouth they sounded more like a threat. Daisy had a soft voice, and almost sang as she spoke. She had a way of winning people around and God knows I tried, but it wasn't in my nature. I could copy her for a while, but not long enough to be myself. I lunged towards him, determined to drive home my point.

'What are you doing?' Jimmy gasped, just as I grabbed his arms.

'Take me,' I said with abandon. 'So we can be together forever.' I'd read it in one of Daisy's old Mills & Boon novels and had hoped that it would work with Jimmy. But instead, he blurted a laugh.

My mouth dropped open in horror. He was laughing at *me*.

'Sorry.' He blinked, as he tried to repair the damage he had caused. 'But you don't want to be with me. Find yourself someone nice. There must be plenty of young lads in the village your own age.' He shuffled awkwardly and looked at his watch, then back down the road where he obviously wanted to be. A cluster of gulls wheeled overhead, their cries sharp and gleeful as they danced on the wind.

'Fine,' I said sulkily, my feelings hurt beyond repair. 'I know when I'm not wanted. Just go.'

He opened his mouth to speak, then closed it again. Then he was gone.

A tremor of anger ran through me that day. It was my sister's fault. She ruined everything without a care for me. Jimmy was too attached to Daisy to think about being with me now. I just needed to show him that I was better than her. I smoothed down my sister's jumper. Yes, I could do better, try harder to be what he wanted. But the only way I could make it happen to begin with was to make him think I was her.

CHAPTER 15

FINN

I hobble into the kitchen, supporting Saoirse with one arm, but Maura doesn't seem to notice that we're here. Spending time with Aiden was the tonic I needed, but now he's gone it feels like the joy has been sucked out of the room. Maura is bustling about, crashing crockery in the sink as she washes up. I feel like I've offended her, but I don't know what I've done. I watch her, head down while she mumbles to herself. She often talks to herself, her tone sharp when she criticises whoever has annoyed her that day. It could be the postman, who'd delivered a bill damp from the rain, or the milkman for waking her up. Her behaviour surprised me at first, because she's so unlike Mum, who found the good in everyone. I blur my eyes out of focus, picking out the facial resemblances as I pretend that she's here. But as Maura shuffles flat-footed around the kitchen, my imagination refuses to stretch that far. It was easier in the early days when she was on her best behaviour, but now her guard has dropped. No wonder Aiden couldn't get out of here quickly enough.

'You don't need a man in your life,' she mutters. 'Much less that one.'

I look up from baby Saoirse, who is busy chewing on a soft toy. 'Sorry, what?'

She looks surprised to see me. She was either talking to herself or rehearsing what she was going to say. 'Nothing. Just . . . be careful who you let into your life.'

My lips tighten and I shift my gaze away from Maura. Sometimes she's too possessive for her own good. 'What has Aiden done to upset you? We were only chatting. He's nice.'

'He's a man, isn't he?' She rounds on me, her dark eyes filled with fury. 'And they're only out for what they can get.'

I cradle my daughter closer, wondering what happened in Maura's life to make her this way. I watch as she busies herself wiping down the sides with a blue J-cloth.

'I appreciate your concern, Aunt Maura. But not all men are like that.'

'Oh yes?' She glares at me, cloth in hand. 'Where's *your* babby's daddy then? No doubt he disappeared the minute he got the job done!'

My mouth drops open in surprise as I absorb the sting of her words. She may as well have slapped me in the face. She throws the dish cloth into the sink, spins around and marches out of the kitchen. Cautiously, I follow her, just in time to hear her bedroom door shut with a resounding crack. Her disapproval has shocked me. I recall Aiden's discomfort in her presence. There's a story behind it. A bad one.

I hear her scream from behind the door. Saoirse is sleepy in my arms and I wince as I struggle to stand. I've never felt so uncomfortable beneath Maura's roof. A crash follows, the sound of shattering glass. What's going on in there? 'Fecking bastards!' Maura roars, along with a string of expletives that have never left my mother's mouth. Mum, whose worst swear word was 'flip' when something went wrong. I limp to the bedroom, laying Saoirse back down. I'm checking her nappy when I notice a red mark the size of a ten-pence piece on her leg. How did that get there? I make a mental note to ask the health visitor about it later on.

I sigh with relief as Saoirse falls back into the realms of sleep in her cot. Every muscle in my body is aching, and sleep calls me too. But I can't rest, not when Maura is throwing a fit. I take my crutches from next to my bed. They hurt my arms and chafe the skin on my hands, but right now I can't move very far without them. They clack rhythmically against the floor when I make my way to Maura's bedroom door.

'Are you alright, Maura?' I ask, listening for the slightest sound. It's fallen silent. *Sod it,* I think, leaning on one crutch as I open her door. It's an invasion of privacy but she doesn't mind telling *me* what to do. I need to have this out with her. If I've worn out my welcome then I'll pack our bags and go.

As I swing the door open, she hastily yanks the sleeve of her woollen jumper down, but not before I catch sight of the three crimson gashes in her arm. The fresh, vivid blood contrasts starkly against her pale flesh.

'Sorry . . .' I pause as she turns away from me. She's staring out of the window now, still and silent in the gloomy space. I've never seen her like this before. 'Is . . . Is everything alright?' It's clearly not, but I don't know how to talk to her when she's like this.

'Fine. Just a bit chilly.' Maura forces a smile, resting her hand on the pane as she often does. 'You know how these old cottages can be.'

I nod, but my gaze lingers on the smashed vase on the floor. It was an ugly thing to begin with. A navy-blue monstrosity with yellow blobs that represented flowers. I take a step towards it.

'Leave it be!' she shouts, without turning in my direction.

'Sorry, I—'

'You're going to leave me, aren't you? You'll take the little one away and I'll never see either of you again.' She bows her head. 'Daisy and I . . . we didn't speak. But I always knew that she was there. Things feel different now. Empty.' Her breath trembles as she sighs.

My gaze lingers on Maura as she stands in solitude in the wake of her twin's passing. It's barely been six months. I've been so wrapped up in my own grief that I have forgotten hers. She seems adrift, untethered from her soulmate, and visibly marked by her loss. Is there a term that captures the void left by an identical twin's departure? I feel a sudden need to offer reassurance.

'We're not going anywhere, Maura. You've done so much for us both. I don't know what I would have done without you.'

Her fingers are steepled so hard against the glass that I hear it creak in its frame. 'Then stay here permanently.' Her expression is hollow and drawn as she turns to face me at last. The room falls quiet and the pat, pat of droplets of her fresh blood hit the floor in a steady rhythm as she awaits my response. She stands rigid and unblinking, haloed by the last of the sun.

'You're hurt.' I nod towards her injured arm. 'Did you cut yourself on the vase?' The blood beneath her fingernails suggests otherwise, but I'm giving her a way out. I'm also avoiding her offer of us staying here permanently. Maura needs more help than I'm equipped to give right now.

'Please,' Maura whines. 'Don't go. Don't leave me alone.'

My sigh is heavy with emotion as I take two laboured steps towards her. 'I'm not leaving. Look at me . . .' I chuckle, trying to lighten the mood. 'I can barely walk. But we need more than just each other. We need connections, friends, people who care.' I take another tentative step. 'Let's get this arm cleaned up, eh?'

'No need.' Her voice is flat and she turns to her bedroom cabinet. 'I have everything I need here.'

As she opens the cabinet, I stare in awe. It's filled to the brim with medical supplies: gauzes, surgical scissors, bandages – way beyond your average first-aid kit. I stare at the sepia-coloured bottles with tinctures contained within. Then there are the tablets – prescription, by the look of them. She closes the cabinet door. 'For emergencies,' she says, by means of response. She opens another thin drawer and pulls out an envelope. 'These are yours.' Her expression hardens as she thrusts it clumsily into my hand before turning back to her supplies. I stare at her bloodied thumb print before opening the envelope. There are receipts, lots of them, dating back from the day of my accident.

'I've done a tally,' she says, her hair shadowing her face. 'I'll take a bank transfer if you don't have the cash.'

Only then do I realise that the receipts are for every penny that she's spent on us. I'd offered to reimburse her as soon as I was well enough, but she'd waved it away at the time.

'Of course . . .' is all I can manage to say.

Maura stands in silence, her gaze filled with silent judgement, as if she's fallen under a dark spell. It's not just her making me uneasy. As shadows move across the room, a creeping sense of discomfort takes hold. The thick stone walls seem to absorb both light and warmth, and my skin crawls with unease. Each gust of wind against the rattling windowpanes feels like a whispered warning. I am overcome with a need to leave this inhospitable room.

'How about I put the kettle on? Make us a nice cup of tea.' Anything to get out of this space.

'I'm going to bed.'

'But, Maura . . . it's only six o'clock. Can I get you anything?' Silence has returned. 'Would you like me to call Geraldine?' No response. I stand in the doorway while she bandages her arm. 'Have I done something wrong?'

'Just leave me. I'm . . . I'm tired. You can sort out the babby tonight.'

I'm more than happy to get up for my daughter. It's Maura who has always insisted on taking the night feed. 'Well, if you need anything, you know where I am.' But my words feel hollow. My arms ache as I return to the living room. It's strange, as sometimes my medication takes my senses as well as my pain, but tonight it's had little effect. All of this, because I invited Aiden in. I have so many unanswered questions. Why does she have a cupboard full of medical supplies? Is she a chronic self-harmer? How often does she hurt herself and where has it stemmed from? But the biggest question is one bound to keep me awake at night. Are we safe under her roof?

CHAPTER 16

MAURA

Sunlight creeps through the cracks in my curtains, casting a pale glow across my pillow. My mind is busy with the ghost of a thousand bad memories that refuse to leave me be. In the quiet stillness of the cottage, I hear Saoirse's distant cries. My heart twists with every whimper. I cannot go to her. Not today. I don't trust myself.

'Can't go on like this.'

I hear the words leave my mouth as I force my body out of bed, but it feels dark and distant, like it's coming from someone else. I'm wearing yesterday's clothes, and I catch sight of myself in the mirror, my hair a bird's nest on my head. I should run a comb through it but I can't bring myself to care. I plug my feet into my slippers and force myself to shuffle forward, only because I'm desperate to urinate.

'Morning,' Finn calls as she appears from the kitchen, Saoirse strapped to her chest. 'Enjoy your lie-in?' She's wearing a dress and a little make-up, perhaps in the hope that Aiden will show his face. The thought draws the darkness towards me and I keep my gaze on the floor.

'Fine, just fine,' I hear myself mutter, avoiding eye contact while I head to the bathroom. Saoirse gives a little coo of amusement. Any other day it would melt my heart, but now it's an annoyance that I can do without.

'Are you sure?' Finn probes gently, concern lacing her words. 'You don't seem yourself.'

'Never mind about me!' I shout a response in the hope she will leave me in peace. I haven't bothered locking the bathroom door and my voice carries through to the kitchen as I pull down my thick woollen tights. My legs are itchy from having worn them all night and the smell of stale sweat rises from my clothes.

I flush the toilet automatically, running my tongue over the plaque on my teeth because I forgot to brush them last night. Everything is an effort when the darkness closes in. I'm about to wash my hands when I notice the blood encrusted beneath my fingernails. Dammit. I forgot about that. Slowly, I pull up my sleeves, wincing as they stick to the dressing. The gouges will heal but I feel like doing it all over again. I eye Finn's razor in the bathroom cabinet. No. It's too much. I'm not going down that road. This habit of self-destruction formed the day my sister left and has stayed with me ever since. Clinging on to the porcelain sink, I close my eyes and keep breathing deeply until the bad thoughts fade. The water is warm as I wash my hands. Finn must have lit the fire in the range. She's a good girl, really. Tears prick my eyes and I wipe them away. I'm riding a wave of emotions and struggling to keep afloat.

'Maura?' Finn's voice rises from the doorway. 'Would you like a cup of tea? It's gone twelve. You must be parched.'

I push past her, biting the side of my tongue to stop ugly words from spilling out. *Bitch. Whore. Floozy. Bastard brat.*

Why must she follow me into the kitchen? My stomach growls in contempt while I consider returning to my room. If I lived on my own this wouldn't be an issue. I'd stay in my cottage until it passes, just as I've done a hundred . . . no, a thousand times before. But then there are the nights . . . the times when I stare out of the window at the winding road and the drivers foolish enough to drive up Misery Hill. Some drive up. Not all drive down.

Finn sets Saoirse down in her highchair and gives her a toy. 'We're family. Let me help.'

'Family.' I repeat the word, tasting the coppery sweetness of my blood as it drizzles from my tongue. 'Fam-i-ly.' My resolve wavers for a moment, my secrets threatening to spill. The moment passes and the floorboard creaks beneath Finn's advancing step. 'Stay away.' My voice is brittle. I barely recognise it. Food. I need food. Then I can return to my room, where it's safe and I can hurt nobody but myself.

I set about making breakfast. I glance at the clock. No . . . it's lunchtime now. I close my eyes as I try to ground myself to the present day. Today is Wednesday, the fifteenth of November. As I open my eyes, I know what I need. Free-range eggs, smoked bacon, brown bread and butter. I grab them from the cupboard and heat the pan and the kettle on the range. I crack two eggs and drop them into the sizzling fat. Finn can feed herself. She's had enough out of me already.

Finn stares at me, hurt and confusion clouding her eyes. 'Aunt Maura, please talk to me. We can work through whatever's going on.'

'Leave it be!' I slam a plate on to the kitchen counter with such force that ceramic shards scatter like the pieces of my fractured life. I stare at the carnage, the violence of the moment hanging in the air. A sudden wail erupts from Saoirse and I return my attention to the smoking pan. Hot fat spits out on to my hand as I give the bubbling eggs a shake.

As the sun rises higher in the sky, I stand over the cooker, the sizzle of frying eggs and bacon filling the kitchen. I take another plate from the cupboard and slide the cooked food upon a slab of bread. I don't need butter, there's enough grease on the pan. I take the biggest teapot – the brown one that my father used to use – from the shelf and fill it with three Lyons teabags. They're costly, sure enough, but I need it for the day ahead. Finn is too busy pacifying Saoirse to say anything as I retreat to my room with the tray. I can't look at either of them. I don't want them in my thoughts. Because, today, my mind is not a safe place to be.

CHAPTER 17

Finn

A soft mist has settled on the road leading up to Misery Hill, but I can still see the Lego-like village of Doolin below. Saoirse sits quietly in her pushchair, focused on the string of toy ducks hanging from the hood. Her face has grown chubby, and while I feel guilty for not being well enough to breastfeed, it seems formula milk has agreed with her. Her downy black hair grows thicker by the day and maybe it's my imagination, but if I look at her in a certain way, I see her daddy looking back at me. My encounter with her father, the dark and alluring Mikka, was never meant to last. Now he's back home in Russia, in blissful ignorance of his daughter's existence. It's just me and her from now on. Anxiety tightens my chest as I realise that the sentiment isn't strictly true. It's me, Saoirse and Maura, which is why I had to get out of the cottage to clear my thoughts. I still can't get over her outburst. The acrid smell of burnt bacon and eggs lingers in the kitchen, along with the chilling memory of Maura's vacant stare.

I gaze down at Doolin, where the colourful cottages seem to huddle together for warmth, strings of smoke mingling with the mist rolling in off the sea. It's a beautiful view. The peak of Misery

Hill seems eerie in comparison and, for the first time since arriving, I feel a shiver of unease standing here. Something tells me that the children from the village didn't visit to trick or treat. But now the focus is on Christmas, and even though it's only November, a couple of premises in Doolin are decorated with twinkling lights. Given that we are in mourning, I don't expect Maura to be very festive this year. I ease myself on to the moss-covered wall that surrounds Maura's dull stone cottage, wincing as I rest my throbbing leg. I fish a stuffed toy rabbit from the pushchair and offer it to Saoirse, admiring her long lashes which frame her sea-blue eyes. Love swells in my heart, then curdles into anxiety. Can I trust Maura with her any more? The red mark on Saoirse's leg has turned into a bruise. An unwelcome thought lingers in my mind. Maura carrying Saoirse out to me, plump tears trickling down my daughter's cheeks. She couldn't have . . . Could she?

I stare at the darkening clouds above, as if they hold answers to Maura's behaviour. It's obvious that she is suffering – the gouges on her arm, the broken vase in her bedroom, the shattered plate left on the floor today. Her expression was eerily empty, unsettling in its hollowness. It was as though she had retreated deep within herself, leaving room for someone else to take the reins.

I glance over my shoulder to the kitchen window where I often see Maura's face. On my way out, I noticed the gouges in the plaster on the inside window ledge. I thought it was wear and tear, but upon closer examination, I realised they were made from fingernails digging in. Most likely Maura's fingernails, which were stained with dried blood when she came out of her room. I tuck the blanket around my daughter, so vulnerable and precious. I need to do something. I slip my phone out of my dungarees pocket and dial the number of the one person who knows my aunt better than anyone.

'Hullo?' Geraldine's concerned voice comes through. It sounds like she's driving and the signal isn't clear.

'Hi, it's Finn, Maura's niece.' I hesitate, glancing up at the window one more time. 'Sorry to trouble you, but I'm worried about Maura. She seems . . . out of sorts.'

'Ah, the poor soul. She's always been troubled.' Geraldine doesn't sound in the least bit surprised.

I chew on my bottom lip, knowing Maura would hate to hear me talking about her. But I can't go inside without speaking to someone about it first. 'I think she's upset because I asked Aiden in for a cup of tea.'

'Aiden? Do you mean Aiden Walsh from the village?'

'Yes, why?' I hear a car radio being turned down as well as a shift in Geraldine's tone.

'Oh, um, well, Maura's not one for spontaneity. She likes her routines.'

I'm well aware of Maura's routines, which have been thrown out of kilter today. 'She's really upset.' I lower my voice. 'She's thrown stuff around.'

Geraldine's tone is that of someone who's heard it all before. 'Sounds like she's in one of her moods. It'll pass in a day or two. Just . . .' She pauses. 'Just give her some space. Maura's not at the wheel today.'

Not at the wheel? My fingers grip my phone. 'Do I need to be worried? Should I stay in Doolin tonight?'

'God, no. Sure, that will make her a thousand times worse. She's really brightened since you've come to stay. Just make sure she takes her medication. She'll be grand in no time.' *Brightened?* I wonder. *What was she like before?*

I exhale sharply as the signal begins to break up. 'What medication?'

'For her nerves. Though it doesn't always help, I'm afraid.'

I want to ask her about Maura's self-harming but the signal is bad and I don't want to be overheard.

'Could she . . .' I glance back at the cottage for the umpteenth time. 'Could she hurt Saoirse?'

Geraldine's reply is instant. 'Oh goodness, no. Only herself, poor dear.' She heaves a hefty sigh and I catch words that don't sound like they're meant for me. 'Maura's no harm to the living, at least.'

I press the phone close to my ear as her voice cuts out. 'Geraldine? You're breaking up.'

'Away . . . the night . . . back . . . tomorrow.' Geraldine's words come intermittently. Then she's gone, the broken signal preventing me from saying any more.

Our conversation has done little to relieve my unease. I have to get my daughter away from this place, but how, when Maura has done so much for me? I feel like I owe her a debt after Mum abandoned her like that. But Mum was a kind and loving person – why did she leave?

Glancing down at the sleeping Saoirse, I make a decision. I won't leave my daughter's side. I'll find out what happened here so I can help Maura and go. Geraldine's voice didn't sound right on the phone – she was clearly reluctant to bring up the past.

I tuck the phone into my pocket as I stand, sucking air between my teeth as I suffer a dart of pain from my leg. It's so bloody frustrating, and makes me feel uncomfortably vulnerable. I grip the pushchair handles, breathing through the pain. The dark peak of Misery Hill casts shadows on the earth as I quietly wheel Saoirse back towards the whitewashed cottage. But it's not white. It's streaked by ugly green stains from the rain leaking through the guttering, and the roof is dotted with thick clumps of moss. The place is suddenly colder, more foreboding. It feels like I'm seeing it for the first time. Just what's going on with Maura? What secrets lurk within these walls?

I pause outside the front door of the cottage listening keenly for signs of life. There is nothing but the sound of the wind and a distant tractor chugging up the road. I slowly turn the knob and open the door, pushing Saoirse ahead of me. The walls are thick stone, providing adequate soundproofing. I'd hate for Maura to have heard my call.

The stink of burnt grease still permeates the air. I miss my modern home in Lincoln, and the sound of the cathedral bells. The place holds so many memories. On Sundays, Mum and I would go to Sudbrooke for a stroll in the woods. Then we'd pop into The Plough in Nettleham for a drink before heading back to the city, where we'd treat ourselves to dinner in the Duke William pub. Mum had built up quite the community for herself. She had friends all over, but few knew of her life in Ireland and she'd avoid the subject when it came up.

My place is back in England, but equally I can't stand to be there without Mum. Being here has given me respite from the worst of my grief. What would Mum say if she were here now? Would she tell me to accept Maura's help, or would she urge me to pack my bags and go?

Blinking, I grow accustomed to the gloom, and stiffen at the quiet shuffling sound behind Maura's door. Maybe if I could find her medication, it might help. My gaze lands on a dresser drawer, slightly ajar. These tall imposing mahogany dressers are in almost every room. I park Saoirse's pushchair and put on the brake. Her chubby cheeks are slapped pink from the cold, but she is content in her slumber, her long black lashes brushing against her face. The ocean air has knocked her out.

The cabinet drawer creaks stiffly on its runners and I stare at the pile of faded newspaper clippings inside. It doesn't surprise me.

This cottage is like a museum of the past. I don't think anything has been thrown out in the last fifty years. I'm about to close the drawer tight when the headlines catch my attention. They all have one thing in common – the tragic accidents on Misery Hill.

A series of questions tumble into my mind. Why has Maura kept these? I gaze in wonder as I realise that these accidents go back to before I was born. So many people have lost their lives on Misery Hill. What was it that Geraldine said? Something about Maura being no harm to the living. I check on my daughter before squinting in the dim light. The newspaper reports on a couple who describe a bright flashing light that made their car come off the road. The article goes on to say that the investigation continues, but something tells me that no explanation was found. My frown deepens as I find another article reported years later that mentions an oil slick on the road. There's movement in Maura's bedroom, and I quickly slip the newspaper clippings back into the drawer. What a macabre collection. I catch a glimpse of the most recent clipping – the article mentions two mothers, with just one surviving child. One of the mothers is me. I can't bear to look at it. It pains me to imagine what the other mum is going through. Life can be so cruel. Why did my baby survive and not hers?

I exhale a shaky breath. It's over – for now. But a sinking feeling tells me that mine won't be the last accident on Misery Hill.

CHAPTER 18

KATHRYN

'Dammit,' I utter to my reflection in the dressing table mirror as I smudge my eyeliner. I'm shaking like an alcoholic with a case of the jitters. Closing my eyes, I take a breath, and count to four before releasing it. I never used to be this nervous at the prospect of speaking to my father, but a lot of water has passed under the bridge. I manage to apply the last touches of make-up, concealing the dark circles beneath my eyes. I smooth over my designer blouse and adjust the skirt which is a little too big for me. I haven't worn make-up since before the accident. Hell, I've barely washed my hair up until now. But today, I have a plan – one that could change everything. Because thanks to the insurance company, I now have the identity of the other woman in the accident – and I know what I must do. They had to be involved in taking my baby. I've spent sleepless hours trying to work it out.

I quickly tidy my room as I prepare to leave. It is lavishly furnished, with the softest carpets and designer wallpaper. Everything has been chosen by my father, a controlling man with an iron grip. He's got decent taste, given where he came from. He's worked hard to better himself since leaving his poverty-stricken background behind. His inability to communicate with his family is something that has passed down to me. It's no wonder my mother is so hard. Any woman with an ounce of sense wouldn't have married him. I prepare myself for our meeting. I've got ten minutes to win him around. I check my reflection. It's amazing what a little bit of make-up can do. Dad has many sayings, some he has heard from others, and some he has claimed as his own. 'Don't just enter the room, own it,' he used to advise my brothers when they lived in the family home. 'Your power should speak volumes before your lips part,' was another. I need to appear in control if I'm to win my father around. Weakness is like blood in the water, and in the Toíbín household, we're all circling sharks.

I can't tell him that I think my baby is alive; he'd have me committed in a flash. I need to go about this differently if I'm going to get my own way. I used to be a daddy's girl, but the moment I hit my teens, everything changed. In his eyes, no man on earth will ever be good enough for me. My hip flask is nestled in the bottom drawer of my dresser table. It's a challenge to find some alone time to fill the thing with Yvonne constantly watching me. Thankfully my father's drinks cabinets are always unlocked, and for now, I can self-medicate with vodka. I prefer whiskey, but there's no masking the smell of a fine malt on your breath.

I stand outside my father's home office door and hesitate before knocking. Our relationship has turned formal since he discovered who I was seeing behind his back. My father is a self-made millionaire, but he didn't get there through honest labour. The high-end furniture in his warehouses has been a useful front. There are many ways to get drugs over the border; packing it in secret compartments in designer Italian furniture is just one.

I've barely knocked before he barks at me to come in. Dad doesn't speak in a neutral tone. He shouts, he roars, he barks, he grumbles. When he gets really angry, his words are laced with spittle as he swears himself breathless.

I push the double doors open, revealing a room heavy with cigar smoke. It's an elaborate space. Like every room in this house, it lacks the cosiness of normal households and is all about show. The walls are lined with photos of Dad shaking hands with all kinds of celebrities, musicians and politicians over the years. There's even a picture of him and his brother Joseph in between the Krays, from when he and Joe lived in England in their younger days. The loss of his brother five years ago hardened him, but left him cautious too. But you live by the sword, you die by the sword. He wasn't shot during a raid, or by a rival gang. No, it was nothing exciting like that. He did it to himself. The gun went off in his hand when he was messing about. His picture hangs on the wall, perhaps as a warning against complacency. My father's office is a testament to that. The floor-to-ceiling bookshelves are filled with law books, which help him stay one step ahead. Dad sits behind the wide Italian designer desk and stubs out his cigar, his piercing gaze fixed on me. I feel sorry for his mistresses, who are younger than me. My father will use violence when he deems it necessary. He doesn't differentiate between men or women. But what about babies? I swallow back my nerves as I exude an illusion of composure.

'Sit down,' he commands.

Obediently, I take a perch on the edge of the leather chair before his desk. Back rigid, I clasp my hands together on my lap. The scent of cigar smoke fills my nostrils and memories of past abuse flood my mind. I remember the last time I lashed out at him, only to be met with a swift punch to the stomach. I never gave him cheek again.

With a deep breath, I gather my strength. 'I want to go back to Doolin.'

My voice betrays me as it wavers. I must be careful with my words, while convincing him to support my plan. The silence in the room is suffocating as he studies me. I feel like a rat in a lab, ready to run the gauntlet for the next piece of cheese. I have a long way to go before he'll forgive me for my indiscretion and I will never forget the cruelty of his words when I lay in my hospital bed.

'Do you, now?' He leans back in his chair, pressing his steepled fingers to his chin.

I convey my thoughts in a steady tone, careful not to reveal too much. I speak of facing my past and finding closure, all the while feeling my father's judgemental gaze. Perhaps by appealing to his own experiences with violence and pain, I can persuade him.

'Imagine reliving your worst memories every day,' I implore, my voice barely above a whisper. 'It's torture.' I meet his cold stare. 'I didn't get to my baby's funeral. And I know that you said she's no loss but . . . I need to say my goodbyes. I need to go back to where she died.' My voice trembles slightly, and this isn't put on. The accident has scarred me, both mentally and physically, for life. I push forward with my plan. 'Two weeks. That's all I need. Long enough for me to come to terms with it.'

'You think that damn village will help you now?' He raises an eyebrow. 'What if it sets you back to square one?' His words aren't said out of concern for me. Everything is about appearances. 'Show them the gold, but not the sweat that polished it,' is another one of his mantras. He wants me back in the limelight, in a united family front.

'It won't be easy,' I admit. 'But my therapist said it would help me move forward.' Thankfully, what's said in my therapist's office is confidential. It's why I chose her. Claudia is one of the few people in our orbit who can't be bought.

My father's eyes narrow, but I continue. 'The flashbacks are unbearable. I keep reliving the accident. It's hell.'

He ponders my words, then finally nods. 'Alright. You can go, but your carer goes too. Two weeks, then I want you home, back to your old self. Understand?'

I exhale the breath that's locked in my lungs. 'Yes . . . thanks,' I whisper, as the first part of my plan clicks into place. The phone rings on his desk and he dismisses me with a flick of the wrist.

My heart is pounding in my chest as I return to my room and power up my laptop. I waste no time booking a cottage in Doolin under Yvonne's name. Hope and fear rise within me in equal measures. My mind is racing with dark thoughts as I allow myself to indulge in the possibility of reuniting with my child. I will do whatever it takes, no matter how twisted or dangerous, to get my daughter back. I am my father's daughter, after all. The details of the plan settle in my mind, my fear replaced with resolve.

The door creaks open, and Yvonne steps into the room. Her owlish eyes peer through her thick glasses beneath her ruler-straight fringe. I'm guessing she's spoken to Dad. It's funny how her posture changes whenever he is around, a subtle sign of fear.

'I hear we're going to Doolin for two weeks.' Her voice is tense as she rests her brown leather handbag on the floor. It's a huge big thing, and it drops to the floor with a clunk.

'Do you want to go?' I ask, looking up from my MacBook Air. I'm asking out of politeness because all my focus is on finding my child.

'Not really.' Yvonne sighs heavily. 'But I've not been given much choice, have I?'

I've begun to notice more of Yvonne's personality emerging lately. These days she seems distant and uncaring, probably due to her recent break-up from her boyfriend of five years. I often pretend to be asleep so I can listen in to her phone conversations. It's amazing what you can glean from a few snatched words. This works in my favour because Yvonne's lack of attention allows me the freedom I need to pursue my plan.

'The break will do you good.' I try to sound sympathetic, but it's a relief to climb out of the depressing hole I've found myself in. Grief has made me weak. I'm taking back control.

Yvonne mutters something under her breath about getting my medication before leaving the room. Alone again, my mind turns to Fionnuala Claffey, the other woman in the accident. She's called Finn, according to my father's sources. She used to live in Lincoln with her mother, who died recently. But I have no sympathy for this woman, because had she not been on Misery Hill that night, none of this would have occurred. There's also a chance that she's rearing my child. I need to see for myself before I will know for sure. And I will know, won't I? A mother's bond is strong. How could I not recognise my own daughter? Because Kiera is alive. The memory of her presence at the scene of the accident has returned even stronger than before. I'm not imagining it. I heard her cry. She was there.

I never wanted children. They didn't fit into my lifestyle. But Kiera made me feel complete. I open my dresser drawer and fish out her small stuffed pink bear. I lift it to my nose, inhaling deeply. The faint scent of my baby still clings to the worn fabric. It's coming to Doolin, along with a few other cherished items for when Kiera is back in my arms. Finn won't see me coming. I'm bringing my baby home.

CHAPTER 19

THEN

MAURA

It took me a long time to convince myself to go through with it. Years, in fact. Jimmy never really got over Daisy, but he did move on. It broke my heart to see him talking to other women. It was only a matter of time until he got wed. I don't know what triggered the plan. I was fed up, I suppose. I couldn't see any future for myself. Not one I wanted, anyway. I was in my early twenties when I built up the courage to go for what I both wanted and deserved. I did not want to be a nursemaid to my parents. Neither did I want to live alone for the rest of my days. And what I did want, was Jimmy, more than anything in the world. I dwelled on the ache of my unreturned affections night and day. Surrendering my feelings for Jimmy wasn't an option yet; in my heart, we were destined to be together, just like in the Mills & Boon novels that lined our bookshelf at home. I clung to the belief that, one day, we would view this as nothing more than a bump in the road. I wanted him enough to make me become my sister to begin with. And for a while, it worked.

I paved the way for that day, being careful not to see Jimmy as I lost the weight I needed to transform. Christmas came and went, and Daisy barely made an appearance, staying for long enough to deliver our presents. Luckily for me, she didn't go into town. It took weeks for me to lose enough weight to pass myself off as her. It wasn't easy but my cravings for sweets and chocolates subsided. Gradually, I got better at applying make-up, and I rang my sister often so I could listen to the tone of her voice. She was always full of chatter, too wrapped up in telling me about her nursing role to be suspicious of my sudden affection. It's funny, I'd never noticed it before. She had all these friends, John and Marie, William and Kerry, and a whole host of others whose names I can't remember, but I instinctively knew that she was homesick too. Not enough to come and visit, but enough that she kept me on the phone. We talked about her hair and make-up, and she gave me her best tips. She asked if I had a boyfriend. I told her not to be silly, that I was just taking care of myself. She said that she was proud of me and I thought that was absurd. Proud of learning how to put rollers in my hair and apply blusher without looking like a clown? I smiled through her condescending chatter and took what I needed to make my plan work.

A week before my planned 'date' I told Geraldine that my sister was coming home for the weekend. Given she was Daisy's number one fan, I knew she wouldn't be able to hold it in. Jimmy was the village doctor, after all. Daisy had changed her phone number so he couldn't contact her back then. I waited until the house was empty and everyone was out. There was a show in the cinema that everyone had to go and see. Even Granny Maura, the miserable old goat. Dad knew how much I valued my time alone in the house and he did not pressure me to accompany them.

That night, I took everything of Daisy's and laid it on the bed. I would become her from the ground up. First, I soaked myself in her favourite bubble bath. Her apple shampoo made my hair smell better than it ever had before. Her conditioner smoothed my wiry strands of hair, and the rollers gave it a wave. My skin felt nice from her lotion and a tiny dab of perfume was enough to help me step into her shoes. The night before, I used a face pack and, thanks to my healthier diet, my skin was clear like hers. I drank lots of water, so my eyes sparkled, and I even took a multivitamin, although it didn't agree with my stomach, so I stopped a few days before I carried out my plan. I painted my toenails the same shade as my sister's and manicured and painted my fingernails too. I had been practising and had got a lot better over the last two weeks. Although Dad was always complaining about the smell of nail polish remover coming from my room. Daisy's clothes hugged my figure, and even her lowest heels made me wobble a little when I walked. I tried not to make it obvious that I was reinventing myself, although one night he asked if I was missing my sister and then mumbled something about twins. I told him I was bored and just playing around with Daisy's things. He gave me a gentle pat on the back and left me to it. My father was a good man, if a little soft. He liked to give hugs, but I drew the line at that. I felt a bit like a dog when he patted me in encouragement and told me I was a 'good girl'. I stopped being a girl when I hit my twenties, as far as I was concerned. I never doubted my father's love. I wanted to find a good man who was kind like him, and Jimmy was the only one who fitted the bill.

I inhaled a sudden breath when I looked at myself in the mirror and saw my sister staring back at me. The people of Doolin wouldn't shut up about how proud they all were of her, especially when she made the newspaper for saving someone's life. They said she went above and beyond, whatever that meant, and I was sick to the teeth of hearing about it.

Jimmy was my future, and I saw us in full colour, him coming home, then to the cottage where it was just the two of us and our three children, two boys and a girl. Everyone would love us. Everyone would love *me* because I was married to him. All the women in the village would be jealous because I ended up with him, the village doctor, no less.

He would be so dedicated to his family, and on his days off he'd bring me and the kids to the beach. We'd have dogs – two of them, and a pony for the kids. They'd get great sport out of that. But I had to make sacrifices first. There was a dark side to my plans. I worried about my soul. I fretted about breaking my Catholic vow of chastity before marriage, but then I told myself there were very few people in Doolin who hadn't broken that. A lifetime of good deeds would make up for it, and if I wasn't with Jimmy, then I didn't want to be with anyone. The thought of living without him scared me more than eternal damnation, if indeed that was a thing. It took several deep breaths for me to rid myself of the tremble in my voice. I told myself that I was stepping into a role. I wasn't Maura, I was Daisy, and I stared at myself in the mirror until I believed that it was true. Then I made the call. I knew that he'd be available, hoping she'd get in touch. Sure enough, he picked up after just two rings of the phone. 'Hullo?'

His deep voice made me weak inside. I took another breath, put on a 'Daisy' smile. 'Hello, Jim. It's me. Are you free to talk?' I didn't have to explain who I was. Nobody spoke like her. And nobody else called him Jim.

'Yeah . . .' He cleared his throat. 'You know I'm always free for you, Daisy.'

It was a little too desperate for my liking. But then again, maybe desperate people don't say no to second best.

'I know it's late notice . . .' I curled my finger around the winding telephone cord just as Daisy used to do. 'But I was wondering, could we meet? In our usual spot on Misery Hill?'

Silence. He either couldn't believe his luck or I was too late. Or maybe he knew that it was me. *Don't say anything,* I told myself, as I listened to him breathe. It was tempting to fill the silence but I forced myself to give him time.

'Alright then,' he replied. 'When?'

'In half an hour.'

'Okay. See you there.'

Our meeting time was sealed. There was no backing out now. I slowly replaced the phone receiver and smoothed over my dress. I tried to swallow but my throat was bone dry. Could I really go through with my plans? I strode into my bedroom and knelt next to my bed, hands clasped in prayer as I squeezed my eyes tightly shut. I said ten Hail Marys and three Our Fathers and I begged for what should have been mine all along.

'I'll live a good life after this,' I promised. 'Please. Please make this work.'

I'd calculated my fertility cycle. I only had one shot.

CHAPTER 20

Finn

My brain feels thick with sleep as I pad into the kitchen in my thick woollen socks. The remnants of last night's worries still haunt my thoughts. Saoirse must have picked up on my unease as she was awake for most of the night too. The same questions keep rising in my mind. Why has Maura kept all those newspaper clippings about Misery Hill? Some of those news articles stretch back for years. Do I know her at all? Sometimes I think that it was a mistake coming here. But then I think of my mother, and how she would have wanted me to reconnect – wouldn't she? What happened between them to make Mum cut off all contact with her twin? I shiver, rubbing my arms against the chill that permeates the room. The range must have gone out, and the radiators have been turned off in an effort to save oil.

'Damn,' I mutter, bending to clean the open fire. Clumps of ash crumble under my fingers as I scoop them out with the dustpan, the cold, dusty remains sticking to my plaid pyjamas. Sighing, I place the lid on the metal bucket. Only now do I realise how much I've been taking her for granted. Maura's been doing this every morning and I've never offered to take over. The weight of the ash bucket sends tiny arrows of pain as I limp to the back door.

I've worked hard on my rehabilitation over the last few weeks by doing all the recommended exercises on my app, but I can't see a time when I'll ever be able to walk normally again. It's a relief to drop the bucket of ash by the back door. The morning is damp and misty as I peer into Maura's unkempt back garden. Thorny bushes erupt from the rocky ground, and at the far end of the rotting fence, I make out the outline of a solitary magpie perching on the barren branches of a tree. One for sorrow . . . The superstitious chant rises in my mind. Up until today, I've only seen seagulls hover around Maura's cottage, and its presence feels like an omen. I throw the bird a wary glance while I make my way to Maura's humble shed, which once housed an outdoor toilet, many years ago. Wasting no time, I carry turf and kindling inside.

The cottage feels even colder when I return, and the hems of my pyjamas are damp as I crouch down. I hesitate before adding a second firelighter to the kindling. Guilt gnaws at me – Maura is frugal, every item rationed and reused. But today, warmth matters more than saving pennies. The state she's in, she'll never know.

Maybe I'm overthinking this. Maura is a hoarder, after all. She kept the shop receipts for Saoirse's things because she can't throw anything away. But then again, the cottage is usually clean and she sticks to a routine. It's not like her to abandon the housekeeping. Everything feels off-kilter without her at the helm.

'I'll make some tea,' I whisper, as if saying the words too loud will disturb the fragile balance of the cottage. Then I set to lighting the range. Maura's got her own peat bog so there's no need to spare the turf. Soon, the kettle is softly whistling, steam curling around the numerous teapots perched on the shelves. My hands move mechanically, pouring water into a small red teapot. I wait for it to brew.

I glance around the kitchen, which holds the power to transport me back in time. Thick wooden furniture, sturdy and worn, anchors the room. Cupboards overflow with relics from decades past. There's an unfinished Rubik's Cube in the drawer, and gold-trimmed plates featuring Ireland's numerous visits from different popes. Records by Daniel O'Donnell fill the shelves in the corner of the room next to an old-fashioned record player which is housed in a bright orange box. It's still in working order, although you have to lift the needle to gently rest it on the record as the mechanism is stiff. I imagine Maura, sitting at the table, tapping her sensible black leather shoe against the worn grey flagstones as she drinks her tea. What is life like for her, alone and cut off from the villagers? I don't know much about Mum's past, but she had a happy childhood with friends in the village, of that I'm aware. Has Maura always been like this?

I remember the way she looked at me and Saoirse yesterday, the intensity of her gaze palpable. I can't help but shudder. If looks could kill . . . *Stop being so melodramatic,* I scold myself, as I approach Maura's bedroom.

'Knock-knock,' I say softly. My knuckles tap lightly on her thick wooden door.

But no response comes. Panic rises in my chest. What if she's hurt herself? A chill sweeps through me as my imagination conjures up an image of her lying on her bed, wrists cut.

'Maura?' I wait, praying for a reply. I sigh in relief when I hear a thump, then the sound of footsteps from within.

A lock is turned and the door creaks open, revealing Maura in a dishevelled state. Her usual neat appearance has given way to a mess of tangled hair, bloodshot eyes, and the slight taint of body odour rises from the clothes that she has obviously slept in. I take in my aunt's haggard appearance, wishing Mum was here because she'd know what to do.

'Maura? Are you okay?'

Maura stares without seeing, her pinprick pupils betraying her medicated state. Fear gives way to concern when I realise she is barely coherent.

'Have you taken your medication, Maura?'

I wait for the backlash but there's none. Maura is a private person. She'd want to know who told me about her meds.

She nods robotically, her movements slow and uncoordinated. 'Had to.'

A sliver of drool leaves the corner of her chapped lips and she wipes it away.

Okay. I can help her when she's calm.

'Come on.' My voice is laced with compassion. 'Let's go into the kitchen. I'll make you some breakfast. You look like you need it.'

Maura takes my arm like a three-year-old who has lost her mother in the supermarket. Her movements are uncoordinated and she walks in a drunken fashion. We shuffle through the cottage, me with my limp, her in a drug-induced state. What a pair we make.

The kitchen is comfortably warm now, and I guide Maura to a chair and encourage her to sit. Soon I've whipped up a plate of creamy scrambled eggs and hot buttered toast, steaming and inviting, to go with the tea that I've topped up. I leave her long enough to check up on Saoirse, who snoozes contentedly in her cot.

When I return, Maura's plate is clean and she looks a little brighter. She blinks as I approach, slowly emerging from her haze.

'The babby?' she mumbles, her voice weak. 'Is she . . .' She looks at me earnestly, emotion returning to her eyes. 'Is she alright?'

'Saoirse's fine.' I'm happy to reassure her if it helps. I recall Geraldine's comment about Maura not being at the wheel before. What did she mean? Relief washes over Maura's face after I tell her that Saoirse is sleeping because she was awake most of the night.

Maura's chin trembles and I can see that she's fighting tears. In that moment, I make the connection. She is the other half of my mother that I never got to see. Mum didn't get into bad moods. She never seemed to worry about anything. She got through life with a smile, loved being in company and always encouraged me to be the best that I could be. It's like Maura took on all the negativity and sorrow so Mum could lead a happy life. Perhaps that's why Mum never returned to this place.

'What's wrong, Maura?' I say, because it's probably been a very long time since someone asked her that.

I've watched Maura interact with the townsfolk of Doolin on the rare occasion that myself and Saoirse accompanied her into town. It's strange, how they ignore her bad manners as she snaps at them. It's like they all hold a shared secret. They know that Maura's behaviour is wrong but in her case, they make exceptions.

'I'm just glad you're . . . both alright,' Maura sobs, her voice barely audible. 'You *are* alright, aren't you?' Her eyes are filled with such sorrow and regret that it almost takes my breath away. I nod, my own emotions threatening to surface.

'Yes, we're fine. More than fine. And *I'm* going to take care of *you* now.'

I hand Maura a tissue and she dabs at her tears. I can't help but feel a sense of responsibility for my aunt, this woman who is like my mother in appearance but so different in spirit. As Maura sips her second mug of tea, I silently vow to do everything in my power to heal the wounds that have driven her to such a desperate state. That starts with finding out just what the hell went on with Maura in this house on Misery Hill.

CHAPTER 21

KATHRYN

The winding cliffside road unfurls before us like a serpent. I grip the passenger door handle while memories of my car crash merge with the gloomy scenery. Doesn't the sun ever shine in this godforsaken place?

'You alright?' Yvonne asks, not taking her eyes off the road. Her nose is almost touching the steering wheel as she grips it.

'I'm fine,' I say through gritted teeth. But my stomach is churning with anticipation. Kiera is out there somewhere. I know it. As my memory strengthens, all I can hear is the sound of her cry. I'm relieved that we won't be driving up the hill today. Yvonne has talked for most of the journey, relaying her relationship woes. Joseph, her ex-boyfriend, is seeing someone else. I've counselled her as we drove, not because I particularly cared, but because a change of subject has helped keep my nerves at bay. I need a drink to ease my growing anxiety, but we are almost in Doolin and I breathe long and slow, determined to keep myself in the present moment.

Doolin emerges around the bend, quaint and picturesque. I scan the hills and cottages. Do any of the people living there know where my baby is? The voice of the satnav delivers another command, bringing us to our rental home near the foot of Misery Hill. It's situated at the edge of the small village, a short walk from the shops but far enough from the pubs to provide peace. Yvonne parks the car next to the pavement and starts unloading our bags. I get out and stretch my legs, recalling the dark days when I wished that I'd gone over the cliff with my baby on the evening of the crash. But now fragile hope burns in my chest. No, not hope. A knowing. I *know* she's alive and I'm getting her back, whatever it takes.

My gaze drifts up to Misery Hill. There, swaddled in mist, perches a lone thatched cottage. The current home of Finn Claffey, if the insurance documents are correct. Is that where they're keeping my baby?

Yvonne's voice snaps me back to reality. 'Are you coming in? Looks like rain.'

Dutifully, I follow her into the two-bedroom cottage, fists clenched. Nobody is keeping me from my child. My heart burns with anger and possessiveness. I'm still a Toíbín, and Toíbíns don't share. Whoever took my baby doesn't know who they're dealing with. But they will, soon enough.

'Well now.' Yvonne gives me a rare smile as she wheels our suitcases to one side. 'This is nice.' With its plush sofas and soft woven throws, the living room exudes warmth. An open fireplace stands in the heart of the room, the mantelpiece above a collage of homeliness – framed photos, scented candles and the odd religious relic. The windows, framed by thick patterned curtains, offer views of the street. I walk into the newly renovated kitchen, which is decorated with framed floral prints and a vase of fresh flowers on the table, next to the welcome pack of milk, eggs, coffee, tea and bread.

'Yes, it will do,' I eventually reply. My mind is taken up with plans. 'Yvonne.' I turn towards her. 'I want some freedom while we're here.'

She hesitates. 'I . . . I don't know if that's a good idea . . .'

'Look.' I rest my phone and purse on the table. 'I'm quite happy to leave these here when I pop out. It's not as if I'll get far without them now, is it?'

Yvonne nibbles on her bottom lip. I imagine Dad issuing stern instructions not to let me out of her sight.

'My father isn't here, Yvonne,' I continue. 'You deserve a break after the hours you've been putting in.'

She looks at me, torn between her need for respite and her duty to monitor me. Finally, she nods.

'Well, I won't say it hasn't been tough.'

'That's settled then.' I smile. 'There's money in my purse. Get some wine and snacks from that supermarket down the road. We'll have a girly night in.'

She doesn't need much persuading. I slip out of the cottage just as she gets back. 'To clear my head,' I tell her as I greet her in the hall. I don't expect to find out anything straight away. I'll extend my stay if I have to. As long as Yvonne is saying all the right things, Dad will be happy.

'It's getting dark.' She looks at me with magnified eyes. Her glasses are starting to steam up, and I hear the clink of two bottles as she rests her bag of groceries on the floor. 'Why don't you stay in tonight? We can check out that Beckham documentary on Netflix. I've been meaning to watch it for months.'

'Dad's called, hasn't he?'

There's new caution in her eyes. She takes off her glasses and cleans them with the sleeve of her thick woollen cardigan. 'He was just checking that we got here okay. Your dad cares about you, Kathryn. I told him we were having a night in.'

'And we will.' I pat her on the arm. 'It's a lot . . . coming here. I just need an hour to clear my head.'

I could just walk out, but I wait for her approval. I need to keep her on side for what I've planned.

'Alright.' She presses her glasses back on to her face. 'I'll stick a pizza in the oven. Don't be long.'

The village of Doolin is tiny compared to my home in Dublin, but the countryside surrounding it is so vast. Its craggy, mountainous landscape is so different to my Dublin abode. Everything is scattered. There are a string of pubs down the road, a few restaurants, a couple of hotels. Some brightly painted buildings add a splash of colour. The pier is on the western edge of Doolin, about a kilometre away. There's a ferry that takes people to the Cliffs of Moher, and a campsite up the road from here. But it's what lies on the side of Misery Hill that interests me the most. A cloud of mist is settling over the village and I stare up at the small cube of glowing light coming from the cottage.

'Can I bring sweets for the baby?'

I'm shaken out of my thoughts as a little girl walks past. Instinctively, I follow as she chatters excitedly. She's strikingly pretty with shiny black hair. I'm guessing she's six or seven, and she skips along as she holds her dad's hand.

'Saoirse's too little for sweets,' the man chuckles, and his words make my heart skip a beat. 'Hullo,' the man says, as he passes me, and I'm so taken aback that I barely manage a smile and a nod of acknowledgement. I always forget how much friendlier people are in the countryside.

'But why?' the little girl replies to her father, filled with the curiosity of a child. 'Why can't she have sweets? What about marshmallows?'

'You only want them for yourself,' her father laughs, as their voices fade.

Slowly, I follow them in the opposite direction of Misery Hill. Saoirse is the name of the surviving baby – at least, that's what people have been led to believe. This can't be a coincidence.

'When can I see her, Daddy?' The little girl tugs on his hand.

'I told you. Tomorrow. I need to ask Finn first.'

Finn. The name of the other mother. The one who walked away with *my* child. The thought hits me like a bolt of lightning as every instinct screams at me that this is the case. Because I can feel Kiera's presence. It's all around me. The pull is strong. If only I'd stayed conscious, I would have been awake when they pulled us from the wreckage. But the paramedics couldn't have mixed up our babies. The other infant died. So who? And how? Did Finn swap our babies? But she was in hospital too. My head is buzzing with questions. The man and his daughter cross the road, and I watch as he gets her into the car. He throws a cautious glance in my direction and I break my stare and look away.

I should keep walking, but I can't, because I'm shaking with fury. Anger consumes me when I think of the pain of my grief that I've suffered since the accident. Grief for my Kiera. Grief for moments like these between a parent and child that somebody has snatched away. Grief for the child that was fathered by the first man I've ever loved. That accident wasn't my fault, it was Finn who crashed into me. And now she's taken my child. It must be her. Only one baby survived that day. Not Saoirse. Kiera. I'm bringing my baby home. And whatever way you look at it, someone has to pay.

CHAPTER 22

Finn

The early evening sky hangs heavy with grey clouds, casting a murky pallor over the landscape. I limp outside, my pain evident in every step. My meds make my head too foggy, and I need to be focused now. Up until recently, I've trusted Maura when she's handed me my tablets, but now, I'm wondering if they're the right dose. I don't want to become hooked. What use will I be to Saoirse then? I've spent the day caring for both my daughter and my aunt – feeding and changing Saoirse, then gently encouraging Maura to wash, and changing the dressings on her arm.

As Saoirse played happily in her travel cot in the living room, I asked Maura about her injuries. I'm not going to be like the villagers, ignoring what's in front of me. But Maura simply shrugged. At least she allowed me to help her dry her hair and provide her with fresh, clean clothes. After eating some reheated chicken soup from the fridge, she said she was going back to bed, and barely lifted her feet as she shuffled back to her room. I set to work laundering the soiled garments in the old-fashioned twin tub washing machine in the kitchen.

It's grown dark in the cottage already, and I've lit every lamp in the living room to chase the shadows away. Supplies are running low, but with Geraldine away, I can't leave Maura and Saoirse alone to fetch what we need. Even if my leg didn't hinder my ability to drive, I couldn't face getting behind the wheel. Not yet.

I stare out of the window of the little cottage, wishing we were nearer to town. It's a twenty-minute walk to the shops for regular people, but for me, it feels like a lifetime away. I touch the claw-like grooves on the windowsill and an involuntary shudder runs down my spine. I resolve to call Aiden. He's texted me a couple of times, offering to help.

'Howeya, Finn.' Aiden answers on the second call. His soft Cork accent is warm and cheerful. 'How's it going?'

'Oh, you know, not so bad.' I inhale a small, sharp breath as a bolt of pain shoots up my leg. 'Actually . . .' I pause. 'I hate to ask, but could you spare me a few minutes today?'

'Sure thing. I was going to call in on you to see if you needed a hand getting any messages. How are things up there on Misery Hill?'

In Ireland, messages mean groceries, and I'm grateful for his response. 'Not great, if I'm honest. Maura isn't well, and I'm almost out of food. Would you mind bringing up some bread, eggs, milk, sugar and a packet of ham? I was hoping to make ham and tomato sandwiches for tea. Geraldine's not about, so I don't know who else to ask.'

'Sure thing,' Aiden replies kindly. 'Can I bring Joy along? She has a thing for babies. She's dying to meet the little one.'

I don't expect this. I hesitate, not wanting to upset Maura but unable to say no. 'Yeah, of course. I'd love to meet her.' We should be undisturbed. Maura took a strong sleeping tablet after her soup. I run a hand over my hair. I must look a state. 'Just be careful driving up the hill. The mist is coming down,' I add as an after-thought. Misery Hill is not claiming any more souls. Not today.

Aiden responds with a chuckle as he calls me 'an outsider' telling him to drive carefully in a place he's lived in all of his life. I'm not sure what to make of his tone as the humour seems to leave his voice. Is that what it's like in Doolin?

I search the corridors of my memories for clues as to why Mum left this place. She said it was because of me, that she'd had to keep her pregnancy a secret because she was an unmarried mother. Was she scared that the people of Doolin might turn on her? But they seem so nice. Mum never married, but she had a few male friends over the years. Always successful men, often married too. Once I asked her why she never got married and she said that no man could make her as happy as when it was just us. God, I miss her so much that it hurts.

Saoirse has fallen asleep, still clutching her soft chew toy. I gently rest a blanket over her tummy, and watch as her legs twitch. Do babies dream? Is she reliving the accident? I hope she doesn't carry the trauma for the rest of her life. Gratitude flows through me at the sight of her. She's alive, and that's all that counts. I return to the window and the foreboding sky. I hope Maura doesn't spot Aiden's car – she was so weird about him last time, but she's fast asleep now . . . I think. I smile as a text comes in from my friend Taylor. He's off to some big hairdressing convention in the States and I quickly text him a reply, wishing him the best.

Anxiously, I watch Aiden's car approach along the winding road to Misery Hill.

'Here goes nothing,' I mutter under my breath, absently running my fingers over the grooves in the plaster Maura had left behind. In this moment, I feel a strange bond with my troubled aunt. She may not be my mother but she's a living reminder that I'm not prepared to let go. The cadence of her voice is flat and steady, while Mum's speech bubbled with vivacity and warmth. Maura's fashion choices speak of times past, and as for her eccentricities . . . they are unique to her alone. But her eyes . . . they're the mirror image of Mum's. Sometimes when Maura is talking to me, I allow myself a few precious moments to believe that Mum is back in my life.

Rain patters against the small, deep-set windows. We get rain and mist in Lincoln, but not to this extent. As Aiden parks up on the gravel drive outside, I can't help but feel nervous about having him here. I'm tempted to ask him what he thinks about Maura's reaction from when he was here before, but I don't want to put him off as he's a lifeline right now. If Maura wants me to stay, she can't stop me from making friends. I run my fingers through my hair, which is unruly but clean. It's the one thing about myself that I'm happy with.

Aiden's smile is warm as I open the door to greet him. He's carrying two bags of shopping and his daughter is at his side.

'Come in,' I say, my voice low. It's not Saoirse I'm worried about waking, it's Maura.

Aiden must be feeling it too, as he glances cautiously inside.

'She's in bed,' I say, and watch him visibly relax.

'This is Joy.' He nods at the little girl. 'Say hello, Joy.'

She giggles at the instruction. 'Hello, Joy!' she says, delivering the most adorable smile.

'Nice to meet you, Joy,' I say, as she studies the room with wide, curious eyes. Her silky black hair is pulled into a neat ponytail. Her inquisitive nature is evident as she issues a series of quick-fire questions. 'Is that a real fireplace? Why are the windows so small? What's that smell? Where's the baby?' She gasps when she catches sight of the travel cot in the corner of the room. 'Oh! Is she asleep? Can I hold her?'

'Joy, let Finn catch her breath, okay?' Aiden gently chides his daughter. 'C'mon. Into the kitchen with you first.'

'She's okay,' I say, but Aiden hands me a bag. 'I'd keep an eye on her. She thinks babies are like dolls.'

'I'm not silly, Daddy,' Joy protests, following us into the kitchen.

Aiden sets down the groceries on the worn wooden table. 'If there's anything else you need, you only have to ask.'

'You're a star, thanks.' I glance at the bags. 'How much do I owe you?'

He waves a dismissive hand. 'Won't hear tell of it. Just happy to help.'

'No, I can't let you . . .' But my argument is dismissed.

'Come to the pub some evening and you can buy me a drink,' he eventually relents.

'Would you like a cup of tea?' I ask, putting the kettle on the range. He nods and I look to his daughter. 'And what about you, Joy? Would you like some squash?'

'Yes, please!' Joy says with great enthusiasm. She glances down at her pink corduroy skirt, her eyes brightening as she returns my gaze. 'Do you like my outfit? Daddy bought it in Dunnes Stores.'

'I love it,' I replied, grinning. 'Especially those mini Doc Martens. You're very cool.'

'Thanks!' Her face lights up. 'You're pretty.'

I grin. 'That's lovely of you to say.' I can see why Aiden called her Joy – she radiates happiness and warmth.

Aiden ushers me to sit down while he prepares the tea, along with sandwiches and a Victoria sponge cake he's bought from the local shops. Their freshly baked homemade products are so much nicer than supermarket processed food. I peep in on Saoirse, and put some turf on the fire. When I return, Aiden and Joy are sitting at the table with a gorgeous spread of food before them. The homely scene makes me melt a little bit inside. It's nice to be able to sit and relax before Saoirse awakes.

'Do you like cake? I like cake. I don't like butter icing though. Do you like butter icing?'

I answer Joy's questions and Aiden gives me an apologetic smile.

As we eat, Joy chats animatedly about her day at school, mentioning how Carly O'Connell had told her she couldn't sing. 'But I *can* sing,' she insists. 'I don't know why she's so mean.'

Aiden and I exchange amused glances before he addresses his daughter. 'You're right, Joy. You have a beautiful voice. Don't listen to anyone who tries to tell you otherwise.'

'Thanks, Daddy.' She beams. 'Can I hold the baby now?'

'Finish your cake.' Aiden pushes the plate towards her. His gaze is filled with love and pride while he talks to me about his daughter and how well she's doing in school. I don't know how her mother could leave such an adorable little girl, but it's not my place to ask why.

By the time we've finished our tea, Saoirse is awake. I check my watch. It's gone six o'clock. There's no sign of Maura and Saoirse is due a feed. I allow Joy to help as I go through the motions of feeding and changing my baby. She is completely enamoured by my little girl. As Aiden and I talk, my thoughts wander to Maura, who is now snoring in her room. What was it about this place that made her so unhappy?

'Everything okay, Finn?' Aiden asks, concern etched on his face. Saoirse is on her playmat, and Joy is giggling as she chews her toy.

'Uh, yeah. Everything's fine,' I lie, trying to hide my trepidation about digging up the past. But as I look into Aiden's eyes, I know that if I want to help Maura, I need answers – even if my questions are uncomfortable to voice.

Aiden studies my face, sensing the concern in my expression. 'C'mon now, what's wrong?' His voice is gentle and full of genuine worry.

I hesitate, unsure of how to put my thoughts into words. 'It's just . . . Maura,' I begin. 'She's been really down lately, and I can't help but feel like there's something more going on. It feels like everyone knows some big secret about her, except for me.' Frustration creeps into my voice. 'And I don't understand why people are so kind to her when she's rude and snappy in return.'

Aiden nods thoughtfully.

Lowering my voice, I continue to confide in Aiden. 'She's very insecure, and she doesn't want me making friends. She was upset after you left the last time you were here.' I glance over at Joy, who is reading a cloth book to Saoirse, oblivious to our conversation. 'I've lost my independence. I'm stuck here. I can't drive or go home to England while Maura's in this state. I want to help her, but I don't know what to do.' Pausing, I look at Aiden apologetically. 'Sorry, I didn't mean to unload all of this on you. I don't know who else to talk to.'

'Hey, sure there's no need to apologise,' Aiden reassures me, his eyes warm and understanding. He sighs, and I can see the weight of something troubling him. After a moment, he seems to come to a decision. 'I didn't think it was my place to say anything . . .' He casts an eye over his daughter, who is animatedly chatting to Saoirse.

Satisfied she's not listening, he returns his attention to me. 'There's something you need to know.'

CHAPTER 23

THEN

MAURA

I thought my heart would explode as I caught sight of Jimmy, driving up towards Misery Hill. I was shaking so hard that I thought I'd have to take one of Granny Maura's diazepam to calm myself down. The small white tablets rattled in my bag, hidden in their sepia container. Sometimes my feelings got so big that I'd take one of her sleeping tablets before bed. She wouldn't miss them. She was always stockpiling medication, making out she'd lost them so she could get more. I held on tight to my bag while Jimmy's car approached our spot on the hill. Only it wasn't my bag, it was Daisy's. And as I closed my eyes against the glare of Jimmy's headlights, I fell into the role.

Hands in pockets, Jimmy ambled towards me, his expression impossible to read. 'You alright?' he said, in a way he'd never spoken to me before.

'I'm fine,' I said, in my sister's voice. 'Why wouldn't I be?' I bit my bottom lip. Those were my words, too defensive to come from Daisy.

'You look tired, that's all.' It wasn't the grand declaration of love that I had hoped for. 'How's work?' he said, then continued to ask about my nursing role.

As my heart skipped a beat, I reminded myself that he was talking to Daisy, not me. I took a breath, being careful not to stutter as I imagined what my sister would say. 'Same as usual. The hours are long, the pay a pittance.' A Daisy-like smile rose to my lips. 'But no two days are the same, and I work with some great characters. Anyway . . .' I touched his arm. 'I didn't ask you up here to talk about work.' I giggled in a way only Daisy could. 'It's almost Valentine's Day . . . It made me think of you.' I looked at him coyly, from under my fringe. 'Are you still mad at me, Jim? After all this time? I can't bear it.'

The expression on his face changed as his feelings were laid bare. 'You hurt me, Daisy, breaking it off like that.'

I had my answer ready. 'I did it to be kind. I didn't think a long-distance relationship would work.'

'So you're not seeing anyone?'

The flicker of hope in his eyes almost made me feel sorry for him. 'I tried . . .' I sighed, because everyone knew that Daisy couldn't be on her own for long. 'But nobody compared to you.' I inched closer to him as he leaned against his car. I yearned so much for this man that I could barely breathe. This was my whole reason for being Daisy. It gave me licence to touch him, something I could never have done as myself. 'What about you?' My heart pounded as I ran a hand over his muscled chest. Even with his thick jumper, I could feel his toned torso and it took every effort to hold myself back. He must have felt it too.

'There *is* someone. We're going steady . . .' he began, but I didn't want to hear that as I pushed myself against him. I forced myself to stay calm, because I knew I could be rough and impetuous in comparison to my sister's gentle ways. *Slow down. Let him*

116

come to you, I told myself. I watched his expression change while an internal struggle seemed to take place. At last, Jimmy relented with a sigh.

'But it's always been you,' he said, cupping my cheek. 'Only you.' And I could have cried in that moment, had he not been speaking to me. At last, Jimmy Walsh would be mine.

'You're freezing,' he said softly. 'Do you want to get in the car?' And as he looked at the back seat, I knew what it meant. His eyes were so full of hope, and I was only too happy to give him what he wanted.

I nodded, allowing him to guide me on to the back seat. The kissing was nice, but I have to say I didn't care for the rest of it. I got discomfort, a little pain, and a lot of awkwardness. Once it was over, I couldn't see what the big deal was all about. I was expecting fireworks and explosions and all I got was a damp patch. But there had been a connection, and when it was over, I straightened up, fixed my hair and smiled.

'Do you love me, Jimmy?' I reached over to stroke his smooth face.

'You know I do. I always have. But I never said it because I didn't want to scare you off.' He exhaled a long breath, and seemed happy to get it off his chest. 'I've missed you, Daisy. But you can't just click your fingers and expect me to come running. I have a life too.'

I allowed myself a smile because that was exactly what he had done.

'It nearly broke me,' Jimmy continued, staring at his hands.

'You don't have to miss me any more. I'm not going anywhere.' I was testing the waters, seeing if he realised what was really going on. I told myself that perhaps he knew all along.

'Don't you have to go back to Limerick?' The wind whistled through the window of the car as he put the question to me. 'I mean, as much as I want to have you here, your job is important too.'

I couldn't help but grimace. My sister didn't deserve this man's love. I shifted in my seat. 'There won't be any Limerick. I'll always be here with you.' I rested my hand on his knee. 'We can be together now. You'll never be alone again.'

Looking back, I know where I went wrong. I fell back into my ordinary way of speaking. I forgot to use that sing-song voice of my sister's that used to drive me up the wall. Because he stared at me – I mean, really stared, and then his mouth dropped open. He knew my sister wouldn't speak those words. She was never into commitment. Granny Maura called her a 'fly by night', even though she was holding down a good job.

I'll never forget the look on Jimmy's face as he stared at me in horror. He just kept staring, and I didn't know what to say. Tears blurred my vision because I knew what was coming next.

It was too late to back out now. 'I love you, Jimmy,' I said, trying to win him around. 'I'll always love you.'

'No.' He uttered that single, damning word. His rejection was like a knife to my heart.

'No,' he repeated, hurriedly buttoning up his shirt. 'You're not . . .' He closed his mouth and opened it again. He was back, staring at me once more, making me uncomfortable in my skin. He finally pulled himself together. 'You're not Daisy, are you? You're Maura.'

I mirrored his actions as I hastily fixed my clothes. 'And what if I am? I found you before she did.' Then I told him about the day that he rescued the hedgehog, and he stared at me, head tilted, as if I was mad.

'No,' he continued. 'This isn't right. Why are you dressed in Daisy's clothes?' His eyes raked my body. 'Is this what you came here for? Because I never would have . . .'

His words were left hanging in the air and, little by little, all that was good and warm inside me shattered into a thousand pieces like someone had stood on glass and crushed it beneath their foot.

But I wasn't ready to give up yet. 'I can be just like her,' I said. 'Please, Jimmy, I'll be whatever you want me to be.'

But he was shaking his head. 'Look . . .' He ran a hand through hair that I had tousled just moments before. 'I'm sorry. We shouldn't have done that. Was it your first time?' He groaned, then rolled his eyes to the back of his head. 'Oh God, of course it was. Jesus Christ, Maura!'

I jumped as he punched the seat in front with force. 'What the fuck have we just done?' Miserably, he pulled at the car door and got out. Cold wind scooped the smell of our bodies from the car and replaced it with salty sea air. I opened the car door, feeling shaky as I stood on solid ground. I'd never heard him swear, and I didn't like such words leaving his mouth.

'You never would've come here otherwise,' I said, trying to excuse what I'd done. 'We had a nice time, didn't we? If you loved my sister, why can't you love me? What's wrong with that?'

Jimmy's response was instant. 'Everything is wrong with that, and if you can't see it then you're not right in the head!' He was shouting at me from across the car, backing off every time I came near.

Sadness turned to anger as he said the last thing that I could bear to hear. I clenched my fists and punched the bonnet of his car. 'Don't you call me mad!' I bellowed.

He screamed something about denting his beloved car, but I barely heard his words, I was so consumed with fury as my world turned on its side. 'Do you hear me?' I screamed then, venting my frustration. 'If you ever say that to me again, I'll punch your lights out!' And I would.

'Alright, calm down.' As he pulled his car keys from his pocket, Jimmy took two steps back. 'It was a misunderstanding, that's all. Maura . . .' He squeezed my arm. 'We can never talk about this again.'

'But, Jimmy—' I began. He turned on me and held me by the shoulders to force me to listen. But this wasn't a comforting hold. It was a tight grip, and I didn't like it.

'This was a mistake,' he continued. 'I feel terrible. But you shouldn't have pretended to be your sister. It was cruel and nasty and vindictive and I could never be with someone like you.' I tried to pull away, but he stood there, squeezing my shoulders as he drove his point home. 'Don't talk to me again. Don't ring me and don't tell *anyone* what happened here tonight, because if you do, I will tell them what you did.' He raised an eyebrow, nostrils flaring as he glared at me. 'You know what they're like in the village – you'll be gossiped about for all time.'

I hadn't thought this through. My parents would have been so ashamed.

'Fine!' I shouted. 'You're a bastard, Jimmy Walsh. I never want to speak to you again!'

It was the first time I'd sworn aloud, a raw and unfiltered response to the sting of rejection. It wouldn't be the last. As Jimmy and I locked eyes, there was a wordless exchange, a damning finality. When he turned his back, his silence sliced through me sharper than any goodbye.

CHAPTER 24

FINN

Half an hour has passed since Aiden was about to open up to me. Joy is a delight, but her interruption couldn't have come at a worse time. I've enjoyed getting to know her but, selfishly, I want the answers he can't give while she's by his side. I've put Saoirse in her bouncer and managed to find some cartoons on Maura's old-fashioned video cassette player. Joy is mesmerised before the screen, one hand on the bouncer as she gently rocks my daughter.

'She's a credit to you,' I say to Aiden as we settle back on the sofa, watching them both. 'Aiden . . .' I give him an imploring look. 'You were about to tell me about Maura.' He's been here a while and I'm worried she might wake up.

He heaves a resigned sigh and crosses his legs. It's nice to have a new friend. My world feels a little less lonely than it did before.

'Maura's parents – your grandparents – were amazing people,' he begins. 'Kind-hearted, generous and loved by all. They did a lot for charity, and at Christmas they took in anyone who needed a seat at the table. This place was a lot different back then.'

I imagine the contrast between that happy scene and the current gloomy state of the cottage. 'That sounds exactly like my mum.' My voice is tinged with nostalgia. She loved Christmas and often took people in.

'Aye. I'm sure. But according to my dad, the place changed after your mam moved out. Your great-grandmother Maura died. Then your grandparents fell ill, and Maura was left to care for them both.' Aiden's tone grows sombre. It's obviously something that he's discussed with his dad. 'Then Maura's father passed away, and her mam became bedridden. People tried to help, but Maura wouldn't let anyone in. She became her full-time carer, and the village rallied around her, leaving food on the doorstep when she wouldn't open the door.'

I feel ashamed that I didn't know any of this. I'm also surprised that Mum would abandon her parents in favour of her job. I steady myself as I listen, because I don't know the truth. I nod at Aiden to continue. His daughter coos at Saoirse, who seems enamoured by her new friend.

'She's always wanted a little sister.' Aiden speaks with more than a hint of regret in his voice. I want to ask about his wife, but this isn't the time. 'Where were we?' he says, as the clock on the wall passes the hour. The air is turning cold and rain pats against the windowpane outside.

'Maura was a full-time carer,' I prompt.

'Oh yeah, that's right. She was. Eventually, her mother passed away too. Maura wasn't the same after that. But everyone remembered the kindness of her parents and, for their sake, kept an eye out for her.' He trails off, his story coming to an end.

But this doesn't explain everything. 'What else happened, Aiden? What are you keeping from me?'

Aiden hesitates, glancing briefly at Joy to make sure she's not listening. He lowers his tone and leans in so close that I can barely concentrate on his words. 'I don't want to be disrespect-ful. But there are . . . rumours.' He sighs, rubbing the back of his neck.

'Go on.' Time is running out. I need answers now. But I don't expect what comes next.

'There are a lot of car crashes on Misery Hill. The steep, wind-ing road and the fog that comes down can make it dangerous.' He gives me a regretful look. 'But of course, I don't need to tell you that.'

A sense of dread rises within me. Is he implying that Maura has something to do with the accidents? 'Go on,' I say, because as much as I hate talking about that cursed hill, I need to know what he's getting at.

'Apparently,' he says cautiously, 'Maura is usually the first on the scene of an accident. She doesn't always call the police. People say . . .' Aiden crosses his long legs once more as he shifts on the sofa. This isn't easy for him. 'Well . . . they say that she harvests things from the crashes. Some call her The Reaper.'

To my surprise, I find myself exhaling a breath of relief. It isn't quite what I'd feared, and the tension drains from my shoulders.

Aiden raises an eyebrow, studying me. 'You're taking this better than I thought.'

My voice is just above a whisper. 'I was worried you were going to say she *caused* the accidents.'

'God, no!' Aiden shakes his head. 'There wouldn't be so many crashes if the drivers weren't all heading to Lover's Leap.'

'Lover's Leap?'

I inhale the spice of Aiden's aftershave as he leans in a little closer still. 'It's a beauty spot further up from here. It has a look-out point and stunning scenery, but lots of people drive up there to . . . well, have it off. It was named Lover's Leap because of some unrequited love story years ago. Apparently some spurned woman jumped off the cliff and killed herself.'

'Ah. Okay. Never a dull moment around here.' I imagine Maura standing at the window, watching people drive to the secret rendezvous.

Aiden's face clouds over. 'My wife, Chantana . . . She used to visit Lover's Leap. That's where she had her . . . affair.'

A sudden wave of compassion washes over me. He's referenced his wife once already. 'Need to talk about it?' I offer. 'You must miss her.' I speak quietly, careful not to disturb Joy.

I'm not surprised when he nods. 'Yeah, I do, despite everything. I should have known she'd never settle in Doolin. It was too much of a culture shock. She used to work in a bank in Pattaya. That's how we met.' A sad smile rests on his face. 'People around here are so ignorant sometimes. They all said she was a mail-order bride.'

I snort in response. 'That's pretty outdated. Do such things even exist?'

Aiden shrugs. 'I was travelling around Thailand for a month. We dated, and after I came home, we kept in touch. I went out there a few more times, and a year after we got married. I suppose things moved pretty fast.'

'And she came to live in Doolin?' I ask, feeling the edge of his pain.

Aiden nodded. 'She got pregnant fairly quickly. But she never . . .' He checks that his daughter isn't listening. 'She never bonded with Joy. And Doolin was . . . *is* far too quiet for her.' Aiden swallows hard, his eyes distant. 'Then I found out that she was carrying on with my best friend.'

'God, that's awful.'

Aiden stares into the distance. 'Maura caught them both up there. She knocked on the car window and tore a strip off them both.'

The revelation surprises me. Maura, with all her quirks and secrets, was the one to expose Aiden's wife.

'God, what am I doing hounding you with questions? You've enough on your plate.' I watch as he turns sombre. 'Have you not heard from her then? Aren't you worried?' He raises an eyebrow and I realise that I've gone too far. 'Sorry.' I clear my throat. 'It's none of my business.'

But Aiden appears deep in thought as he shakes his head. 'It's not the first time she's taken off. She'll be back, full of apologies. It's only made the local gossip because Maura caught them at it in the back seat of the car.'

'God. I'm so sorry. Me and my big mouth.'

Aiden attempts a smile. 'Not at all. It's good to talk, as they say.' I'm surprised at how frank he's being, but then haven't I been the same with him? It's like we've known each other forever.

'Who told you about Maura?' The question pops out of my mouth before I have time to think. Because I can't imagine Maura telling Aiden about her scandalous discovery.

'Geraldine. It was all around the town by then.' He shakes his head. 'Chantana took off after that. I suppose it was the push she needed.' He exhales a bitter laugh, which is understandable, given the circumstances.

'And you've no idea where she is now?' I can't help but wonder how she could leave a daughter as delightful as Joy.

Aiden shakes his head. 'I reported her missing to the gardaí and told them everything I know. She's not been spending on her card but she sent money to her family every month . . .' He meets my gaze. 'She could have squirrelled it away for herself, for all I know.'

'And her family? Have you spoken to them?'

'They said they've not heard from her but who knows?' He nods towards his daughter. 'I've told her that her mum's away on holiday.'

'And the gardaí? What did they say?'

'Only that they're looking into it. It doesn't help that Chantana was having an affair. Apparently, it gives me a motive to hurt my wife. But then again, I went to them first.' He sighs. 'I'm not under arrest or anything like that, but still, it's a worry. If she doesn't come back soon, they might start blaming me.' He pauses as a thought seems to cross his mind. 'You won't say anything, will you? If the gossips hear that the police are involved, I'll be suspect number one.' He speaks in a light-hearted manner, but there's a world of worry behind his eyes.

'God, no, of course not. It's none of their business. I hope she turns up soon.'

'So do I,' Aiden sighs. 'For everyone's sake.'

Saoirse starts to grow restless and Joy bounces her a little too enthusiastically. I stretch my stiff legs as I stand. 'Go easy there, hon, we don't want her to throw up her milk.'

'We should get going now, anyway.' Aiden rises from the sofa. 'We've taken up enough of your time.'

I hear movement in Maura's room and I don't disagree. 'Thanks so much for everything, Aiden. You've been a lifesaver.'

'Anytime.' He beckons to his daughter. 'C'mon, me lady, bath and bed.'

I shepherd a dozen more questions from Joy before she leaves. It's been nice having such a cheery soul in the house.

As the door clicks shut behind them, a feeling of worry settles over me. I wasn't expecting a connection between Maura and Aiden's wife. I imagine her tearing a strip off Chantana as she catches her in the act. I'm surprised that she went that far. Judging from what Aiden said, there are plenty of other couples meeting on

Misery Hill. Maura can't be watching them all. Chantana's sudden disappearance gnaws at me as I hold Saoirse close. I watch Aiden drive down the road, the rain pelting against the cottage window-panes like a thousand tiny whispers. In the depths of the gloomy cottage, I can't shake the feeling that there is still so much more to uncover.

CHAPTER 25

MAURA

I stare at the pale morning light filtering through the yellowed lace. I've been lying here since dawn, grateful that the fog in my mind has cleared. It seems Saint Jude has answered my prayers. How could he not? If anyone is a lost cause, it is me. I throw back the heavy wool blankets and swing my legs on to the cold floor. It's not the first time that this has happened. Sometimes, when I get stressed, my head fills with blackness and shuts down. Only now do I realise that I'm wearing yesterday's clothes. Yesterday was Thursday, wasn't it?

I sniff in the direction of my right armpit and wrinkle my nose as the stench of stale sweat is returned. A hot bath is called for, and that dear conditioner that I bought in Dunnes Stores, the one that cost nearly ten euros that I got for three in the sale. It smells like a tropical garden and I always use it sparingly, which isn't easy with my long hair. Jojoba, indeed. When I was a child, I was lucky if I was spared a bit of washing-up liquid for my hair. It gave it a grand sheen, although the knots were a devil to tease out afterwards. But then Mammy would give me a heel of bread sprinkled with sugar and milk. It was enough to buy my cooperation as she patiently tugged the knots free.

I slip my feet into my worn-flat shoes, dragging myself back to the present. But it's hard, when so much of my life is anchored in the past. Seeing Aiden has brought up all sorts of bad memories. I even dreamed about him yesterday and thought I heard him laugh in the living room. Aiden looks so much like his father . . . thoughts of the only man I've ever loved are prised from me yet again. It's a dreadful feeling, like an invisible hand digging into my chest and having a good root around. I briefly close my eyes, turning my mind to something, anything, until it passes. I shift my attention to the window, and the fog that is taking its time to lift.

The kitchen looks different. The jar of instant coffee is on the counter, not in the cupboard where I normally keep it. Some of the plates have been moved around and two mugs lie upside down on the draining board by the sink. I've watched Finn. She always uses the same cup and washes up afterwards.

Someone has been here.

Aiden. I didn't dream his laughter. It was real. Geraldine is away. Who else could our mystery guest be?

My hands curl into fists. Finn and the baby will stay here with me, where they belong. Wasn't it me who brought them both here? That letter wasn't an easy one to write. When I first heard of my twin's death I took to my bed. Only Geraldine could make me get out of it again. I didn't want to face the world without Daisy in it. Even though we didn't speak, I keenly felt her absence. I'd been feeling quare all week, and then the call came from a cousin on my father's side who had heard the news.

I missed my sister's funeral. I lost all sense of time. But then Geraldine suggested that I write a letter to Finn and invite her over to stay. I didn't know what to say, but Geraldine helped me piece it together, word by word. She made me drink a bowl of soup before we wrote the first paragraph, then suggested I get a bath before we finished it off. By the time I got out of the bath, Geraldine had lit the fire and changed the sheets on my bed. We finished the letter and she made me get out of the cottage and walk to the post office to deliver it. If it wasn't for her . . . I wouldn't have found the strength to carry on.

I gaze around the kitchen, looking for any other traces of Aiden's unwanted presence. She couldn't wait, could she? Couldn't fend for herself for a couple of days. I stare in dismay at the fresh groceries in the fridge. Milk, cake, tomatoes, ham, coleslaw and . . . chocolate milk. So the little one has been here too. Joy, the motherless child. She's better off without her. The harlot. That Chantana was flouncing around with any man from the island who'd as much as give her a second glance.

Now I have Finn and Saoirse to worry about. A bloom of guilt rises. I suppose it can't have been easy, her stuck here with no food while I was in my bed. But I'm back now. It won't happen again. Not when I have things clear in my mind. She doesn't need Aiden. She doesn't need anyone but me. A thought enters my head. It's dark and ugly, but somewhat necessary if I'm not to be abandoned once again. But I can't rush into it. I need time to contemplate what I'm about to do.

I'm barely out of my room when I bump into Finn. I should explain my behaviour, but I can't. The thought of opening up about personal feelings raises a lump to my throat. I hate that I've had another one of my episodes, but it's too late to fix it now. She looks me up and down, a hint of wariness in her stance. Her hair is wild but pretty, and she's still in her pyjamas, her fluffy dressing gown tied tight to ward off the cold. She clutches a bottle of milk, on her way back to her bedroom. 'Sorry, did I wake you? Are you feeling better?'

It's barely light outside but I need to take myself away. 'I'm going for a walk. Be back in an hour.'

'An hour?' Finn calls after me. 'Take a flashlight.'

I snort a response. I know every inch of this island with my eyes closed. I know the places that are safe to walk, and the spots on the cliff edge that guarantee quick entry into the sea. I wait for Finn to return to her room. I have one small job to do before I leave.

CHAPTER 26

KATHRYN

Three times, I got out of bed last night and went to the front door. But the rain always drove me back. I've been wearing the same old grey tracksuit for the last few weeks. I suppose you could call them my mourning clothes. I bought them in Primark, the cheapest, crappiest, most comfortable clothing I could find. It was my way of becoming anonymous, the sort of person men wouldn't look twice at.

The transformation was a complete 360 compared to who I was before I fell pregnant. I don't even recognise the old me now. Back then, I enjoyed spending my father's money on parties, booze and travelling around the world. I admit, there was coke involved too. I mean, it's not as if I didn't get it for free. But the buzz of a socialite lifestyle faded when I met David, Kiera's dad. God, if there was ever an ill-fated relationship, it was ours. But I never imagined that it would end this way. I suppose you could call it a rebellious streak that I was going through. I didn't mean to fall in love. I sigh at the memory of him, his short black hair, his strong jawline, his nature so caring and thoughtful that it felt odd to me at first. I'd never been treated with such compassion in my life. He saw behind my fake persona. I could be myself with him. I should have known better. Our love was as fragile as a flower in a stiff winter breeze. Nothing that beautiful was ever built to last. We've both paid the price for going against our parents' wishes.

I can't risk seeing David again. Neither can I bear to see what I've done to him. But I won't be on my own. Not when I get my baby back. She calls to me. There's an unrelenting pain in my chest at the injustice of it all. Nobody takes what is mine. She is near. I can feel her presence all around me. I won't rest until I get her back. A quick swig from my hip flask eases my growing irritation. I place the tracksuit on the radiator and pull on my black jeans and jumper. I pull the belt an extra notch to make up for the weight I've lost.

I creep down to the living room, where evidence of Yvonne's blow-out remains. It seems that she continued drinking after I went to bed. Two empty wine bottles, a giant-sized Minstrels wrapper and an empty tub of Ben and Jerry's on the side. Her break-up couldn't have come at a better time.

My stomach grumbles as I grab my coat in the hall. I pocket the spare set of front door keys and slip out. It's just as well that I didn't make it all the way up Misery Hill last night. I mean, what good would it have done, turning up at Finn's door, my hair stuck to my face and a mad glint in my eye? They probably would have called the police, and that would have been the end of that. '*Slowly, slowly, catchy monkey,*' I whisper to myself as I turn right and head towards the quaint pubs and shops that line the small main street. I take in the postcard views, using them to calm my nerves. I can't blow this. Not now.

But the scenic distractions only work for so long and the coffee shop doesn't open until 9 a.m. I'm beginning to feel more desperate with each step. Visions of my baby's face float in my mind. Sod it. I turn on my heel and head towards Misery Hill. The plan had been to speak to the locals. To put some feelers out. But I can't wait another minute. I need to know if Kiera is there.

Zipping up my coat, I quicken my pace. I will search every corner of this damned village if I have to, but I can see no better place to start than Finn's current abode in Misery Hill. I've tried to work out how this came to be. Were both babies thrown from our cars and mixed up by mistake? But I didn't imagine my baby's cry. She was with me when I passed out. Was there a mix-up in the ambulance? But surely Finn would have known that the baby wasn't hers. Unless she couldn't face the prospect of being motherless . . . A sigh leaves my lips as my thoughts raise more questions.

I'm breathless as I take the shortcut, leaning into the wind as my lack of fitness becomes apparent. The road ahead is narrow and winding, lined with stone walls and ancient hedges. The sound of the sea in my ears brings with it a sense of dread. Am I ready for what awaits me?

The cottage looms ahead, its deep-set windows like beady black eyes glaring down upon me. It gives off a vibration of negativity, and the string of smoke wisping from the chimney tells me that someone is home. A battered old Ford Cortina is parked in the neglected yard.

I realise that I'm trembling as I approach the house. My stomach is doing somersaults. I need to catch my breath. I walk to the side of the cottage, taking shelter against a tall oak tree. The thick body of wood gives me time to collect my thoughts because I haven't rehearsed what I'm going to say. It's not as if they're just going to hand Kiera over, is it?

I slip behind a crumbling stone wall to observe, but I'm not there long when an older woman emerges from up the hill, her greying brown hair pulled back from her weather-beaten face. Her eyebrows are knitted together in determination as she observes me watching her, a few feet from the cottage.

My breath catches in my throat while she walks towards me, slowly negotiating the stony path. I hear a soft whimper from inside the cottage and my heart skips a beat in response. It's her. It's my Kiera. I straighten myself as I approach the path leading up to the cottage but the woman rounds on me, her words filled with aggression. 'What do you want? And why are you hanging around outside my house?'

Her house? She must be related to Finn. For once, I am unable to vocalise my words. 'I wasn't . . . I'm not . . .'

I don't know what I'm trying to say because all I can focus on is my baby, who is now crying within the cottage.

'Liar. I saw you watching.' The woman is fierce in her accusation as she points a finger at me. 'What do you want?' But the look in her bloodshot eyes tells me that she already knows.

'Hang on, who are you?' I counter. 'I'm here to see Finn Claffey.'

'I'm her Aunt Maura,' the woman snaps. 'You're on my property. What do you want with Finn?'

'She has my baby.' And my heart sings with the conviction of these words. Because she is my baby. I may not have seen her but I can hear her and she's crying to be with me. That's my little girl.

Maura straightens her posture and I meet her cold, hard stare. '*Your* baby? Who are you, coming here making . . . making . . .' Her face grows redder while she tries to find the word. 'Insinuations!' she blurts, her hands forming into fists.

'I'm Kathryn Toíbín. Finn crashed into my car and sent me off the road.'

'She did no such thing. And you have no place here, so off with you, on your way.'

But I sense trepidation in her words. I've hit a nerve. Hands trembling, I approach the cottage. But Maura is quick in her movements and she pushes with such force that it lands me on my back.

I gasp as the air is stolen from my lungs. I can't . . . I can't breathe. A warm tear runs down my face, the wind whips around me and the gravel digs into my back.

The woman waves a fist in my direction, shouting spittle-laced words. 'Come near here again and I'll send you into next week.'

I am beyond anger as I struggle to catch my breath. How dare she attack me, a Tóibín, for wanting to see my own child? She has no idea who she's dealing with. But the sudden act of violence has taken me by surprise. By the time I get off the hard ground, Maura is heading into the cottage. It's not the first time I've been winded, but it's never taken me this long to recover before.

Get it together, I tell myself, finally steadying my breathing.

I wipe my dirty hands on the back of my jeans and trot after Maura, who is a complete unknown entity. I won't back down now, not after coming this far.

'Hey! You!' I shout after her, the wind taking my words. 'Who the fuck do you think you are?' Rage flares inside me. If we were near the edge of the cliff, I'd push the bitch off.

'I should have known you'd come here eventually, looking for someone to blame.' Maura's voice is low and hard. 'Get off my property before I call the gardaí. She's not your babby, however much you tell yourself that she is.'

I'm shocked by her reaction as she manhandles me down the path. The fact she's acknowledged how I'm feeling has validated what I've known. My motherly instincts are powerful as they come to the fore. The sound of Keira's faint cries is tearing me in two.

'Kiera,' I whisper. 'I'm here.' I meet Maura's eyes, as anger and fear wraps around me. 'You can't stop me getting a DNA test.' After endless nights of torment, my baby is there, almost within touching distance. I'll find a way.

But there is no understanding from Maura, whose fists are clenched. There is an element of danger surrounding this woman. I underestimated her. Then it hits me.

Finn didn't steal my baby. Her aunt did.

'Why?' I ask in a choked voice. 'Why did you take her?'

Maura meets my gaze unflinchingly. 'Your babby is in the grave. Now off with ya, go home.' We stare each other down. The fate of a child hangs in the balance. I'm trying to hold it together, but the urge to storm into the cottage and grab my child is strong. I clench my fists, my nails making crescents in my palms as I fight my instincts to act.

'You have no business in Doolin,' Maura shouts. 'There's nothing for you here.'

'I'll smash every window in this cottage until you let me in!'

'Then the babby will pay the price as she freezes for the night.' Maura glares at me one more time before she opens the small cottage door.

Tension coils in my stomach. I can't bear it. 'You don't know who you're dealing with!' I shout after her as I try to push my way inside. 'I'm Kathryn Tóibín, do you hear? Danny Tóibín's daughter. I'm giving you one last chance. Give my baby back, or I'll make you regret it!'

'Do your worst!' Maura bellows. 'I'm not afraid of Dublin scum!'

Her arrogance amazes me. I try to push my way inside, but Maura is too strong for me and she slams the door in my face. I bang with my fists until splinters pierce my skin. I'm spent. Fine. If that's the way she wants it. I turn back towards my cottage because Yvonne will be worried about me.

The next time I meet Maura Claffey, I will be prepared.

CHAPTER 27

Thirty Minutes Earlier

Finn

I shake my head in amazement as I recall Maura's behaviour. She really is a strange one. I've no idea what's going on in her head. First, she took to her room to escape me, then when she finally emerged, she marched outside to clear her head. Has she always been this moody? Perhaps my presence is doing more harm than good.

'C'mon, sweetie.' I kiss Saoirse's forehead and make her comfortable in her travel cot, where she's safe. She's getting heavy. I must be doing something right. But then again, am I? Is it safe to have her here? I throw a glance towards Maura's bedroom door. There are secrets in there. I can feel it.

My heart picks up a steady rhythm as I approach. I will myself to keep moving. I've tried the cupboards in the cottage, and apart from the newspaper clippings all I've found is a collection of plates, knick-knacks and old Irish cookbooks she's not been able to throw out. Nervous energy flows through me and I wrap my fingers around her doorknob. Cold air meets me as I open the door, as if the room is whispering dark secrets of its own.

It is eerily quiet. I can't shake the feeling that something is off. My fingertips graze the cold, rough dresser and I build up the courage to search. *Maybe it's just nerves,* I tell myself, pushing away the unsettling atmosphere. I glance out of Maura's window, half-expecting to see her disapproving face staring back. But the windows remain empty, the dark panes reflecting nothing but my own apprehension. The air smells stale as Maura rarely opens the window because these rooms get so cold at this time of year.

I don't have time to waste. I pull open drawers, rifling through aged letters and old prescriptions that she's never thrown out. There has to be something.

My ears prick up at the faintest sound outside – leaves rustling, branches swaying – but no sound of the scrunch of Maura's footsteps on the gravel path. She said she'd be gone for an hour but I can't take anything for granted and I certainly don't want to get caught. I open her cabinet doors, which reveal row upon row of old medications, some dating back decades. I gaze at the first-aid kits, just like the one I used to have in the back of my car. I remember Aiden's words. Has she taken these from accident scenes?

Methodically, I search the shelves, looking into an old shoe-box containing old wallet-sized photos of people I don't know. I work through the rest of the cabinet, examining each item I find and discarding it with growing impatience. Every second spent in this room heightens my nerves, the fear of Maura's return looming over me like a dark cloud. Every creak, every distant sound ignites a fresh wave of panic. I quickly check on Saoirse, still snoozing in her travel cot.

I return to the bedroom, my search growing more frantic with each passing minute. Clothes are checked and closets emptied and carefully replenished as I check every square inch of the room. The seconds tick by, each one a reminder that time is running out. I tidy as I go, so Maura won't suspect that I've been rifling through her things. I can't leave until I know what secrets she's hiding.

As I continue my search, my fingers brush against something hidden in a drawer beneath a pile of bobbled woollen sweaters. A glimmer of hope rises within.

'Finally,' I breathe, pulling out a small leather-bound journal. I hesitate for a moment, sensing the gravity of what lies within its pages. As I begin to read, I'm on high alert.

I leaf through Maura's journal, my eyes widening at the bent-up old photos that fall out. Each snapshot depicts a twisted car wreck, shattered glass glistening like confetti on the ground.

'Where did you get these?' I whisper to myself, my voice barely audible. A cold chill snakes its way down my spine, and for a moment, the world seems to stand still. There are times and dates in each page of the journal, almost like police reports, except they've been written by Maura's hand. I'd recognise the scrawl of her writing anywhere. I scan the words that log each accident by weather, date and place. There are ticks, wiggles and crosses – some sort of secret code that I'm unable to decipher. I close the journal and return it to its hiding space. I need to move on. Maura could walk in any minute now.

It takes a lot of effort but I manage to get down on my hands and knees and check beneath Maura's bed. In the farthest reaches, nestled amid old newspapers and forgotten trinkets, I find something that stops me cold: a high-power battery lamp and a pair of binoculars. The implications of their presence are murky at best. I can't shake the feeling that I'm treading on melting ice. I dig deeper into Maura's belongings, unearthing a dusty box containing a bizarre collection of trinkets: small, intricate carvings of animals – each with unsettling sharp teeth; worn antique keys, their purposes long forgotten; an old curved pipe that stinks of tobacco and a jar filled with what appears to be false teeth, carefully labelled with dates.

'Who collects these things?' I mutter under my breath, shivering involuntarily as I pick up a carved cat that seems to stare right at me. I place it back in the box when a red leather designer purse catches my eye. This isn't Maura's style at all. I'm not ready for the discovery when I open it. Inside, I find some Irish bank notes, some euros in change, and a couple of loyalty cards. But it's the driver's licence that floors me. My breath comes in short, shallow gasps. I glare at the licence. A pretty Thai woman stares blankly from the photographic ID. The name is clear – Chantana Walsh. It belongs to Aiden's wife.

I return to the kitchen in a daze and swallow my pain meds without thinking. Did Maura kill Chantana? *My* Aunt Maura? I can barely comprehend the thought. But then I think about her strange behaviour. I don't really know her – or what she's capable of.

CHAPTER 28

MAURA

I can't believe that woman, thinking she could barge her way in here. I barely recognised her from the accident, but she's left me in no doubt as to who she is. Her family are well known. That big lump of a father of hers has been in court so many times that they may as well install a revolving door. I've seen him on RTÉ News. His fancy Dublin lawyers always get him off. Drugs, kidnapping, even murder charges have been thrown at him. They called him and his brother Joseph the 'Irish Kray twins', until Joseph accidentally shot himself a few years back. That cooled his brother's jets. He's quietened down a bit now. Like father, like daughter, by the sound of it. But I'm not afraid of her.

I rub Saoirse's back, and she emits a burp of wind that brings her immediate relief. It feels good to hold her warm body in my arms. There's no way I'm letting her go. I stand at the cottage window, watching that Kathryn make her descent down Misery Hill. The front door is locked, the windows bolted. I wait until Saoirse is settled before looking for Finn, who I find asleep on her bed. I pull a blanket over her shoulders. The rest will do her good. I did her a kindness, swapping her pain meds for sleeping tablets before I left.

The angels must have been looking out for me today. Everything is clear in my mind now. I know what I have to do.

'Let's get you in your pushchair,' I say softly to Saoirse as she waves her arms in the air. She's wearing a fleecy pink onesie, which has bunny rabbit feet and a stick-on tail. She plays with the string of ducks before her and I slip a pink dummy into her mouth.

I put the kettle on the range before pushing Saoirse into my bedroom. My armpits are sticky with sweat, but this can't wait. The well-stocked cabinet in my bedroom calls to me. It'll take more than a sleeping tablet to gain Finn's acceptance of the situation now.

I narrow my eyes as I glance around my room. Something's changed. I have so many things scattered around this house, and it wasn't a problem until Finn came to stay. Nothing is private now. I open my wardrobe doors, casting an eye over my neatly folded clothes. Too neat.

Carefully, I slide the crash diary from its resting place. But the photos inside aren't in the right order. So she's been in here, snooping through my private things. Finn needs to be re-educated. I turn to my bed and check one more hiding place. Surely not. I'm not easily shaken, but as I pull out my box of things, my heart beats a little faster. I hold the red purse close to my chest. At least it's still here. But has Finn seen it? I'll have to deal with this. Groaning, I rise from the floor and smile at Saoirse as she watches me cross the room.

The dresser door creaks open and I stare at the stockpile of medication I've accumulated. Some belonged to Granny Maura from years ago. Some I've stockpiled for myself. Others I've taken from accident scenes. It's surprising what you can find when you have a quick rifle through a handbag or the glove box of a dented car. I've only been caught twice, and on both occasions I've said that I was looking for a phone to call for help. I run a finger over the other boxes of medication – the ones the doctor in Dublin prescribed. Powerful sleeping tablets that help Finn to be compliant until she sees things my way. The small round white pills are thankfully similar to her painkiller meds. I don't know why my hands are trembling, it's not as if I haven't done this before, but doubling the dose could push her into a sleep from which she'll never awake. The trick is to give her just enough to weaken her resolve. This is for her own good.

Humming under my breath, I carefully count out two pills and place them in a small blue mortar bowl. I pummel them with a pestle until the powder is as fine as dust. Cradling the mortar in one hand, I push Saoirse to the kitchen with the other, humming a tune as I tell myself that everything is under control. There won't be any DNA tests, not on my watch. I transfer the fine powder into a cheerful yellow mug. Finn can have it with some Ovaltine later on. Needs must.

I can't help but picture Finn's trusting face as she drinks my special brew.

Family.

I repeat the one-word mantra in my mind. It's all that matters now. I won't be abandoned again.

CHAPTER 29

THEN

MAURA

They say in Ireland that if there's a traffic jam it's either from a GAA match or a funeral. The whole town came to bid Jimmy's mother farewell. The village was dotted with May bushes decorated in colourful crêpe paper and painted eggshells, which were strangely at odds with the hearse as it trundled slowly down the road. Everyone came out to pay a tribute, standing with heads bowed, hands clasped in reverence as it passed. Nannie was a liked and respected lady, that's for sure. Her death came suddenly. Her heart, by all accounts.

The wake was held in the Grand Hotel and the food was full and plenty, catering for everyone. Daisy did not come home for the funeral, despite knowing the woman well. She was abroad on holiday and Daddy said that she was to be left to enjoy herself. He'd joked that perhaps I could get changed halfway through and pretend to be her. His comment was close to the bone.

I was glad Daisy didn't come home. I couldn't bear to see the look on Jimmy's face when he saw her again. He never looked at me like that. Well, only once, when he thought I was her.

Jimmy went out of his way to avoid me since the incident in the car. He'd cross the street, or duck behind one of the aisles in the supermarket and make a quick exit. Anything to escape time in my company. Even if he passed me in the car, he would look the other way. I'm surprised he didn't crash. If we were both to keep living in Doolin, we couldn't go on like that. Of course, I was fierce upset with him, and hard done by. I was just as upset with myself for committing the sin of fornication before marriage. Sometimes I'd fantasise that he knew it was me all along and was putting on a front because he couldn't bear to have his heart broken again. Common sense told me that nobody could fake his blatant horror that day. But real love does not evaporate beneath the cruelty of rejection. I still loved him and I had to speak to him again.

It took a while, but I waited until he had a few drinks in him during the wake. Jimmy was a lot more pliable with a few whiskeys down his throat. I waited until he slipped out the back of the building for a cigarette. He was smoking back then and I worried about his health and how Daisy's behaviour had left him a wreck. If only she had done the right thing. It always came back to that day in our cottage when I told her that he was mine. Did the bond of our twinship mean nothing to her? A decent sister would have made her excuses and left. Then when Jimmy turned up, *I* would have been the one to make him tea and giggle at his jokes, not her. But then, jokes have to be explained to me three times before I understand. I'm a boring version of Daisy. She was a butterfly, bringing joy as she flitted into people's lives, while I was the earth-bound caterpillar, ploughing through the dirt, never destined to fly. But I would have been a good wife to Jimmy, had he given me the chance. Sure, I worshipped the ground he walked on, more fool me. The more I thought about it that day, the angrier it made me. She never gave us a chance. Then she went and ruined him for anyone else.

I crept out the back of the hotel in search of the man who plagued my thoughts. My long mousey brown hair was tied back in two French plaits, but somehow I knew that the gentle speckle of rain would instantly make it frizz. My mourner's outfit consisted of a black jacket, a black jumper over a white blouse, and a knee-length elasticated black skirt with thick woollen tights and flat-soled black leather shoes. I bought it in Clerys in Dublin, and while it was a little on the expensive side, I consoled myself that as long as I didn't put on weight, I'd get a wear out of it. There weren't many funerals in Doolin, as the population was small, but it would do for my parents' farewells when the time came. I remember wishing I'd worn my coat as the spring weather had yet to make itself known. The back of the hotel was a dingy spot, with its damp walls, dirty floor and the questionable smell of urine rising from the alley off the back door.

The sight of Jimmy standing in the alleyway made my heart lurch in my chest. His suit was fitted to perfection, complimenting his athletic build.

'Jimmy,' I whispered, making him almost jump out of his skin. Coughing, he waved the smoke away. I smiled, my heart dancing in my chest because I hadn't spoken to him in weeks.

'Jesus.' He looked left and right before taking another drag. 'What are you doing, sneaking around?' His words were harsh and peppered with smoke.

'Sorry for your loss,' I blurted, as I needed to get the sympathies out of the way. I offered a hand as was the custom, but he didn't shake it.

'Thanks.' He looked at me with that regretful expression that I'd come to hate.

I excused him because he had whiskey in his belly and had probably not eaten much. 'Why are you avoiding me?'

He didn't deny it. 'It's awkward.' He flicked the ash from his cigarette, unable to meet my eye. 'I feel bad, although it's more your fault than mine.' He shook his head, the corners of his mouth raising in an ugly smile. 'Daisy said you liked me, but I never thought you'd go that far.'

It was my turn to be embarrassed. I imagined them laughing about my so-called crush when they were alone. 'What's that got to do with the price of potatoes?' I retorted. 'It's water under the bridge now,' I lied. I hadn't moved on.

He stubbed out the butt of his cigarette with the heel of his black leather shoe. My emotions swelled up in my chest. I was angry at him and my sister, but I loved the pair of them too. I wished I could be tough like Granny Maura. Perhaps she had the right idea all along. But equally, I wanted to kiss him, like he kissed me that night in the back of his car.

'I'm going in.' He glanced at me. 'This isn't the day for it.'

'You don't need to feel guilty about Daisy.' I followed. 'She's never coming back here. She couldn't even make it for the funeral. Do you hear me? Jimmy . . .' I touched his arm, but he pulled away. 'Why are you being so horrible? Don't I look just like her? I can wear her clothes if you want.'

He looked at me in disbelief. 'You're too clingy, Maura. You can dress up like Daisy all you like, but you're a different person inside and we're not compatible.'

'Why aren't we compatible?' I whined, a lump forming in my throat as I tried not to cry.

'Because you don't even realise that what you did was wrong.' He leaned towards me, a threat carrying on his voice. 'I could call the guards. That's if I could stand the embarrassment. What you did . . . it was wrong.'

148

I stared at him, agog. What was he talking about? A door opened from within the hotel and closed again as someone went to the bathroom.

'This . . . fixation,' Jimmy whispered. 'It's not love. You don't even know me. It's all in your head.'

It was true, I didn't know him, but I loved him just the same.

'Wait,' I called, because the life I'd planned was disintegrating. My parents weren't well, and Granny Maura was demanding. And all I could see was years of being a carer stretching out ahead of me. Jimmy was meant to take me away from this, and now he was walking away. 'You can't leave me, Jimmy Walsh, do you hear?'

'Go home, Maura.' He turned back towards me. 'Leave me alone, I mean it this time. If you come after me again, I'll tell everyone what you did, and you have a lot more to lose than me.' The whiskey-laced words leaving his mouth almost made me cry. Where was my Jimmy? The kind one, the one who rescued animals and told off bullies. He was in there somewhere. I could fix him, bring him back to what he was. It wasn't his fault. *She* made him like this. Daisy was to blame. I grabbed on to his shirt but he pushed me away.

Instinctively, I knew what I had to do. I opened my coat and lay my hand on my stomach. 'I'm pregnant.'

'What?' He looked at me as if the devil himself had prodded him in the arse with his fork.

'I'm pregnant,' I repeated. 'Three months gone . . . and it's yours.'

CHAPTER 30

KATHRYN

I approach the bend leading to the crash site, my body pulsating with rage. I can't return to Yvonne yet, not with Maura's taunts echoing in my mind. I need to calm down first. The shiny new section of the metal road barrier catches the light. This bend in the road is horrendous, narrowing dangerously as it curves around the wide cliff edge. Judging by the faded plastic flowers and ribbons flapping in the wind, other people have lost their lives here. I don't want to look at the names etched on the cards tied to the older guard-rails. I can't absorb other people's grief right now. I climb over the repaired road barrier, as I try to tease memories from my fractured brain. But all I still feel is the need to lash out at something, anything to ease my growing frustration.

'Damn these shoes!' I hiss, limping to the patch of ground where my car came to its final rest. The Italian leather footwear may be fine for the streets of Dublin, but not here.

The cliff isn't on a sharp precipice, but rather a slow decline to the edge. My car rolled three times. My body is a scarred road map of each bump and twist. Had it rolled for a fourth time, I wouldn't be alive today. I wince as the tight leather of my shoes cuts into my heels with every step.

'Crazy bitch!' I scream at the wind.

There is nobody to witness my outburst. Nothing but the wind and the sea, and the gulls dive-bombing the foamy waters below. I touch the broken earth, driven by the burning desire to make sense of it all and find the truth.

Kiera's alive. She has to be. Despite the pain and the fury of the moment, the possibility steadies my focus. The terrain becomes rugged as I walk the scene, sharp stones stabbing the soles of my shoes. But the pain pales in comparison to the fury, hope and disbelief that overwhelms me. I never expected Maura to attack me like that. She's as mad as a box of frogs, and she's in charge of my child.

Somewhere in my mind, there is a voice of caution. *You didn't see Kiera. How can you be sure?*

I am absolutely sure. I should have hit the old cow back, and carried out my threat to smash her windows in. Hot tears of disappointment sting my eyes. I was so close to my baby. What held me back? I can almost hear David's voice saying violence isn't the way forward, that things have a way of working themselves out. I rifle in my pocket for a tissue and blow my runny nose. My hip flask is empty already. I haven't even had my breakfast yet.

I look back up at the barrier and a vivid image of the accident flashes before my eyes – a memory that feels both distant and painfully close. The swirling mist, the dark cliff's edge, and the sickening crunch of metal against hillside rock as I'm thrown around in my car. My camera, bouncing from its resting place on the passenger seat and hitting me on the forehead. My open handbag, emptying its contents, each one a missile as I'm thrown around with force. The sudden wham of the airbag releasing against my chest.

Painful memories surge through me like electric currents as I recall Kiera in the back, bundled in blankets and strapped into her car seat. Did it . . . ? I recall . . . her passenger door coming loose as it was smashed against the rocky cliff. The chaos was overwhelming, but there had been one sound that pierced through it all – Kiera's cries.

I succumb to the memory and close my eyes. The smell of petrol. A wisp of smoke. A wheel still spinning as the car lay on its side. Blood . . . my blood . . . running warm and thick down my face and hand. But there's something else.

A human presence at the scene. Footsteps approaching. Not the hurried approach of the emergency services. This was silent and cautious. A blurry figure in the dark, checking the wreckage. A thick tweed skirt. A pair of sensible shoes. Is it . . . ? Was it her? But as soon as the question rises in my mind, the memory is gone. My back molars press against each other hard.

It was Maura. It had to be. She lives just minutes from the scene. The village is at least half a mile away.

My mind races while I try to replay the events of that awful night. The twisted metal, the shattered glass, the helpless cries . . . Kiera's cries. They were coming from the back of my car. I'm not imagining it. She *was* alive. She wasn't thrown clear of the wreckage like the police investigators said. Did Maura take my baby from her car seat and swap her with Finn's dead child? Because it's the only explanation that I can come up with. My mind has been clouded with grief and alcohol abuse, but for the first time in weeks, I feel clarity.

Where is Finn now? Does she even know?

I touch the cold, damp earth, slowly coming to ground.

Maura had a maddened glint in her eye. Perhaps this is her doing alone. Finn wouldn't want to raise someone else's child, would she? All it would take is a simple DNA test. She'd want to be sure, too, wouldn't she? Rain spits from the sky as the sound of crashing waves below echoes through the eerie silence, their relentless rhythm a haunting reminder of the power of nature. The sea looks both beautiful and powerful when it hits the cliff edge with force. So many times I've felt like coming back here and walking off the edge but now I have something to live for.

My baby wasn't thrown clear from the wreckage. She was still in the car after the crash, crying out for me. But she was taken. And I know who by.

CHAPTER 31

FINN

I only meant to close my eyes for a minute, but hours have passed. I was having the strangest of dreams. Someone was banging, screaming, threatening. Saoirse was crying but I couldn't lift myself out of the fog to find her. It feels like after the accident all over again. My head throbs as I try to make sense of my surroundings. The room swims in and out of focus, shadows stretching and contracting like living things. I'd taken the medication from the little sepia bottle that I'd left on the kitchen table, but something about the dose feels all wrong.

I blink, forcing my eyes to adjust. For a moment, I convince myself that I'm at home. Home, with Mum downstairs, singing along to Phil Collins on the radio. But this room is cold and unwelcoming, the blankets coarse on my skin. Something stirs deep within, a connection tugging at the edges of my memory. Then it dawns on me, and my spirits fall. I'm at Misery Hill. Mum isn't with me any more.

I glance at the cot. It's empty. Maura must have taken care of her. An alarm bell is raised in the back of my mind. Something. There is something wrong . . . I remember searching Maura's room.

The photos. The purse. My senses are dulled as I pull myself out of bed. I tug on my dressing gown, rubbing the sleep from my eyes.

'Maura?' The word forms slowly in my mouth. Where is Saoirse? Even speaking is an effort. Groaning, I approach my bedroom door, my left leg protesting every movement. Stumbling, I lean against the frame for support. What the hell is wrong with me?

As I shuffle into the hallway, a wave of vertigo washes over me. 'Steady,' I whisper, touching the wall. I make a pit stop to the toilet before going to the living room.

The soft glow of sunlight filters through the curtains, casting warm, golden hues across the floor. Dust motes dance lazily in the beams, creating a sense of serenity in contrast with my growing anxiety. A faint sound reaches my ears. Maura's singing; a haunting melody weaves itself into the fabric of the room.

'*O, ro, sheanduine, o, ro . . .*'

The words are unfamiliar, but they carry an emotional weight that sends shivers down my spine. I take another step, my eyes drawn to the source of the song. There, in the corner, sits Maura in a rocking chair, swaying gently back and forth as she cradles my baby in her arms. She gazes down, lost in the lilting rhythm of the lullaby, seemingly oblivious to my presence. 'C'mon now, little one,' she softly says, my baby whimpering in her arms. 'Take it.'

'What the . . . ?' My voice falters as my vision clears. Disbelief renders me speechless while I struggle to process the scene. Maura is gently guiding my baby towards her exposed breast. 'Wh-what are you doing?' I stand, aghast.

Maura jumps, her jaw slack as she is caught in a forbidden act. For a moment, neither of us speak, and the tension in the room grows thick.

'Finn.' Her grip on Saoirse tightens ever so slightly. 'You're awake.'

'Give her to me.' I limp towards her. 'Now.'

With a sigh, Maura covers herself up, her eyes never leaving my face. 'I was just . . . I was just helping.'

'Helping?' I'm incredulous as I take my baby from her arms. 'By trying to breastfeed her?'

'I just wanted to feel close to her,' Maura admits, her voice laced with desperation. 'I never got the chance with my own child.'

I stare in disbelief, torn between sympathy and outrage. She had a baby?

This isn't a ploy to get off the hook. There is a raw honesty in Maura's words. But this is not the time for understanding or compassion; my priority is Saoirse's safety. I rub my baby's back as I position her on my shoulder, leaning on my right foot.

'Stay away from us,' I warn, my voice cold and unwavering. 'Stay away, or I'll . . . I'll leave and I won't come back.'

'You can't go.' Maura is defensive as she rises from the rocking chair. She fixes the buttons on her blouse, her mouth downturned, her face an expression of hurt. 'I only want to help.'

'Help?' I blurt a laugh. 'By trying to nurse her? She's not your child, Maura! It's abuse, that's what it is.'

Saoirse emits a whimper, caught in the centre of the storm. I turn to leave but a wave of dizziness holds me back.

'Let me explain,' Maura follows. 'You don't understand.'

I stare at the clock on the wall. It's gone 2 p.m. I've been out for hours.

'Did you touch my medication?' She stares at me with a blank expression. 'This morning,' I continue, as Saoirse fusses in my arms. 'I left my tablets on the kitchen table. Did you touch them?' I think about the stockpile of medication in Maura's room and another warning bell chimes.

'Now why would I do that? I went out for a walk after you left, remember?'

But I'm thinking of those early days when I first came here and was out of it. I should challenge her about what I've found in her room, but I don't feel safe here. 'I've had enough of this place.' I glance around the room. 'Where's my phone?' I'll call a taxi, get a lift to the train station. I just need to gather up my things first.

'I lost my own babby,' Maura whispers, her voice barely audible, as if the words themselves are too painful to speak. 'And ever since, I've been trying to fill that void, find something to ease the ache.'

'By taking mine?' My protective instincts flare to life. 'That doesn't justify what you did.'

'Please,' Maura begs, gripping my arm tighter than is comfortable. 'It's not just about Saoirse. I need you both.' Her chin trembles with emotion. 'Daisy . . . She would've wanted us to be a family. Don't take that away from me, Finn.'

'Mum wanted nothing to do with you!' I try to pull away but her grip is too strong.

'Please,' Maura pleads, desperation making her reckless. 'I can't lose you both.'

'Get off me!' I stagger back as I try to escape her grip. 'I need to go!'

'Let me take her. You're not well!' Maura demands.

Saoirse's cries pierce the air as we tussle. Maura's too strong from me as she wrenches my baby from my arms. I'm caught off guard by Maura's sudden aggression and she pushes me away. My legs buckle beneath me as Maura's shove sends me careening towards the edge of the room. I grasp at the air for something – anything – to break my fall. But there is nothing. The corner of a wooden coffee table looms in my peripheral vision, and then—

Crack.

My head collides with the unforgiving surface. Searing pain explodes behind my eyes. The world tilts and spins as I try to call out to Saoirse, but my voice is just a drizzle from my lips.

'Finn!' Maura's voice falters, a distant echo.

Darkness presses in, suffocating, relentless.

'Get . . . away . . . from her.' I try to force the words through gritted teeth, but they emerge as a whisper.

Consciousness slips away like sand through my fingers. The last thing I register is blood running down my cheek, before darkness closes in.

CHAPTER 32

FINN

'Finn. Are you alright, my love?' Maura's face looms above me. She is red-faced from a stress rash as it creeps up her throat and cheeks. I look around. I'm back in my bedroom.

'What? What happened?' I touch my head.

'You don't remember?'

'No, I . . .' My frown deepens. 'I don't. Everything's a blank.'

'When you say everything . . .' Anxiety is streaked across her face.

'The accident. I was in an accident. You looked after me, then . . .' I strain to speak. 'That's all. How long have I been here?'

But Maura presses on. 'What about Aiden? Do ya remember him?'

'Who?'

'Aiden, from the village. He was here, with the young one.' She nibbles on her bottom lip as she waits for my response.

'No, I . . .' I feel a bandage. 'What happened to my head?'

Maura exhales, her relief evident. But I won't ask why she's questioning me. I need to keep Saoirse safe.

'You were in an accident, pet. Your crutch slipped, you lost your footing and hit your head on the coffee table.' She looks me up and down. 'The doctor's been. He's given you a prescription and said you need lots of bed rest.'

The doctor? This is news to me. 'Where's Saoirse?'

'She's grand.' Maura smiles. 'Fed, changed and played with. Don't worry about her. It's getting late. Get some sleep.'

'I'm stiff.' I grimace. My head throbs as I sit up in bed. 'I need to stretch.'

She helps me pull on my dressing gown. I need to see my baby for myself. I glance at the end of the bed at the old-fashioned men's ties resting on top of the blanket. 'What are they doing here?'

The flush in Maura's cheeks deepens to crimson.

'Oh nothing,' she flusters, snatching them from the blanket. 'I was . . . um . . . just going through some of my father's old things. I asked Doctor Flanagan if he'd like them.' She exhales a small laugh. 'But he only wears the narrow ones, not these big kippers.'

The ties are another part of the treasure trove she's accumulated over the years. I haven't forgotten a thing. I know all about Maura's hoarding, and I know what's under her bed. But knowledge can be a dangerous thing when you're as vulnerable as I am right now. I need to keep my baby safe, and I can only do that when Maura's on side. Her moods need to be managed. I can't risk tipping her over the edge.

I catch sight of my clumsily bandaged head in the mirror. The doctor wasn't here. Concussion is taken more seriously than that. I would have woken up in a hospital, not in my bed. As for the ties . . . Was Maura ready to restrain me if I kicked off? She's a strong woman and I'm recovering from my injuries. The fact that she's knocked me unconscious shows she's desperate for me to stay – at any cost. I don't know this woman at all. I'll get to my phone, I'll call Aiden for help. He'll get me and Saoirse out of here. I can't believe that it's come to this. No wonder Mum wanted nothing to do with Maura. She must have known that her twin was unhinged. But what about Aiden's wife? What has become of her? Because if Maura is capable of murder, what plans does she have for me and my baby?

CHAPTER 33

THEN

MAURA

When I revealed my unexpected pregnancy, I'd hoped Jimmy would step forward with a proposal of marriage. That was the unwritten rule in those days. I was only three months gone. There was time to get wed before the baby arrived. Anything to save face. Doolin had seen its share of rushed weddings. In my tight-knit village, appearances meant everything. But beneath the surface, undercurrents of gossip carried the truth. In this place of hushed whispers, the unspoken agreement was clear: guard my family secret, and I'll guard yours.

I expected Jimmy's shocked reaction. He wasn't exactly kind to me the first time around. It turned out that when under the influence of drink he wasn't so pliable after all, especially at his mother's funeral. I admit, it was bad timing on my behalf. But what was I supposed to do, given he avoided me at every turn? I told myself that he'd come around. That he left me standing there because he was at a loss for words. But he was not the man I thought he was. Daisy was right. I didn't know him at all.

I couldn't turn up at his surgery because he'd passed me on to old Doctor Tyrell. If I called to his house, I'd be the talk of Doolin, especially given he still had a steady girlfriend. As Granny Maura used to say about the town gossips: 'If a mouse crossed the road in Doolin, it would be an elephant by the time it got to the other side.' I couldn't bear for anyone to know what I had done. In the end, I took myself off to Limerick for a break.

I remember stepping off the train and wrinkling my nose as I inhaled the city air. Summer had come at last, although you wouldn't know it to look at my pale skin. The humidity seemed worse than back home, and the air lacked the fresh saltiness of the sea. You only miss things when you suffer from their absence. That would hit me in a colossal way later on.

Clutching my small suitcase, I scanned the platform for the way out. When someone's hand tried to grab it, I cried out in fright.

'It's only me,' Daisy laughed as she claimed my suitcase. It took me a second to recognise her. Her bottle-blonde hair was cut into a shoulder-length bob, and with her red lipstick and figure-hugging clothes, she looked the most beautiful that I'd ever seen her.

'You frightened the life out of me . . .' The rest of my words were stolen as she dropped the case and squeezed me tight.

'Sis . . . I know you don't like hugs, but I'm giving you one anyway.' She spoke into my hair. The sweet smell of her signature perfume made my shoulders drop an inch. She was our Daisy and I couldn't help but bask in the warmth of her company. As angry as I'd been, I was equally lost without her. Without Daisy's guidance, I was a leaf in a storm.

I watched her smile crease into a frown as she stepped back from our hug. I was getting bigger, and while Mam and Granny Maura may not have noticed what was behind my thick woollen jumpers, Daisy did. Twins are like that. They sense things. But then again, she was also a nurse, and I was dressed in too many layers for such a sunny day.

'Maura . . .' she said uncertainly. 'Have you . . . ?' She looked at me with intensity, trying to read my expression. My cheeks grew warm beneath her scrutiny. I gave her a pleading look. This wasn't the time or place.

'Have you put on a bit of weight? God . . .' She exhaled a nervous laugh. 'I sound like old Granny Maura.'

I wound the window down as she drove us back to her apartment in a little Citroën car that she bought 'for a steal'. I told her I was grand and that the house was quiet without her. Then she talked about the friends she'd met in work. But in the gaps between our sentences, silent words passed.

My sister carried my suitcase into her flat. She wouldn't let me pick it up. She carefully escorted me up the stairs and asked me if I was alright. She sat me down and got me a drink of water and told me to take off my shoes because my ankles were swollen. The jumper came off too, because I was sweating buckets by then. When I was fed and settled with a cup of tea on her small but comfortable two-seater sofa, that was when she finally asked. But her first question surprised me as she stared at me with eyes that seemed so much bluer than my own. 'Tell me the truth. Has someone hurt you? Are you in trouble?'

Back in the day, 'are you in trouble' meant 'are you pregnant?'

I nodded, the ugly feelings of jealousy and annoyance returning. Why did she think that the only way I'd get pregnant would be if I was attacked?

'I'm six months gone,' I said, tightly gripping my cup. 'And I wasn't forced into anything, if you must know.' I was barely able to believe the words leaving my mouth. I'd paid to go private to see a female doctor in Dublin for the pregnancy test. Dublin isn't like

Doolin. In the city, they don't give two hoots who you are and what sort of trouble you're in.

'Does anyone else know?'

My sister's voice snapped me out of my thoughts. I shook my head. 'And you're not to tell anyone. This would kill Mammy and Daddy. As far as they know, I'm here on me summer holidays.'

Daisy cleared her throat. 'Okay. You can stay with me until you have it, and then after the baby is born, you can go home.'

She didn't ask me if I wanted to keep it. Given that I was a single mother and hadn't told a soul, she presumed that I wanted rid. Then came the question that I dreaded the most.

'Who's the father?'

I didn't want to hear it because I didn't know how she would react. But as it turned out, she had already guessed.

'It's Jim, isn't it? You've always had a thing for him. God, I thought it was just a little crush. Have you told him?'

I nodded, each bow of my head filling me with shame. 'He took it very badly. He doesn't want to know.'

'Typical.' Daisy rolled her eyes. 'He's always been a bit odd.'

A pause stretched between us because I didn't know how to respond. I'd always thought of their relationship as some tragic romance. I never for a second thought Jimmy was 'a bit odd'.

'You're not angry with me?' I checked in case this was all a front.

'Why would I be angry with you?' Daisy gave me a weak smile. 'Worried, yes. Pissed off with Jim for taking advantage – absolutely. But you're my sister and we'll work it out. If you want to keep the baby you can move to Limerick. In the city, nobody cares.'

It was such a lot to take in. My sister's show of support, her offer to care for me. I could've cried. But instead I agreed that Jimmy was indeed a bit odd, and tended to drink too much.

My sister touched my hand and I didn't pull away. 'Oh Maura, you are always the sensible one. How did you end up like this?'

I couldn't tell her because I was ashamed.

Jimmy wasn't such a prize after all. But now I had a big decision to make.

CHAPTER 34

FINN

Maura seems abnormally cheery as she bustles about the kitchen. I force a smile when she puts on the kettle to make some Ovaltine. My thoughts keep returning to her bedroom. She doesn't know that I've been there, does she? I folded and replaced her clothes. I shut the cupboard doors. And the things under her bed . . . they were in such a mess anyway she wouldn't have known. Would she? I glance at the clock on the wall. It's gone 10 p.m.

'Hungry?' she says, not waiting for a reply. 'You've not eaten for hours. Of course you are.'

Within minutes she is placing hot buttered toast and jam and a steamy mug of Ovaltine before me. But is it safe to drink? This is crazy. She's family. But then I think about the red purse under her bed, and I'm scared. I sniff the toast before taking a bite. What am I doing? If Maura's going to drug me, it will be in my drink. I stare at the swirling Ovaltine as she rests the mug before me.

'Thanks.' I chew my toast, listening out for my daughter who is peacefully slumbering in the living room. I need to get us both out of here.

'Where are you going?' Maura is immediately upon me as I begin to rise from my seat.

'My phone . . . I left it in the sitting room.'

'I'll get it for you.'

She's gone before I can disagree. I want to throw the Ovaltine down the sink but I don't have time. Without my crutches, my movements are slow. I have time to swap Maura's mug with my own. I settle back into my chair, taking another bite of toast as she returns. Her movements are rushed, which means she's scared to leave me alone.

'You haven't touched your Ovaltine.' She sits in the chair across from me.

'Did you get my phone?' I choose to ignore her comment.

'Finish your drink and I'll give it to you, that's a good girl.'

The sigh has left my lips before I can contain it. I take a sip from my mug.

'All of it.' Maura produces my phone from her skirt pocket.

'I'm not twelve,' I snap.

I can't help it. But I instantly regret my outburst as the lines on her face deepen into a frown.

'Sorry. It's lovely, really. I just don't feel too good.'

'All the more reason to look after yourself. You're dehydrated. Drink up.'

I do as I'm told, grateful that I had the foresight to swap the mugs. The Ovaltine is lukewarm, so it doesn't take me long to knock it back.

'Good girl.' Maura delivers a cold, unnerving grin that chills me to the bone. I'll wait until she's not looking and send Aiden a text for help.

'You miss her, don't you?' Maura crosses her legs. She's not touching her Ovaltine. Her gaze is solidly on me. 'Daisy,' she clarifies. 'You miss her.'

'Don't *you*?' I peer at my phone but the screen is blank.

'Everybody loved Daisy,' she says wistfully. 'Would you stay if she came back?'

'What?' I can't have heard her right. I press the power button on my iPhone. Why isn't it coming on?

'I know you're not happy here, Finn. But it doesn't need to be this way.'

But I'm not giving Maura my full attention because my phone won't come on. 'I charged it,' I mutter, as my annoyance grows.

Maura picks up my plate and brings it to the sink.

'Aren't you going to drink your Ovaltine?' I ask. I suddenly have a bad feeling about this.

'Heavens, no.' She picks up the mug, turns and pours its contents down the sink. I straighten in my chair as I hear Saoirse awake. I push the heels of my hands against the table for support and I stand.

'Where are you going, dear?' Maura's voice sounds different as she calls after me in a sing-song tone.

'To get Saoirse,' I reply. Because all I want to do now is to take my daughter, strap her into her pushchair and go. But I only get as far as the hall when my legs give way. That's when I realise that Maura drugged both mugs.

CHAPTER 35

MAURA

Humming beneath my breath, I drag Finn back to her room. She's a slight girl, which isn't surprising, given what she's been through. I heft her on to the bed, and her right slipper falls to the floor. I move her left foot and take her other slipper off. As I stare at her slender feet, I think how much easier life would have been had she been wheelchair bound. Completely dependent on me, she never would have wanted to leave.

Moving one leg over the other, I ease her into the recovery position. I can't afford for her to choke in her sleep. Drugs affect people differently, but it has to be done. At least, until she comes around to my way of thinking. I push her long hair from her face, my thoughts growing dark. I'd presumed that when she came here from the hospital she'd be grateful. After everything I've done for her . . . A sigh escapes my lips. I might have believed her bout of amnesia had I not seen her switch the cups of Ovaltine. Another test failed. Had she not been so mistrustful, she wouldn't have been drugged. As for her fake memory loss . . . Am I really such an ogre to her?

Family.

The word haunts me. What if it's too late for Finn?

I think of Saoirse in her cot, always happy to see my face.

Finn's head thumps back on to the mattress as I pull out the pillow from beneath her and lay her flat on her back. She makes a small, choking noise and I momentarily pause. I'm still holding her pillow when her breathing resumes.

What am I doing?

I blink as I realise that her position has changed. My thoughts have run away with me, just as they've done so many times before. I resume my humming, placing the pillow back beneath her head.

CHAPTER 36

KATHRYN

Yvonne opens the door to meet me. She's wearing her puffa coat and looks like she's on her way out.

'Where have you been? I thought you did a runner! I was about to go looking for you.'

'Has he called?' I glance at the phone in her hand. I don't need to elaborate. My father is the reason why she looks so scared.

She audibly swallows. 'Not yet.'

My father is a busy man but still finds time to keep tabs on me. He never used to be this bad, but my dalliance with a rival clan hasn't helped.

'Look at the state of you,' Yvonne says, with new-found compassion. 'Come in. You look frozen.'

She ushers me inside and it's bliss to kick off my tight-fitting shoes. Yvonne follows me into the living room, which seems tiny compared to my father's abode. 'What happened? Where did you go?'

I rub my lower back because more than my pride is bruised. 'Do you care? Or are you asking for Dad?'

Yvonne sighs, then nibbles her bottom lip, her trademark habit when she's nervous. 'You've been kind to me, Kathryn, listening to me babble on about my ex the whole way here in the car.'

I feel bad now, as I wasn't really listening but concocting plans of my own. 'Then spending time with me last night . . .' she continues. 'It was just what I needed. I don't get on with my sisters.' She begins to pick at a jagged thumbnail. 'It's the first bit of kindness anyone has shown me in years.'

Oh God. I've been so wrapped up in myself that I've not given her feelings a second thought. She's been by my side since the accident and I've never asked her how she was. 'Hey, that's okay. That's what cousins are for.'

Her face crumples a little and she looks like she's going to cry, but instead she pulls a tissue from beneath the sleeve of her jumper and blows her nose. 'That means a lot, thanks.' She shoves her damp tissue back up her sleeve. 'Now. What's going on, because there's a lot more to this than you're letting on, isn't there?'

I follow her lead as she takes a seat in the living room. Against my better judgement, I tell her everything that's happened up until now. Not because I trust her, but because I need her advice.

Yvonne listens to every word. She doesn't say that I'm being stupid, or tell me I should up my meds. Only now do I realise that I like her. I have no real friends. I have lots of hangers-on and socialites who have lost touch, but not one person in the world who cares.

'I feel like going up there with a baseball bat,' I confess, as my Toíbín nature comes to the fore. I'm restless and hungry for retribution. 'Nobody, and I mean nobody outside of the family, has ever laid a finger on me before. If Dad finds out . . .' I imagine Maura's cottage in flames.

'Best we keep your father out of this,' Yvonne hastily replies. 'But there is someone who can help.'

'Who?' Because unless it's one of his heavies, I can't imagine who it is. 'You're not calling the gardaí, are you?' I touch her skinny wrist as she slips her phone from her pocket.

The whites of her eyes flash and she looks at me in surprise. 'Me call the cops? Do I look like I've got a death wish?'

We both laugh at the absurdity of the situation. My father is the lawmaker of our family. To involve the police is an insult to his name.

'I'm calling your mam,' she adds, before I say another word.

I slowly shake my head as I spy my mother's name on Yvonne's phone.

'Trust me,' she mouths, as the call picks up on the other end.

I can't bear to listen. I take myself into the kitchen, put the kettle on and take two mugs from the cupboard. I should never have told Yvonne. I was stupid to trust her. I'm halfway through making plans to disappear when Yvonne joins me.

'All sorted.' She smiles brightly. 'Your mam is on her way.'

'On her way to what?' I retort. 'To have me committed? To bring me home?' What am I thinking, of course she wouldn't come here herself. Which of Dad's cronies is bringing me back? I narrow my eyes at Yvonne. 'You should have said that you didn't believe me. There's no need for this.'

But Yvonne gently reaches across and touches my arm. 'It's not like that at all. Your mam wants to build bridges . . . She just doesn't know how.'

'How do *you* know?' I snap because this is painful to listen to. Mam has been so distant, I can't leave myself open to further hurt.

'Because she talks to me, Kathryn. She's told me loads.' Yvonne looks me square in the eye. 'Give her a chance. She wants to help.'

'What about Dad?' I squeeze the teabags and leave them to one side.

'He's away on business. He doesn't need to know.'

I give Yvonne her tea and cradle my own cup. 'I can't see what good it's going to do, getting Mam over here.'

'Then you underestimate her.' Yvonne smiles. 'Your mam is a force to be reckoned with.'

CHAPTER 37

THEN

MAURA

I never imagined myself as a mother, at least, not back then. I was too young and foolish to understand the repercussions of what I had done. Daisy never talked about Jimmy and, luckily for me, never spoke to him again. I was too ashamed to tell her the truth. It never occurred to her that I tricked Jimmy into sleeping with me.

She kept trying to force check-ups on me and, given she was a nurse, I suppose it was only natural. In the end, I told her that I had gone private and lost the scan picture. She spent a lot of time worrying about me back then. I couldn't come to terms with the pregnancy. It was a ploy to marry Jimmy, but that had backfired on me. Jimmy had thought that I was Daisy, who of course was on the pill. But he was wrong on both counts.

I returned home to Doolin because I couldn't stand living in the city any more. My sister spent half the day in the hospital and I was bored in the hot flat. I didn't have any friends in Limerick, although she did introduce me to hers, but I had nothing in common with them. I was embarrassed about my situation, and being compared to her. She was clever, slim and beautiful, with personality and charisma, while I was a country girl with brittle hair, red cheeks and zero personality. Back in Doolin, depression closed in as I mourned the loss of the life that had felt painfully real. I should have been happy. I would be the mother of Jimmy's child. But I couldn't relate to my growing unborn baby, could barely stand it when it moved. I tried to imagine his child, just as I'd done a thousand times before I got pregnant. But the cold reality of my situation was nothing like the dream I once had. I should have been victorious, but bitterness and shame coursed through my veins.

Dad was too concerned about Mum's failing health to notice me. But Granny Maura did. I swear that evil woman grew more twisted by the day. Daisy called her an emotional vampire. She fed off misery. I'll never forget the night she cornered me. The rain was coming down hard outside as the weather turned, and we sat warming ourselves by the fire as I kept her company. The clothes were hanging on the wooden clothes horse and the faint smell of detergent hung in the air. Mammy was in the hospital, and while he was there, Dad took a funny turn. It turned out to be angina, and they were both kept in for tests. With the two of them sick, the house was a very glum place indeed. Without Daisy, it seemed like all the joy had been sucked from the world.

The only thing that kept me going was knowing that I had a roof over my head. I thought a lot about the cottage, and what I would do if my parents died. It gave me comfort to know that I would be alright in that way. I was young enough, but I loved the place even then. I loved how it stood on the hill looking down over the people of Doolin. I loved that separation of us and them. I loved it when the mist shrouded us at night apart from that reverent square cube of glowing light from the living room window. I loved the twisty hill and how hard it was for people to visit us. I even felt a guilty pleasure when the cars skidded on the way down.

I was thinking about the cottage when Maura turned her attention on to me. The fire crackled and hissed between us. I recall Maura's eyes narrowing as she took in my appearance. I was wearing my usual elasticated skirt and my brown flat shoes. They weren't trendy but they were comfortable. Geraldine had knocked on my door an hour before to ask if I wanted to go to the cinema. I'd sent her away, telling her that my parents weren't well. I hated talking to her, given how huge I was. I caught her looking at my great big stomach more than once. She'd also told me that if I ever 'needed to talk' she was always there for me. But talking wouldn't get me out of the situation I'd found myself in.

Geraldine asked me about Limerick and what it was like. I described Limerick as a noisy, smelly place to stay. It was Daisy she should've been talking to. I was relieved when Geraldine left. I sat across from Granny and she gave this little funny sneer. It was one of those ugly smiles that were usually reserved for my father.

'So when is the little bastard due?'

My mouth dropped open at the bile in her words. I told myself that she must have been talking about someone in the village.

'Sorry, what?' I leaned my head in closer, and she didn't blink. Her gaze was unyielding and cold.

'You heard me. You must be, what . . . six or seven months gone now.'

My stomach twisted into a knot of embarrassment and fear. Fear because I did not want my parents returning to this in the morning when they got home. I couldn't bear the thought of my father's shameful gaze. He had enough to deal with back then.

I managed to catch my breath. 'Eh? What are you on about?' But my shaky voice betrayed me immediately.

Granny Maura tutted loudly. 'I'm not stupid, nor am I blind. Your parents might be too sick to notice it but I'm not. And if you think you're bringing a bastard into this cottage, you're mistaken.

I won't have it under my roof. The shame of it . . .' she continued, each word a tiny arrow to my heart.

'This is my cottage too,' I said in a small voice. 'It's written in black and white.' I didn't acknowledge the baby, but I *had* to make that clear. Without the cottage, I had nothing.

'Not any more.' Her rasping words turned into a cough and I got up and fetched her a glass of water. After taking a swig, she continued with her threats. 'I'm going down the solicitors tomorrow and I'm changing my will. I'm not leaving my house to a dirty whore.'

It was not the first time I'd heard such filthy language come out of my grandmother's mouth. She had a name for everyone in Doolin and not one of them was pleasant. But I never thought that I would become such a target of hatred. 'Granny, please,' I pleaded. 'Don't be like that. You've always said I'm your favourite.'

'I never thought you'd be so easy!' she barked in return. 'The other one, yes. But I suppose she had more sense and sorted things out. But you . . .' She pointed a bony finger in my direction. 'You're no Catholic. You're just a dirty bitch. And I won't have an unmarried mother under this roof.'

A bloom of pink rose to her face as she became enraged. Perhaps she expected me to deny it, and maybe she thought she could've been wrong. But my silence spoke of my guilt.

She groaned as she rose from her chair, spluttering a tobacco cough. 'Tomorrow, I'm going to the solicitor. Everyone in Doolin will know what you are.'

'Please, Granny,' I pleaded, as she grabbed for her walking stick. 'Don't.'

She slapped away my hand. 'Look at the size of you! *Everybody* is going to know soon. I want you out of here. All of you.'

I couldn't comprehend it. She was threatening to throw us all out. Not just me, but Mam and Dad too. I couldn't allow it. I watched her shuffle into her room, her cane clanking against the floor with force while she mumbled under her breath. She was weak, but there was power in her words.

'I'll make you a cup of tea,' I called after her.

And I did. I made her a special cup of tea. Enough to make her drowsy, but not too strong that she couldn't swallow the medication I gave to her, just to be on the safe side. She was always stockpiling things. She was tight with money, and I suppose I inherited that ugly part of her.

That night as she fell asleep, I sat in her chair by the fire. I would not lose the cottage. Whatever else happened in my life, the house on Misery Hill would remain mine.

CHAPTER 38

FINN

A small tap on my face grows stronger as I emerge from my slumber. My eyelids feel glued together and I rub the sleep away.

'Are ya alright, Finn?'

Maura's voice breaks through the clouds of my confusion. For a second, I thought I was back in the hospital. My body is stiff when I try to sit up in bed but my leg . . . something's not right.

'I had the doctor round again,' Maura explains. I stare at what appears to be a rigid plastic splint forcing my left leg straight. I can't bend it at all, let alone walk out of here.

'What happened?' I gaze at the empty cot. 'Where's Saoirse?'

'In her travel cot.' Maura smiles, like this is the most natural situation in the world. 'It must have been the concussion. You fell and hurt your leg. The doctor's put a splint on it for now.' But a stress rash has crawled up her throat and I know that she's lying to me.

'Take it off, I don't want it.' I try to wriggle off the bed, but a bolt of pain stills my movements.

Maura tilts her head to one side as I suck air between my teeth. 'Are you in pain, dear? Do you want your meds?'

'No more meds!' My response is sharp – I know that's what has landed me here. I glance around the room. Dim light filters through the curtains. 'What time is it?'

'It's almost eight a.m.'

'Eight?' I say in disbelief. 'The next day?' I can't believe how long I've been out for. I want to challenge her about the so-called doctor, but I need to handle Maura with care. 'I need the toilet.' My kidneys are screaming for relief. I'm desperate to see Saoirse too. I don't have my phone, and the pain in my leg is searing as Maura helps me shift it from the bed. When Maura leaves, I presume it's to get my crutches. I baulk at the sight of her pushing an old battered-looking wheelchair towards me.

'Where are my crutches?'

'You're too unsteady for those,' Maura commands.

I stare at the contraption which she positions at the side of the bed. Where did she get that from? But then I remember the travel-sized first-aid boxes that she'd stolen from people's cars. A vision rises of Maura pushing the old wheelchair up the hill, laden with items she's taken from the back of crashed cars.

I accept Maura's help and go to the toilet because I haven't got much choice.

This is temporary, I tell myself. Because she can't keep me here forever. The safest thing I can do right now is to pacify her.

Relief sweeps over me as she pushes me into the living room and I see Saoirse, playing in her travel cot. Her cheeks are a healthy colour and I pray that Maura hasn't slipped some kind of sedative into her milk during the night.

I watch the fingers of Maura's right hand climb up her left arm. She sees me looking and pulls down her sleeve. Is she self-harming? How many scabs and scars is she hiding under there?

My mind races ahead to an escape plan. I need food, my medication and my phone. If I could get the plastic splint off, I could pack a bag and go down into Doolin, or find a local B&B. But a part of me needs to discover the truth. Maura lifts up my baby and hands her to me. I get lost in the smell of freshly changed clothes and baby powder, delivering kisses to her soft pink cheeks. She plays with my hair as I hold her close.

'I'll scramble you some eggs,' Maura says, pushing us both into the kitchen.

I'm famished, but my trust has gone. 'I'll have cornflakes, thanks.' I look up at my aunt, hoping she won't slip anything into the milk.

She wheels me into the kitchen. I'm sitting at the sturdy oak table, holding my daughter close and hoping that my compliance is enough to earn Maura's trust.

'You're homesick, aren't you?' Maura places the bowl of cornflakes in front of me.

I nod, tears not far away.

'Sorry that I've been so hard to live with.' She breathes a heavy sigh and I watch closely as she makes us both a cup of tea. 'I've always had problems with my temper.'

I don't correct her as I hold my daughter and scoop the cornflakes into my mouth. My throat is so dry, cornflakes and chilled milk have never tasted so good. If this sends me under, it will have almost been worth it. Maura hands Saoirse a teething rusk. I wait as Maura places our mugs on the table, along with a teapot and a small jug of milk. I recall how she hadn't touched her Ovaltine last night and am relieved as she takes a long sip of tea.

'Motherhood is hard . . .' Her gaze is so wistful that I don't know if she's talking to me. 'I should have made allowances.' Her eyes are misty with tears when they meet mine.

I rest my spoon on the table. 'What's wrong, Maura?' Because despite everything that's happened, it hurts me to see her in pain.

Besides, I need to win her around if I've any chance of getting out of here.

'It was harder in my day,' she continues without answering my question. 'Single mothers were treated like lepers. People would cross the road rather than talk to you . . .' I'm about to say that things are better now when she adds, 'I kept my pregnancy a secret. I couldn't bear for my parents to live with the shame.'

I can't digest Maura's words. Saoirse is restless, so I allow her on to the floor. There's a blanket already set down, and she plays with her favourite toys.

'What do you mean?' I can't help but ask because I'm hungry for clarification.

'I'm talking about my pregnancy. And if you're asking who was the first person to bring you into Misery Cottage, then you'd be right to think that it was me.'

My mouth drops open at the revelation. What does she mean?

She is resolute, unblinking. It's like she's daring me to challenge her. But she's getting het up again and I dare not say a word. 'Daisy wasn't your mother. She took you away from me.'

'You . . . You're lying!' I stutter. Yet I've always felt that my childhood hasn't been quite right. There were no baby books. No mementos of my birth. Photos are few and far between, and always taken in the UK. Then there were the times when Mum acted strangely when I'd ask about my past. I'd brushed these things aside, but now all my niggles and worries return. I never knew my dad, and Mum was all I'd ever known. But this nightmare unfolding before me . . . I . . . I can't take it in.

My stomach churns as I watch my daughter, happily playing with her toys. Was I like her once, sitting here on the floor under Maura's guidance? It's inconceivable to me now.

'It's why Daisy left so suddenly. She didn't think I was fit to bring you up.'

A sob catches in my throat. 'You're saying . . .' I swallow to strengthen my words. 'You're saying that you are my mother?'

'A mother of sorts . . .' she says, following my gaze. 'I went to stay with your ma—' She's about to say 'mammy' but stalls. 'With Daisy in Limerick for the last couple of months of my pregnancy and had my baby there. Such a beautiful little girl . . .' Her words fade as she becomes lost in the memory. She's referring to me in the third person. Perhaps it helps, to keep me separate. No. I can't accept it. I won't. Though Maura seems terrifyingly sincere as she stares into the middle distance.

'I couldn't cope. I didn't have the temperament to raise a child.' She blinks three times in quick succession while she fights to keep the tears at bay. 'Then, much later, Daisy took you away from me. She never came back. I suppose she thought it was better that way.' Maura gives me a sideways glance. 'Geraldine has always known. It's the one secret she's managed to keep to herself. Your father is a local.'

My stomach churns when I hear her utter the words aloud. The subject of my father is something that Mum . . . *Daisy* has always swerved. She said he was in the army and here for a brief stay. She never saw him again. But now I'm wondering if my real dad is closer to home.

Maura drains the last of her tea and pushes her cup aside. 'It's Aiden's father – Jimmy Walsh. Now do you see?'

Bile rises in my throat. 'Aiden is my half-brother?'

'He's family,' Maura says softly, as she stares at my daughter, happily playing on the blanket. 'Now you see why I was so upset. Seeing him here in my house.'

The revelations hit me like a punch to the gut. We became close so quickly. I thought it was flirting. Was it our familial bond?

A wave of nausea threatens to overcome me. But Maura . . . with her eccentricities and mistrustful ways. I don't want it to be her.

Daisy was my mother. She reared me. She took me away from this awful place and I'm so glad that she did. Her leaving finally makes sense. This is why Mum – and she will always be my mum – didn't want me to come here. Maura gave birth to me, but Mum knew she was too mentally unstable to bring me up, so she fled to England to keep me safe. Had I not been in an accident near Misery Hill I wouldn't have stayed long, but my disability has kept me dependent on Maura. Seeing Aiden again must have triggered her recent outburst and pushed her over the edge.

'Aiden looks so much like his daddy,' Maura sighs. 'He was a very handsome man.'

I glance at the contraption that Maura has tightly fitted to my leg, before returning my attention to the woman before me. 'Maura, you have to let me go. You know that, don't you? I can't stay. It was never meant to be long term.'

I can't acknowledge the fact that she's my biological mother. Not yet.

Her eyes are wet with tears as she meets mine. 'I know. And I'm sorry. Things just ran away with me.' She swallows and I sense that there's a lot more she wants to say, but can't. Not yet. 'Don't leave on a bad note.' She swipes away a tear. Her eyes are bloodshot and I can see the toll that this has taken on her. 'Please. Give me one more day with you both. I'll make us a nice dinner. There's a storm forecast for today. There won't be any ferries or flights. Go tomorrow, once it has passed. You can cook the dinner with me,' she pleads. 'Serve it up yourself.'

'Fine. But I need to speak to Aiden. Tell him that I'm okay.'

'Later.' But there is an edge to her voice.

I imagine Aiden with Joy – who is my niece, I suppose. I don't know how I feel about seeing them again. Mum wouldn't have left Ireland with me without good reason. Ever since I saw those newspaper clippings there has been a nagging sensation in the back of my mind. But I can't ask Maura about it. Her moods are balancing on a tightrope as it is. I compartmentalise the bombshell that has landed on my lap. I cannot accept Maura as my mother. Not now, not ever. Once I leave Misery Hill, I'm never coming back. Maura needs more help than I can give her right now.

'There's something else I need to tell you.' Maura's hand returns to her other arm and she begins to scratch. A feeling of dread rises within me as I realise that there is more.

That's when she relays her run-in with the other woman who crashed into my car. Her name is Kathryn and, according to Maura, she comes from a powerful family. 'The silly woman's got it into her head that Saoirse is her child.' The words are spoken without compassion, just the annoyance of someone trying to swot a persistent fly. 'Fancy coming all the way here. As if you'd just hand her back!'

Maura's words are chilling. She didn't say 'hand her over'. She said, 'hand her back'.

'Why does she want Saoirse?' The tone of my voice has risen a notch but I can't help it. 'She's not her baby . . . is she?'

'Of course not!' Strained laughter leaves Maura's lips. 'But it's best if you both stay in your room for today.' She scratches her cheek, her nails leaving red marks in their wake. 'She said she was coming back. I'll tell her you're not here.'

Now I'm wondering if it's safe to hide away in the bedroom from the woman who will soon be knocking on her door.

'Can I get you anything?' she asks. I try not to flinch when Maura touches my shoulder.

'No . . . thanks. My leg is playing up. I just need to rest.'

She opens her mouth to speak, most likely to offer me painkillers, but then thinks better of it and stops.

'Fine, well, um . . . you know where everything is.' A sudden shower of rain makes its presence known as it taps upon the windowpanes. Does it *ever* stop raining in this godforsaken place?

'Maura, can I have my phone? People will start to worry if they don't hear from me.'

'Goodness, is that all that's bothering you?' Maura's fists clench. 'After everything I've said? I'm your mother! You haven't once asked about what life was like for me!' The outburst is sudden and frightening as she grabs my wheelchair and begins to push. 'Selfish girl . . . Stupid, selfish girl . . .'

'Maura, wait, I . . .' But my words are lost as she continues with her outburst.

'And now this awful woman is coming to take the little one from me. You don't care! You don't give two shits!'

My heart beats hard as she pushes me into the room, and I scream, my outstretched leg bouncing against the side of the door. I tell her that I'm sorry, but my words trail after her as she storms out.

Moments later the sudden sound of Saoirse's cries drill into my brain.

Oh God, I think, and I try to turn the wheelchair around. *What's she doing to my baby?*

CHAPTER 39

THEN

MAURA

Granny Maura was cold and stiff in her bed. I hadn't expected the vomit trailing from her blue lips. Her bony hands clutched the blanket, her eyes open and accusing when I entered her room. I'd slept quite well that night. So well, in fact, that it had all seemed like a dream. But now I was faced with the harsh reality of what I had done. And me, meant to be a Catholic! I wasn't doing very well on that front. What would my parents make of this? And them both ill in the hospital . . . What had I done? I gasped from the force of the kicks inside me. Could babies sense distress? I barely got a wink of sleep back then as my poor ribs were punished from the inside.

With a shaky hand, I picked up the phone receiver and called the doctor's surgery.

'This is Mrs Claffey,' I said, knowing that Jimmy wouldn't speak to me. 'I need to speak to Dr Walsh. It's an emergency.' Back then, you could speak to the doctor directly if you said the right things.

'Mrs Claffey, how can I help you?' Jimmy sounded harried as usual, although his tone was more understanding than it usually was with me.

'Come to the cottage *immediately*.'

A pause. 'Maura.' The word fell from his lips like a stone being dropped into a well.

'Wait,' I continued. 'Don't hang up. It's Granny Maura. She's dead.' I didn't dislike the feeling as I said the words aloud.

'Are your parents there?'

'No . . .' My mind felt clouded and confused. Why was he asking me this? Didn't he trust me? Did he think I was trying to lure him in? 'They're . . . they're at the hospital. Neither of them are well. Daddy has angina and Mammy . . . well, you know what's wrong with her.' Of course he did. He was her doctor. I was babbling because I didn't want him to hang up. 'Granny Maura's dead. You need to come right now.'

'Right. Do you need an ambulance?'

'No. She's quite dead. As stiff as the sheets hung out on a frosty night.'

Perhaps he sensed something in my voice, but Jimmy came alone. My heart danced in my chest as he entered our small cottage and his presence filled the room. Despite everything, I still loved him. His brown leather bag swung from his fingers, his knuckles white. He was wearing his corduroy jacket, the one with the patches that made him look distinguished. He gawked at my expanding waistline and his cheeks turned a light shade of pink that made me forget my sister's warnings about him being a bit quare in the head. At least he had the decency to ask how I was. I pressed my fingernails into my palms and I tried to stay in control. 'I'm not well. This has all been . . .'

'A shock, yes, I can imagine.' He tore his gaze from my stomach. 'I'll have a look, then.'

I followed him into Granny's bedroom. He had been there numerous times, as she liked to call the doctor out as often as she could get away with it. But today was different. Granny Maura wouldn't be calling the doctor any more. He had barely laid hands on her body when I blurted out my confession.

'It's all my fault. That's what I've been trying to say.'

'What's that now?' His brow was furrowed as he glanced at the empty prescription bottle on her bedside. It was well out of date but the drugs had proven effective just the same.

'I did it,' I replied, feeling the weight of my guilt lifting off my chest. 'She said she was going to the solicitors to take me out of her will.'

I shrank a little as Jimmy's eyes grew as big as the saucers on Granny's sideboard. The special ones that she wouldn't let anyone touch. I could touch them all I wanted now. The thought delivered a little bit of warmth. I felt no regret, just fear for what was going to happen next.

'Jesus.' Jimmy's leather bag made a loud thunk as it dropped to Granny Maura's thinly carpeted floor. The rest of us had to make do with cold lino back then. 'I . . . I can't be party to this. You're not serious, are you?'

'Why would I joke about killing my own grandmother?' I stared at him in surprise. He was meant to be a doctor. I'd expected more professional behaviour than this. 'She was going to leave me homeless. She said I was a dirty whore and that I was to pack my bags.'

'Oh God.' The words were muffled as they escaped his cupped hand. He looked like he was about to throw up. 'Does anyone else know?'

I filled him in on the evening's events. How my parents were still at the hospital. My row with Granny Maura. How I crushed up her medication and stirred it into her tea. Then when she was drowsy, how I made her swallow a load more for good measure. All the while, Jimmy was pacing, his face flushed.

'Why did you have to drag me into this?' His eyes were wide and fearful. I felt strangely calm. I suppose I'd had all night to come to terms with it.

'Sure who else would I call? It's as much your mess as mine. If you hadn't abandoned me, I wouldn't have been so desperate for a roof over my head.'

He dragged his hands over his face, as if he could wash the thought away. He took a few breaths and at last, composed himself.

'Okay. Okay. Well, we can't have you going to prison. Not in your condition. She had a bit of dementia. She overdosed herself by accident. Yes, her dementia's on her medical records so that'll stick . . .'

I had a feeling he was talking more to himself than me so I left him to it.

'Where are you going?' he said, as I turned to leave.

'To make a cup of tea.'

He grabbed me by the arm. It was the first time he'd physically touched me since our night in the back of his car seven months before.

'Maura. Do you understand how serious this is? You could go to prison. We both could, now that I'm involved.'

'It was her time,' I simply said. 'Sure she couldn't go on forever. I just helped her along.'

But Jimmy didn't seem very pleased to hear this. 'You're not to say that to anyone, do you hear me? I won't be able to help you if you do.'

'What do you take me for?' I snapped. 'I'm not stupid. Do you think I'm going down to the village to tell everyone I finished her off?' I shook my head. 'You're the father of my child. I *had* to tell you the truth.'

Jimmy gave me a look that said he very much wished I hadn't. 'Well, it was the shock talking, do you hear me? She's not been well. Did you know that she had cancer?'

I shook my head. This was news to me.

'Yes, well, lucky for you there shouldn't be a post-mortem. Get me some clean bedding. We need to make it look like she died in her sleep.'

It wasn't easy, due to the rigor mortis. Her grip on the dirty blankets was tight. I'd have to get rid of them before my parents came home.

'Hurry.' A sheen of sweat had broken out on Jimmy's brow as he checked his watch. 'I've been here a while. Just say that you were upset and I was comforting you.'

I snorted at that. He'd been of little comfort to me of late. But to be fair, he was making up for it now. As soon as the bed was made, he called the surgery and updated them with the news. He told me for a second time that because she'd been ill, there was no need for an autopsy, as long as we stuck to the story that she died in her sleep. We got rid of her stash of tablets, and washed her teacup clean.

I'll always remember the sight of Jimmy standing at that window when he finally turned to me, his face haggard as he spoke.

'What are we going to do about the baby?'

CHAPTER 40

MAURA

A voice in my head is shouting. It's Daisy's voice, but it's distant as she yells at me to calm down.

'I don't know you any more, Maura! What happened to you while I was away?' The ghost of our row plays in my mind. 'You're not cut out to be a mother! You hurt everyone you love!'

Her accusations still pain me, even now. Because they're true. I hurt myself too. My head is wrecked, with all of this coming at me. First losing Daisy, then the challenges of seeing Finn again. Then that awful Toíbín woman from the accident, threatening me with all sorts. I think of my life before Finn arrived, so simple but so lonely. And as I take a few deep breaths, I comfort the babby and tell her everything will be alright. Because she doesn't know any different. She is worth fighting for. I'd hoped that when I told Finn I was her mammy, she might react differently. After everything I did for her . . . It was hardly my fault that Daisy snatched her away. Now Finn is rattling her bedroom door and screaming for Saoirse.

But there's something more worrying on the horizon – the swanky car driving up Misery Hill. It's a Bentley by the look of it. My mouth thins into a cold hard line. Of course it is. If those filthy Dublin scum think they can come to *my* house and order *me* about . . . they can think again.

I turn on my heel, still shushing and soothing the babby as I unlock Finn's bedroom door. 'She's coming,' I warn, thrusting the babby into Finn's open arms. Her tear-streaked face has lost its colour and she accepts her with gratitude. 'That Kathryn woman,' I warn once more. 'She's on her way. Keep the babby quiet.'

I don't waste a second as I close the bedroom door behind me. I trot into the living room, and turn the radio on. Country and western music fills the air. I'm just in time as I hear the crunch of tyres on the gravel outside. She's here.

CHAPTER 41

KATHRYN

My mother likes to make an appearance, wherever she is. Unless she's by my father's side and then she takes a back seat. This morning I watched from the upstairs bedroom window as she exited the chauffeur-driven Bentley. She knows how to drive but stopped doing that years ago. She daintily stepped out of the car, wrapped in a luxurious fur coat, her designer handbag dangling from the crook of her arm. I came downstairs, my nerves on edge with anticipation. Yvonne stepped aside, allowing my mother entry into the hall. The driver waited in the car, a middle-aged man who could be trusted not to talk. All of Dad's staff signed NDAs. Even if they hadn't, none of them would dare blab. People who can't be trusted have a tendency to disappear.

'Mother,' I said, with a polite nod of the head as she entered the hall in a cloud of fragrant perfume.

'Kathryn.' Her eyes appraised me like she was examining a piece of art. Distant as always, but she had come. I only hoped it was for the right reasons.

'Please, come in,' Yvonne beckoned. 'Will I put the kettle on?'

'I'm not staying.'

Mother glided into the room, her stiletto heels echoing on the wooden floor. The air grew thick with tension. I felt like I was suffocating as I waited for her to speak. Was she going to demand that I returned with her? Or worse still, check me into some psychiatric unit because she thought I'd lost the plot? Because I wasn't going. I glanced at the expensive jewellery adorning my mother's fingers, the cold diamonds sparkling in contrast with the warmth of the room. I knew what her priorities were.

'Mum—' I began, but she cut me off.

'Yvonne told me everything. You believe your baby is alive.'

My baby. Not her granddaughter, or Kiera. Just 'my baby', like she's a separate entity to the rest of the Toíbín clan.

'Yes.' I swallowed, feeling angry but small in my mother's presence. 'They said she had been thrown clear of the crash, but I remember hearing her crying inside the car before I passed out. I think there was a mix-up at the crash site.'

'Interesting,' Mother mused, brushing imaginary lint from her coat. 'And what do you plan to do about it?'

'Find the truth.' My response was immediate.

'Good. What have you done so far?' A hint of approval tinted her words. A spark of hope ignited inside me and I dared to believe that maybe my mother cared after all. I told her everything, including details of my run-in with Maura. Her face grew rigid as I described how I was pushed to the ground.

That was when my mother instructed me to put my coat on. She snapped her fingers when I failed to move. 'Come along. I haven't got all day. It's time we straightened this out.'

Yvonne raised a hand, as if she was in school. 'Um . . . Mrs Toíbín . . . do you need me to come along?'

My mother looked down her cosmetically enhanced nose. 'Stay here, and if my husband rings, tell him we've gone for a walk.'

My pulse picked up pace at the mention of Daddy. 'He knows you're here?'

'Just for a visit, nothing more.'

Of course. Because there would be trouble otherwise. I wasn't the only person my father liked to keep an eye on.

I followed my mother out of the Airbnb, trying to keep pace with her brisk, high-heeled stride. As I got into the car, I silently prayed that she wouldn't instruct her driver to turn the car around and head back to Dublin with me inside.

'Drive.' She gave directions to the chauffeur, who immediately started the engine. We pulled away from the kerb and drove towards Misery Hill, the car wipers swishing back and forth as bad weather closed in. I held on tightly to my seat belt while we commenced our ascent.

My breath hitched as the cliff edge guard-rails taunted me. They hadn't been strong enough to stop my car coming off the road.

'Are you okay?' Mother asked, in an uncharacteristic display of concern. I must have looked a sight, clinging on to my safety belt like a raft in the storm.

I delivered a tight nod and forced myself to look away from the scene of the wreckage. It may have been cleaned up, but it was there in my mind. Maura's thatched cottage loomed before us, standing lone in the weather-beaten landscape. In that moment, I hated Misery Hill more than anything.

I wanted to ask Mam why she had come here. I needed to know if she really cared. I never imagined that she'd give Yvonne the time of day, let alone talk to her about me. Was her cold exterior all a front?

'There it is,' I told the chauffeur as Maura's cottage came into view. 'That's Maura Claffey's house.'

My mother's steely gaze locked on to mine. 'Stay strong, Kathryn. Remember, you're a Toíbín.' I responded with a nod, grateful for her support. 'You need answers, and we won't leave until we have them. Don't let these culchies boss you around.'

'Thanks.' I offered my mother a watery smile as the car parked on the small gravel drive.

'Ready?' Mother asked, concentrating on the cottage ahead. Such an ugly little thing, with tiny windows and thick whitewashed stone walls. I gazed past the thatch to see a string of smoke rise from the chimney. Someone was in.

'I'm ready,' I said at last. Taking a deep breath, I got out of the car. I straightened my posture and tried to fix my hair as the rain beat me back. Mam didn't flinch. She just pulled an umbrella from her bag and took dainty steps to the door. Seagulls screamed over our heads, heightening my sense of unease. I tasted salt when I licked my lips to ease the dryness. I hated the sea air. I hated everything about this place that had caused my life to implode.

Now we're standing at the door. It's not even 10 a.m., but I couldn't have waited another minute.

Mother knocks authoritatively and my heart begins to race as footsteps approach from inside.

'What do you want?' A deep female voice rises from the other side of the door.

'If you'll kindly open the door, I'll tell you.' Mam speaks with a force that I didn't know she possessed. But the door doesn't budge. Instead, a small square pane of glass is pushed forward and the window abruptly opens.

Mother sighs, already exasperated with the woman staring out from the other side. 'I'm Mrs Toíbín. I'm with my daughter, Kathryn. Her baby was in the back of the car when your niece drove her off the road down there.'

My mother doesn't mince her words as she points to the accident blackspot on the winding road.

But the woman's waxy face glares at us through the window. 'What do you want? Sympathy? Best you go into town for that. There's nothing for you here.'

'We want answers,' Mother replies bluntly, trying but failing to open the locked door.

The woman's about to close the window when I find my voice at last. 'You've got my baby. I don't know how, and I don't care. I just want her back.'

If I find out that she's stolen my Kiera, she'll regret it until the day she dies. My hands bunch into fists. That day may be closer than she thinks.

CHAPTER 42

FINN

I hold Saoirse tight in my arms. Her long lashes brush her rosy cheeks, and her warmth is a comforting presence against the chill of fear that has settled in my chest. The door had barely closed behind Maura when that woman and her daughter turned up making threats. I listened from my bedroom window, their words carrying a sense of foreboding that pushed my other concerns to the back of my mind. Maura may be desperate to make me stay, but I have no doubt that she'd defend us to her last breath.

Kathryn Toíbín shouts against the rain, demanding to be let inside so she can 'see for herself'. I know about the Toíbín family, now Maura has filled me in. For once, I'm grateful to Maura as she stands her ground. Had she allowed them inside . . . I dare not think about it. I don't want to see Kathryn Toíbín and relive that awful day. I listen keenly while Maura tells them that we're not here.

'She's gone back to England with the babby, not that it's any of your business.' Her words are met with dismay.

'She's mine, do you hear me?' Kathryn's scream pierces the air. 'You've no right to take her away from me!'

'Shhh, shhh.' I comfort my baby as I listen to Kathryn say that she heard her baby cry right before she passed out.

It can't be true. I don't believe it. But yet . . . I recall those hazy days after the crash when I first saw that picture of Saoirse. And then when we were reunited, I didn't recognise her. But then I was dosed up to the eyeballs with drugs. It's only natural to be out of kilter after such a traumatic event.

But what if they are right? What if she isn't mine? Did my baby die in the crash? But all my fears melt away when I look at my beautiful girl, her black hair soft against my fingers as I brush it back from her face. She gazes at me with a calmness that seems to say, 'I'm yours, and you are mine.'

There is movement outside, footsteps on the gravel, and I breathe in the silence while the angry voices fade. I hear something about solicitors and DNA tests. Closing my eyes, I dismiss the pain in my leg and the fear that Maura has instilled in me in the last few days. All I can focus on is keeping my daughter close. They can't take her now . . . can they? I've managed to loosen the home-made splint on my leg but I'm a long way from mobile. I've never felt so helpless in my life.

I try not to cry because I've done enough of that already, and it won't get us anywhere. Cautiously, I push the wheelchair towards the window and watch the two women walk away. The woman in the fur coat leads the way, while the younger of the two waves her hands in the air. So this is the woman who crashed her car into mine. She is thin but pretty, with long blonde hair. She walks with little effort, unlike me. I pull back from the window when she turns around to glance at the cottage. Her presence makes me feel nauseous and I push away the memories of the crash. I can't give it a second viewing. I'm not strong enough to go there again.

I wait for Maura as the car pulls away. What is she doing down there? It feels like she's been gone forever. Our earlier problems have been swept aside while fresh worries take centre stage.

The radio is turned down, and she strides into the bedroom, her gaze never leaving me. 'You're shocking pale. Are you in pain?' She smiles at Saoirse, taking her chubby hand and giving it a kiss.

'Those women.' I hug Saoirse even closer. 'Are they coming back?'

'Don't worry about all that nonsense. That Kathryn Tóibín is mad with grief. And her mother . . . I know her sort. I soon put them in their place.' Her mouth becomes downturned and she mumbles some choice words beneath her breath.

'I heard some of it.' I inhale to ease the tightness in my lungs. 'She said the babies were mixed up after the . . . after the . . .' My emotions threaten to spill over. 'Maybe we should do a DNA test.'

Saoirse babbles in my arms, oblivious that her future lies in the balance.

'Over my dead body,' Maura says firmly. But now the look on her face makes me scared. 'Whatever happens,' Maura continues, 'that babby is yours. Those Dublin tramps won't cross this threshold. You have my word.'

They were hardly tramps. I saw the chauffeur-driven car, and the mother's jewellery-laden fingers. Those people come from money. Money equals power. What if they take my baby away? My daughter claps her hands, and love rushes through me like a tidal wave. I tell myself not to worry, but Maura's behaviour scares me.

'Maura . . .' I say, trying to read her mood. 'Have I anything to worry about?' I watch her closely, aware of the possibility that she might be hiding something. It's not just about Saoirse's identity. What about the other things I found? 'Maura?' I prompt, when she fails to respond. She's standing in front of me like a life-sized mechanical toy that has wound down.

'Nothing,' Maura mutters. 'I'm just annoyed that they came. Who do they think they are? The cheek of it. You should lay low for a while, just in case they try to come back.'

Her words floor me. I wanted her to say that no DNA test in the world could prove anything other than that Saoirse is mine.

Maura's shoulders are hunched as she approaches to wheel me out to the living room. We have a lot to discuss, but we'll do it when Saoirse is asleep. The last thing I need is Maura getting upset and disturbing the baby. My thoughts float to the red purse under her bed. The one belonging to Aiden's wife. How did it get there? And can I report this woman who calls herself my mother to the police?

I wait until after lunch when Saoirse is asleep. Our plates of food are cleared. We have eaten quietly, our minds filled with the events of the last few days.

'Maura . . . we need to talk. I don't want any bad feelings, I just want the truth. Because I need to know what I'm dealing with, now the Toíbíns are involved.'

'And what truth would that be?' A shadow crosses Maura's face. 'You want to know if Saoirse is really yours? Or maybe you're more interested in what's under my bed.'

CHAPTER 43

KATHRYN

Mother sits in the living room and hands her empty cup to Yvonne, as if she's some kind of servant. She's used to being waited on, but she hasn't always been this way. Yvonne almost curtseys as she takes it from her, and I realise that her cosy chats with my mother were an exaggeration. But they brought her here, and that's a start. If I get my baby back, she's going to need a grandmother. But how will Dad feel about that?

I try to break the silence but I don't know what to say. 'Thanks for coming,' I manage eventually. I can't drink my tea. My stomach is in knots.

'Nobody disrespects a Toíbín. That bitch is lucky there was a wall between us.' My mother's features grow stern. 'If your father knew what she did . . .' She shakes her head. 'One way or another, it'll all be over soon.'

I nod. 'And if she's mine?'

'Then we'll deal with it, in our own way.'

The Toíbín way, I think to myself. I'll never escape my family, no matter how hard I try. But today, I am grateful for it. 'But she's gone back to England. What are we going to do now?' I wanted to ask in the car but I was just about holding it together as we made the journey back to the Airbnb.

'We follow her.' Mam's blue eyes shine with determination. 'She's not getting away with this.'

A surge of hope flares in my chest. 'Really? You mean it?'

Mother nods, her features tight as she searches her designer bag for another cigarette. 'I'll sort everything out. I just need to clear the trip with your dad first.' She crosses her elegant legs and I feel like I'm in safe hands.

My father's regime means everything. But my heart is warm. Is this what it's like to feel a mother's love?

I walk her to the door and she relaxes a little as she exhales a stream of smoke. I've liked having her here. No, not liked, that's not the right word. This whole day has filled me with dread. I've *needed* her, and she delivered. The thought of seeing the baby – my baby? – in that creepy little cottage has left me more confused than before. I feel like Alice in Wonderland – forever falling. I don't know which way is up. But her offer to travel with me to England gives me hope.

'Can't you stay a bit longer?' I hate the neediness in my voice.

'I have to make arrangements.' She stands at the front door, waiting for Yvonne to open it for her. She'll do the same with the car. The moment she makes an appearance, the driver will get out and open her door.

'Arrangements for what?' I follow her out. There's an unspoken rule in the Toíbín clan. When someone says they're making arrangements, you don't ask about the details, only know that it will get done. Dad's contacts will track Finn down, I've no doubt of that.

'A DNA test, of course.' My mother's tone is matter-of-fact.

I hadn't expected her answer but it makes sense. There's so much I want to say to her, but I'm taking tentative steps. This has been more about defending our family honour than helping me.

There are no goodbye hugs. She stands at the side of the shiny black car, delivers a nod of acknowledgement and tells me to be strong.

'Remember your roots,' she says. 'You're not alone, Kathryn. You never were. Let us take care of this now.'

Us? Not her. I stand in silence, a drizzle of rain kissing my skin. Father knows about this visit, after all. Is it possible that he's monitoring us from afar? Of course he is. He's protective of his family – to a fault. Now Mam's gone, and I blink against the mist as I watch her car drive away.

'Are you okay?'

Yvonne almost makes me jump out of my skin. I take a deep breath and glance back up at Misery Hill. 'I will be.'

'I hope I didn't overstep the line. Telling your mother.'

'No. You did the right thing.'

Yvonne's face creases into a soft smile. 'Come in then, come in.' She ushers me inside. But a silent warning bell rings in the back of my mind. My situation is desperate. I want my baby back. But am I doing the right thing? Because if that baby is Kiera, I'm bringing her into a family as cold as ice.

CHAPTER 44

THEN

MAURA

If Granny Maura had a big turnout, then Daddy had it three-fold. People came from way beyond Doolin to see him off. Daisy had no choice but to come back. She cried at his graveside – big, fat tears rolling down her cheeks. I stood, in sombre silence as the rain flattened my hair to my face. Nobody offered me an umbrella, but then my sister had gone to such an effort to style herself. Every time she came home, it was like she had something to prove. This time, she turned up driving a BMW. She didn't get that from her nurse's wage. She had an eye for rich men. We had the wake in the Doolin hotel and it was packed to the rafters. It was the same place we'd seen off my mother four short weeks before, after she succumbed to the cancer. Some say Da died of a broken heart.

The last few months had taken its toll on me. I couldn't find anything black to wear but Granny Maura's old funeral dress fitted my expanding waistline. I washed it twice to rid it of the smell of tobacco first. I was mortified, having to go out in public when I was as big as a house. It was hard to walk without waddling, and I wore the biggest coat I could find. But still there were whispers. Tongues were set wagging in Doolin that day. I grew to hate the people who lived there even more. I looked for Jimmy but saw no sign of him. He should have been there with me, we should have been wed. But instead, I was left to face the scandal on my own.

'Are you wearing Mammy's perfume?' Daisy had said when she joined my side.

'So what if I am?' I'd snapped. 'No point in wasting it.'

Then she tilted her head as she stared, and the hairs on the back of my neck prickled. Too much had passed between us for me to be able to read her thoughts. Later, after she'd had a few too many drinks, she took me aside. 'Don't end up like her,' she'd said, unsteady on her high heels.

'Who, Mammy?' Now this confused me, because she was barely in the ground.

'No, Granny Maura.' My sister couldn't hide her disdain as she took in Granny's old dress. 'Don't get like her. Promise me. Take up a hobby. Dress your age. Look for the good in life.' It was at that very moment that Jimmy made an appearance. As he gazed at my stomach with disdain, the meaning in my sister's words withered away. I couldn't bear to see him arm in arm with someone else. Her name was Maria. They'd been dating for over a year, which meant that they were together when he'd slept with me. She was older than him but pretty, with sleek chestnut hair that tumbled down her back in waves.

'Fecking bitch,' I muttered beneath my breath. 'I hope we bury her next.'

Consumed with misery, I turned on a group of three villagers who were obviously talking about me. 'Take a picture, why don't ya? It'll last longer!'

Then I turned and strode out the door, pushing past the people who relayed their condolences. Daisy apologised in my wake. I stomped out of the hotel, stopping to take off the pointed heels that pinched and twisted my poor swollen toes. I vowed to wear sensible shoes from then onwards. I mean, who was going to be looking at my fecking feet?

'Where are you going?' Daisy trotted up the road after me.

'And you with a university degree,' I said coldly. 'Where do you think I'm going? To Buckingham Palace to see the Queen.' Grey clouds rumbled above me, threatening to spit out more rain.

'Don't be like that.' Daisy touched my arm, and I pulled away. I saw the hurt in her eyes and found gratification from it. 'Maura, you can't leave me to face them all on my own.'

My nostrils flared in fury. 'Why? Isn't that what you've done to me for the last few years? Where were you when Mam needed her meds or her backside wiped? I didn't see you when she was moaning in pain but refusing to go to hospital. Where were you when all the villagers came to visit, expecting me to make tea for them, night and day. I've had enough of them and I've had enough of you.'

'Why did you say that about Maria? None of this is her fault. She's not done anything to you.'

Jimmy had wronged Maria too, but I didn't want to hear it. I carried on, enjoying the sensation of the hard ground bruising the soles of my feet as I walked towards Misery Hill.

◆ ◆ ◆

The birth was long and painful, and took place at a private clinic where questions weren't asked. Apart from the village gossips, the only people that knew about my pregnancy could have been counted on one hand. I didn't want my sister there, but Daisy came just the same. Something changed in me the day I gave birth. Little by little, any brightness around me turned grey. I was so distraught about Jimmy's coldness towards me that I couldn't see things clearly. I remember lying in bed and reflecting upon it all, with a cup of tea and an empty belly. Fear washed over me as I thought about motherhood. A good mother would be someone like Daisy, who would socialise with other parents and know exactly how to act. She would manage things like schools, special occasions, birthdays and play dates. Such things were beyond me. I got stressed even thinking about it.

I brought my little girl home at night, when the villagers were in their beds. Nobody knew about her then. We knew the news would come out eventually, but with Granny Maura and my parents gone, it didn't seem to matter as much any more. Those early days were tough. I both loved and hated my baby. She was such a wee thing, but her cries were like a drill to my brain.

The fire was always on, the cottage toasty warm. My inheritance left me comfortable, but I hated the expense just the same. Daisy stocked the shelves so I didn't have to leave the cottage, and told villagers that I was ill and not up for visitors. She'd begged me to go to Limerick with her, but I couldn't live like that. It wasn't long since the death of our parents, and Daisy needed to go back to work.

Home in the cottage with a newborn baby was not a good place for me to be. Daisy had shown me the ropes. I called my little girl Fionnuala after the princess in the Children of Lir. It was a tragic story, but what was life but one big hardship? It felt fitting at the time. I knew how to change my daughter's tiny nappy. But that motherly longing, that desperate *need* wouldn't come until much later on. I was ignorant back then, and ill-equipped to deal with motherhood. No, I wasn't just ignorant, I was angry, and resented the situation I was in. Then came the night when I learned that

Jimmy had got engaged, and a date for the wedding was set. I was alone with the wee one when Geraldine told me over the phone and it couldn't have come at a worse time. My fragile little Fionnuala wasn't safe in my company. Daisy never would have left had she known what I was capable of.

CHAPTER 45

FINN

What have I done? To think, that Kathryn Toíbín was right outside my window and I didn't call for help. I must have been crazy, but my fear of losing my child was stronger than my need for self-preservation. I thought I was getting through to Maura, but her sudden act of violence was impossible to predict. I knew she was unstable, but I can't believe that she's tied my wrists to the metal frame of the bed. I've managed to kick the stupid splint off, but my leg is burning from the exertion. It feels like someone has lit a match to it.

I struggle against my bindings, which consist of two old-fashioned men's ties. I can't believe that it's come to this. I was helpless as she pushed my wheelchair into the bedroom and launched me on to the bed. I can't bear the thought of Saoirse in the living room, alone with this woman who claims to be my mother! The life I've tried to rebuild has come apart at the seams. Now I'm at Maura's mercy. Everything has been about control. She began with drugs, and then the splint. Where does she go after this?

Oh God, she's coming.

There's no mistaking the sounds of her heavy, clumping steps. Those solid shoes she wears. She thunders towards my room, sounding like an elephant on the rampage. I inhale a quick breath as the door opens. Maura's hair is wild, her eyes darting around while she cradles a cup in her hand. She glares at the remnants of the home-made splint and throws it off the bed. 'You . . . ungrateful . . . little . . .' She speaks between clenched teeth.

'Maura. Mum.' I try to act calm, despite my heart beating its way out of my chest. 'Please. Let me go.' I keep my voice low so as not to upset my daughter who is in the other room.

Maura's face darkens. I've said the wrong thing, but it's too late to reclaim the words.

I am met with silence as she raises a cup to my lips. I don't trust Maura's concoctions and I shut my mouth. Maura presses the rim of the cup against my tightly closed lips. 'Drink it. Then I'll untie you.'

My nostrils flare and I fight against my bindings, keeping my mouth shut.

'Take it.' Maura's voice is firm. She presses the cup hard to my lips and I shake my head from side to side, spilling its murky contents on to my blanket.

'Now look what you've done!' She shakes the liquid from her fingers and glares at me. I fight the urge to scream. She wants to drug me into submission but she hasn't thought this through. She can't keep me here permanently. I fight against the ties that attach my wrists to the old-fashioned bed posts. Maura is clearly not in her right mind. I just hope that Aiden calls on me soon. He's not the only one with concerns for Maura's mental health. Geraldine knows too.

'Fine!' There's a fire of fury in her eyes. 'I'm only trying to help.' Small red veins have bloomed on her skin. When she's like this, she's capable of anything. My heart lurches as she turns to leave.

I'm scared for my daughter, who is grizzling in the living room. After everything we've been through, this frightens me the most.

'No, please.' My whispers are pleading as Maura leaves. 'Don't pick her up. Not when you're like this.'

This is madness. I shake and writhe in the bed to try to loosen the ties but the knots are too tight. 'Don't hurt her . . . please.' I want to scream but can't risk Saoirse becoming upset.

The ring of Maura's mobile phone is enough to make her flustered enough to forget to close the bedroom door. I listen intently while she answers the call. I can just about make out her words.

'Yes?' Maura snaps. 'What is it?' A pause. 'What? No, I'm fine. Did she now? Well, there's nothing to worry about, I'm grand. She's not here. She's gone to the hospital for physio.'

What? I think. *Is she telling people I'm gone?* The conversation continues.

'No, no, she had to go to Dublin this time. Her leg was giving her gyp. She's going to stay there for a while. No, don't come. Saoirse has a cold – we both do.'

Please come. I send silent messages of hope into the ether. *I need help. Come now.*

'I have plenty. Aiden dropped off enough food to feed an army. I'll see you when Finn gets back. It hasn't upset me. I told you. I'm grand.'

Given she's mentioned Aiden, I'm guessing Geraldine is on the phone. I hear my daughter cry and the urge to comfort her is strong.

'Well, I am,' Maura continues. 'The babby is hungry. I have to go.'

Silence. I presume she's hung up the phone. Maura never was one for pleasantries. I could be stuck here at least until tomorrow or the day after that before anyone comes to check. It's too long to leave such a disturbed woman alone with my child.

'I need the toilet!' I cry out, my voice measured. 'Please. I'm bursting.'

Maura exhales a heavy sigh as she enters my room. The redness has left her face and she warily regards me.

'This is silly,' I say. 'I'm not going anywhere now, am I? Untie me.'

'Is it a number one or a number two?' Maura says, as if speaking to a child.

'What?' I can't believe what I'm hearing. But she bunches her fists and rests them on her hips.

'You're not going to behave, are you? You don't want the toilet. You just want to leave.'

'I won't. How could I? I'd never leave Saoirse. I can't even walk.'

'But I can't trust you, can I?' She stands at the foot of my bed. Her expression changes as an idea appears to form in her head. 'There's only one thing for it,' she mumbles, turning to leave the room.

'Where are you going?' I call after her. 'Maura? Mum. Please? I won't go anywhere. I know you're only trying to help. Aren't you my real mother, after all?'

She stills. Thinks about it before turning to face me. 'Do you mean it?'

I blink away the tears that threaten to come and force a smile. 'Of course. I'm lucky to have you. Not many people get a second chance.'

I don't even know what I'm saying but my words seem to be sinking in. 'So there's no need for this,' I continue. '. . . Mum.'

She exhales a long sigh before leaving the room. Within minutes, I hear the sound of her footsteps approaching. But this time she's carrying a knife.

CHAPTER 46

THEN

MAURA

Being a mother did not live up to the fantasy. After years of caring for my grandmother and mother, Daisy said that I had carer's fatigue. All I know is that after Daisy left for Limerick, I regressed into myself. Daisy called all the time, and I put on a good show, telling her that the health nurse had been and gone. But I never registered my daughter's birth. Perhaps a small part of me knew that she was never destined to live. It was windy the night she died. We lost a few roof tiles that night. Nobody, not even mountain goats, took the path up Misery Hill.

Maybe if the weather had been better, Geraldine would have called in. Maybe if I'd seen life outside I wouldn't have felt so alone.

I never loved the wee one. I thought I could, but each time I stared at her face Jimmy's likeness taunted me. That wisp of brown hair, her button nose, but it was her eyes that got me. Unmistakably Jimmy. All I felt was my inability to keep the only man I loved near.

I thought about Maria, the woman he'd run off to marry on the sly. The news must have spread around Doolin like wildfire.

I imagined Jimmy . . . *my* Jimmy slipping a wedding ring on his bride's finger, and it made my blood boil. The babby picked up on my fury because she wouldn't stop crying as I paced the room. I smashed some of Granny Maura's precious plates. I even threw some of my little felt hedgehogs in the fire. I broke the leg of the rocking chair with a good swift kick. I screamed. I roared. But nothing could quell my growing rage. My fists shook as I imagined Jimmy and his beloved Maria laughing at me. The baby's cries rebounded around the room as my emotions reached a crescendo. Anger overwhelmed me, just like it had done a hundred times before. But this time was different. Because when I came to, I couldn't remember what I had done . . . at least, not straight away.

She looked like she was sleeping. I hope she went peacefully.

That night the rain felt like needles against my skin as I dug her tiny grave. My shovel slid through the mud next to the roots of the old tree. I put her in a place where she would forever be in my eyeline as a reminder of what I'd done.

Six days later, Daisy returned from Limerick to find me on the floor in my bedroom, next to her old cot. At first, she'd thought that the house had been broken into and I'd been beaten into submission. It was only when she threatened to call the gardaí that I spoke up.

'She fell asleep,' I said, but my words were disjointed, as if being spoken by someone else. I wouldn't let go of the pillow that I knew had ended it all.

Things changed between Daisy and I that day. My sister was never the same with me again.

CHAPTER 47

FINN

The sight of Maura brandishing a knife makes me almost pass out. She looks at me, bewildered as I scream at her to get back. Her puzzled expression tells me that I've made a grave mistake.

'I was going to cut the ties.' She's tilted her head to one side in that unnerving way, as if examining a specimen in a jar. 'You thought I was going to hurt you?'

'Mum,' I say in desperation. 'I'm sorry. Please. Let me go.'

'I'm not your mother . . .' She spits the words. 'I never was.'

Shaking her head in disgust, she turns and leaves, her words falling behind her like stones.

I'm so confused. Why did she say that she was? I try to remember our conversation. She spoke about her pregnancy. I asked if she was my mum . . . didn't I? And then I remember her response. 'A mother of sorts.' What was that supposed to mean?

I call until my throat is hoarse but there is no reply. I need to see my daughter, to know that she's okay. Because Maura is being backed into a corner, and I fear for my little girl. There's no response, but then suddenly she barges into my room, face flushed.

'Whist!' she orders, and I fall silent as I stare at the headscarf in her hands. 'I didn't want to have to do this.'

I shake my head to avoid it, but her hands are strong as she wraps the headscarf around my mouth. I cough, inhaling the stench of old tobacco as I taste the dirty cloth.

'It's only for a few minutes.' Her breath is stale on my face as she leans in and grabs a fistful of my hair. 'Or do you want me to shut you up for good?'

My scalp stings from the small but violent act. Her warning is enough to silence me. This is all getting too much for her. I can't risk tipping her over the edge.

A fine sheen of sweat has broken out on her forehead. She releases me and takes a step back. Closing her eyes, she takes two deep breaths. 'I'll be back in a minute, alright?'

Then she's off thundering out of the bedroom door. Not for the first time she hasn't closed it properly, and I hear it creak open a notch. I sit bolt upright as I hear car tyres roll over the gravel outside. Someone's here. That's why she's silenced me. I try to call out but my throat is ragged and my voice muffled against the force of the headscarf. Panting, I listen as words are exchanged. Whoever it is has come inside, and Maura is none too happy about it.

'I told ya, we're fine. Saoirse's got a cold.'

'She looks fine to me. Hello, pet!' The voice is that of Geraldine. She's come back. I listen as she chatters to Saoirse.

'Yes, well . . . she's much better now.'

'Where's her mam?'

'I told you. At the hospital.'

'You said she was only gone for a while.'

'She is. What's with all the questions? Don't you trust me?'

'Aiden said she's not answering her phone.'

A harsh sigh. 'She forgot it in all the rush. She was late for her train.'

'But most people buy the tickets on their phone. How did she manage without it?' Geraldine is grilling her now, and I'm grateful for her suspicion. She knows that something is up. 'Surely she'd want to call and ask about the little one?'

But Maura is ready with an answer. 'She rang me from the hospital. Several times, in fact. With her phone calls, and Aiden's constant texts, now you calling in uninvited. Can't I have a minute's peace to myself?'

'Alright, alright . . .' Geraldine says calmly. 'Don't get your knickers in a twist. You would say if there was anything wrong, now, wouldn't you? Because all this business with Aiden . . . He looks so much like his da. It's bound to open old wounds.'

I tug on my bindings in an effort to shake the bed, but it only gives out a feeble creak.

'I'm fine!' Maura snaps. 'How many times?'

'Then show me your arms.'

'What?'

'You heard me. Have you been self-harming again?'

'Of course not.' Maura's voice is thick with disgust. 'I scratched my arms on the briars in the back garden. There was a hedgehog, riddled with fleas, he was. I was just trying to help.'

'You and your hedgehogs,' Geraldine snorts.

'Well, if you've finished checking up on me, I'd like some peace.'

'If you need anything, you only have to ask.'

No.

I whimper behind the scarf. She can't go. Not now.

I buck. I squirm. I try to scream.

But the old metal bed is thick and heavy and doesn't move easily beneath my light weight. I pause long enough to catch her final words as she says goodbye.

Saoirse has started crying. I wait, my despair growing as I hear the sound of Geraldine's car driving away. *Please stop crying.* I send silent messages to my daughter, who becomes increasingly upset.

My heart lurches when Maura screams, 'Shut the feck up or I'll shut you up!'

CHAPTER 48

THEN

MAURA

I didn't cause the car crash that brought Finn into my life, it just happened. I never believed in fate until that day. It was the anniversary of my daughter's death. Five years had passed, and I couldn't forgive myself for what I had done. Daisy couldn't bear to look at me but, once a month, she returned from Limerick to Misery Hill to see if I was still alive.

I didn't love Jimmy any more. I couldn't stand the sight of him. Seeing him and Maria in town playing happy families with their little boy made me want to throw up. There would always be a connection between us. The bond of a child is far more powerful than any marriage certificate.

The night of the crash was dismal. I remember seeing the headlights coming up the hill and wondering what anyone would be doing out at such a late hour. Thick mist had closed in like a curtain over Misery Hill. I knew in my gut something was going to happen. Sometimes I get premonitions, and this was one of those nights.

I was ready, with my wellington boots by the door and flashlight. The car was going too fast to safely make the bend. It didn't seem to matter how many warning signs were put out, some foolish drivers seemed oblivious to such things. Perhaps they were used to the city roads and surfaces that never give way. It was the black ice, you see. Black ice gives no warning to its presence. It is the demon of road surfaces. By the time you realise it is there, it is far too late. The car didn't make a sound. It seemed to fly over the barrier before rolling over and falling short of the cliff edge.

I ran, out of breath from excitement, as always when such things occurred. I was fuelled by morbid curiosity and there was a small sense of relief as it took me out of my own world. I could have called the guards but I had to have a gander at it first. Usually the people are shaken but alright as I help them out of the car. There is a small percentage of folk for whom it is too late. These are the times when I gain a trinket or two. It is a guilty pleasure, a small reward for being the first on the scene. It isn't as if they need them any more. First-aid kits, boiled sweets, gift-wrapped presents, or even a little bit of cash.

As I climbed over the bent-up guard-rail, I barely needed my flashlight. I know every inch of that hill. I know it in the summer when we are blessed with soft, warm showers and an occasional blast of sun. I know it in the winter when it is cold and hard and the breeze coming off the sea waters your eyes and chaps your skin.

It was too late for the woman behind the wheel of the small blue Fiat Punto. Her eyes were open as she stared, unseeing, into the night. The gash that had taken away part of her skull would have been enough to finish her off. These old cars weren't built for a tumble down the hard, rocky surface of Misery Hill.

The driver-side door had come off, and the roof of the old car had partially collapsed as it balanced on the cliff edge. I poked around the car, afraid to go too close should the whole thing tumble into the sea. It creaked and groaned and then finally settled down. That was when I heard the babby's soft, feeble cry.

The hairs on the back of my neck stood up because all I could hear were the ghostly cries of my little Fionnuala in the back of my mind. I had a choice. I shouldn't have done it, but it seemed like God himself was giving me a second chance.

I didn't have long. I looked at her precious face, and I melted.

Slowly and carefully, I opened the door of the back of the car. I told myself that it would surely be jammed, and if that was the case, I'd call the authorities. It opened easily. I took this as another sign. I spoke to the baby as I leaned over her car seat, praying that the buckles wouldn't stick. But again, they gave way, and I eased her from it, my heart going like the clappers in my chest.

The car shifted as gravity took hold. I stepped back from the wreckage. After wrapping my coat around the crying babby, I placed her safely on the ground. Then I took a deep breath of strengthening sea air, and managed to extract the pink changing bag from the back. It was a dangerous, precarious situation and I knew that at any second, my luck could run out. I blessed myself and whispered a quiet prayer for the woman who had passed on.

Then I pressed my palms against the cold metal of the car. If it wanted to go over the cliff, then so be it. I was just giving it a helping hand. It made quite the racket as it tumbled down, glass smashing, metal bending, tyres bouncing against the rocky edges, until it finally met its resting place in the sea. The tide was in that night, the dark foamy waters crashing mercilessly against the cliff edge as it took the wreckage into its embrace.

I had no time to lose. I swept up the babby, and held her close to my bosom while I raced up the hill. Her mother was dead. I was doing her a favour by taking her in. That car was ready to go over anyway. I had saved her life.

It was too late to wonder about my actions. There was no coming back from that. I was ready for the gardaí when they knocked on my door.

My dressing gown was tied tightly, and my hair dishevelled. I poured a drop of vinegar into my eyes to make them red and watery, and I gripped a hanky in my hand, sniffling and sneezing when I opened the door.

'What is it?' I said to a man who appeared far too young to be a guard. I knew him from the village and he knew of me. He was one of the little scallywags that used to knock on my door and run away when he was a child. A woman in uniform stood behind him, tall and skinny with beady, mistrustful eyes.

The guard mumbled a little bit and then asked me if I'd seen anything, as a car had come off the road on Misery Hill.

'What do you mean?' I snapped in response. 'You think I've got bionic eyes? How could I see anything in that mist?'

'Now, Maura.' He spoke with a hint of condescension. 'You're usually the first on the scene.' Then he gave me the queer eye, looking me over like I was some kind of suspect.

I told him off good and proper. I shouted at him not to look at me like that, and said that I remembered when he used to run round with his breeches falling down because his mother dressed him in second-hand clothes. He was the last of ten children of the Buggy clan, and by God, I let him know about it. Who did *he* think *he* was, questioning me, when he used to go to school with holes in his shoes?

He cleared his throat and straightened himself, his face flushed as he tried to recover his masculinity in front of his colleague.

I did my best to act remorseful because I needed to get rid of them both.

'I'm not well,' I said, swiping my nose with a tissue. 'I was in bed listening to the radio. I thought I heard a noise, but I didn't get up because I've got the flu. Now can I go back to bed, because you're letting all the heat out.'

The radio was doing a good job of masking the sound of the wee one in my bedroom, but it would only take an ad break for them to notice her tiny cries.

There was some satisfaction as I closed the door because I knew they would not return. Still, it would be best to leave the radio on for the night in case one of them detectives came back.

The crash seemed pretty straightforward to me. The mist was down thick, the car skidded on black ice and came off the road. There was nobody else around. The woman didn't make it, and the assumption would be that the child followed her mother into the Irish Sea.

Three days I had alone with the babby, my little Fionnuala. That's what I named her, because it was as if she hadn't died at all. Three glorious days with what I believed was my second chance. She was such a gift. I hated leaving her to go to town to get supplies but I had little choice. I made an appearance in Geraldine's shop before I drove further out to get the babby milk. Of course, Geraldine was fully briefed on the gossip as she told me all about the accident, and how the poor woman had died and her infant had been washed out to sea. Word had it that she wasn't wearing her glasses when she was driving. Her satnav had brought her the wrong way, and she was trying to find somewhere to turn. I thought I was in the clear. But I was not prepared for what awaited me when I got home.

CHAPTER 49

KATHRYN

The zipper on my make-up bag is cool under my trembling fingers, and I can feel the weight of my cleansers, moisturisers, toners and serums pressing against it as I shove it into my suitcase. I'm all packed for Lincoln now, to track down Fionnuala Claffey and get my baby back. I think of my walk-in wardrobe at home in Dublin, filled with designer clothes, and the rows of cupboards filled with shoes that I hardly ever wear. My parents funded it all, and I never once said thanks.

I've been soul-searching since Mam left. Perhaps my parents showed love in different ways. I've been so busy finding fault that I never appreciated what they did for me. Having my mother by my side felt good. And if Dad's been overprotective then at least it means that I've never been alone. Our family unit is like a fortress and I breached it by letting our enemies in. The Kennys.

God, I need a drink, because I've never felt so conflicted. Just when I thought I was done with my family, I'm finding my way back. My thoughts drift to Kiera and the vow my mother made to get her. I can't shake the image of her tiny face from my mind. A fierce determination grows within me; I swear that when I bring my Kiera home I'll be a better mother.

'Kathryn, do you need a hand?' Yvonne calls from downstairs. We'd decided to leave for Shannon Airport this afternoon to catch a flight to East Midlands Airport, which means we should be hitting Lincoln this evening. But the tug in my gut tells me that I'm not done with Doolin just yet.

I wander out on to the landing. 'Actually, I'm going for a walk first,' I call down. We've got plenty of time. Shannon Airport is only an hour's drive away.

She doesn't try to stop me as I come downstairs and pull on my coat.

'Are you sure you're okay?' She seems a lot brighter now.

'I'm grand.' I zip up my coat and wind my thick woollen scarf around my neck. And I will be. Because I'm not alone any more. Yvonne visibly relaxes and I give her a genuine smile. 'I won't be long.'

Stepping outside, the cold air embraces me, and darkness envelops the landscape. I mean to stay close to the Airbnb, but somehow, I find myself drawn to the cottage on Misery Hill.

Walking up the rocky path, the smell of the sea fills my nostrils. The landscape seems so vast compared to Dublin's city streets. I've tried to immerse myself in the countryside, but I've missed city life. For the first time in a long time, I want to go home.

I just need to satisfy myself with one more visit to the cottage first. There was something about the way Maura wouldn't come to the door. She doesn't strike me as a woman who is afraid of anyone. So what – or who – was she hiding? But now I'm at the cottage, something is different. Maura's car is gone. Curiosity piqued, I circle the house and spot a faint light flickering inside. I can't help but feel that I have unfinished business here.

Every one of my senses is on alert. Is it a crime to go into someone's back garden? Do I care? Would that crazy bitch call the guards on me? Well, she's not here right now, so. I climb over the mossy stone wall into an overgrown yard, being careful not to dirty my designer jeans. In the corner, a tree with bare branches sways, its limbs groaning in the wind. There's an air of creepiness about this place that makes me feel cold inside.

The back door catches my attention – it's set low within the deep stone walls of the cottage. I tell myself that I've seen and done worse things than this. I'm a Toíbín, after all.

The cottage is old and insecure, practically inviting me in. In the unlikely event of Maura being inside, I'm ready for her. There's no point in knocking, because she won't let me in. *Fuck it,* I think, picking up a rock near the back door.

I peer through the window to check that the kitchen is empty before breaking the pane of glass. I pull my jacket over my hand and reach inside to unlock the door. I move cautiously, so as not to walk on the glass on the other side.

The kitchen looks like something out of the seventies. I press my hand against the kettle. It's cold. Slowly, I check the drawers, rifling through their contents as I look for clues.

I push open the kitchen door, half expecting to run into Maura, but she's not here. The living room smells of smoke and the fact that there's a fireguard in place suggests that Maura has definitely left.

I involuntarily shudder as I stand in the middle of the room. Foreboding weighs heavily on me – what am I doing here? I turn and am about to leave when a baby's cry pierces the silence. My breath catches in my throat. Is it in my head?

'Kiera?'

The name slips from my lips before I can stop it. I stand there, frozen in time. There it is again. I wasn't imagining it.

Heart pounding, I inch towards the room on the left, the floorboards groaning beneath my cautious steps. The chill in the air intensifies as I reach for the doorknob, my hand trembling with a mixture of anticipation and dread. What lies beyond this door could change everything.

Maura could return at any moment; every second is precious.

The door is locked. I grip the cold metal key and turn. I push the door wide and my mouth falls open when I see what's inside the room.

CHAPTER 50

Thirty minutes earlier

Finn

I fear for the worst as Maura approaches, cup in hand. Her expression is stony, her mouth pressed into a bloodless white line.

'Drink it,' she commands, pressing the cup to my lips. But as usual, I shake my head.

'Drink it, and I'll give you the babby.' She stares at me, unblinking. 'I'm leaving. Things are . . . they're getting the better of me. I don't trust myself with the child.'

A plan forms in my head. The sound of Saoirse crying her heart out in the living room is killing me. 'Untie me first,' I beg. 'Please. I can't look after her like this.'

Maura exhales a harsh sigh. After placing the cup on the rickety bedside table, she leaves the room. Then she's back, holding a knife. 'Maura . . . please . . .' I manage to say, before she slices one of my bindings, leaving one arm free as she turns and brings my daughter to me. I could cry with relief as I hold out my arm to comfort my distressed daughter.

Maura narrows her eyes and she holds Saoirse at bay. 'Not until you drink your Ovaltine.'

I grasp the cup, its warmth doing nothing to chase away the cold dread. I gulp it down, the taste bitter and unfamiliar, hoping to appease her demands.

There is no further reasoning to be had as she stands before me, her haggard face twisted in a frown. Each time Saoirse cries, she visibly winces. Her left eyelid spasms. My baby is getting to her. Maura paces as I drink, and now she virtually throws my baby into my free arm after I lay the cup aside. Satisfied with my obedience, Maura returns with the changing bag.

'Shh, shh, shhh . . .' I comfort my daughter, whose nappy is sopping wet. I figure that Maura has given me enough drugs to sedate me, but not to render me unconscious. Maura closes the door behind her and I lean over the side of the bed and force my fingers down my throat. I gag and spit as the contents of my stomach slap against the floor.

I juggle my daughter, whose cries have subsided to sobs. Plump tears rest on her chubby red cheeks, and I wipe my mouth with the back of my hand before holding her close.

'It's okay, sweetie,' I whisper, thumbing away her tears before getting her dummy and a fresh nappy from the bag. But it's not okay, not until I get us both out of here. I recognise the rev of Maura's old car engine as it leaves the gravel drive. Thank God. She's gone. But how long for? Cradling Saoirse with my knees, I tug and pull at my bound arm. But pins and needles fizz through my bound hand. It's tied so tightly that it's restricting my bloodstream.

Somehow, I manage to remove Saoirse's wet nappy with one arm. My daughter stares up at me as I quickly fasten her fresh nappy and make her comfortable. I stiffen when I hear movement. I swear I heard glass breaking. There's someone in the house, outside my door. It's not Maura, is it? I didn't hear the car return, but she could be parked down the road. A wave of wooziness overcomes me as the drugs take hold. I was foolish to think I'd got rid of it all. My limbs are heavy, my eyelids like lead. I force myself to stay awake and I hold Saoirse close. As her hands rest on my chest, I dread to think what effect this is all having on her. I've tried to undo my other binding, but the knots are too tight. I have little to defend myself with as the floorboards creak outside the room.

Has Maura returned to finish us off? I imagine her coming back with a newly purchased shovel in the boot of her car.

I hold my breath as the key turns in the lock and the bedroom door opens.

I blink, barely able to take in the sight of the thin blonde woman standing at my open bedroom door. *Thank God,* it's not Maura after all.

We assess each other for a moment, and I realise that it's Kathryn Toíbín, the woman I saw outside my bedroom window. Is she friend or foe? Her cold blue eyes assess the room with calculated precision as she steps inside. A new wave of fear washes over me.

'Help me,' I croak, the drug's effects making it difficult to stay alert. 'Maura . . . she could come back at any minute. Untie me. Please.'

I watch shock register on her face, because it's not until she steps closer that she sees I am restrained. She looks me up and down, taking in the homemade splint on my leg, and the navy-blue tie attaching me to the bed. But her gaze locks on to my baby, and she seems hypnotized by her innocence as she approaches us both. Her voice is distant, detached. 'Kiera?' She raises a hand mid-air.

No. The word turns my blood cold.

'She's mine.' I instinctively tighten my hold on Saoirse.

But my drowsy limbs betray me, and I cry out as Kathryn slowly takes my baby from my arms. Saoirse glances at the woman taking her, before reaching back for me.

'Kathryn . . . whatever you think about my baby . . . you're wrong,' I manage to say, straining against my binding. 'Let us *both* go. Maura's dangerous. She's killed before.'

Saoirse grizzles in the woman's arms as she continues to reach out for me.

'I found a purse . . . hidden in her room,' I continue, frantically trying to convince Kathryn. 'I think Maura killed the woman who owned it. Please. Call the guards. Maura could come back any second.'

Kathryn's eyes flicker to me, weighing the truth of my words. 'You'll agree to a DNA test?'

'Yes.' I nod. 'Of course! Now, please . . . give her back and cut . . .' I inhale a breath to control a wave of nausea. 'Cut this damned tie.'

But Kathryn does not look convinced. She stands there, holding Saoirse in her arms and glancing at the door. And then it hits me. She's taking my baby. I'll never see her again.

CHAPTER 51

MAURA

I lean against my car bonnet and suck in a lungful of cold sea air. I had to get out of the cottage. This has all been a big mistake. These evil urges . . . they make me do desperate things. Like the urge that drove me to pretend to be my sister and have it off with Jimmy in the back of his car. Or the urge that made me drug Granny Maura before she wrote me out of her will. Then there was the decision to keep my pregnancy a secret, which is why nobody missed my helpless little girl after she died. It's monstrous. I am a monster. This has to stop.

I left Finn to drive to Lover's Leap on Misery Hill. I couldn't face Geraldine, not today. As I stepped out of my car I embraced my isolation and the sharp chill of the wind. So much has come to pass in this spot. I recall the night that I watched Chantana, Aiden's wife, drive past my cottage to meet that fellah she was carrying on with from town . . . I couldn't help myself. I followed her up the hill. The look on their faces was a picture as I caught them both in the act. By God, did I give him a piece of my mind. She won't do that again. Aiden deserves better. I shake my head in disgust. That Joy is better off without her for a mother.

I've made such a mess of things with Finn. I was foolish to think that we could begin again. All these years, I've blamed my sister for taking her from me. But she wasn't mine to begin with. And I know in my heart that had Daisy not taken her to England, she may not be alive today.

The problem is, what do I do now? For a while, I thought that maybe I could raise wee Saoirse as my own. I can't bear the thought of being abandoned again. But I'm getting old and I'm tired of anything life has to give. There's no way forward for us, whatever way you look at it. I stare out to sea, recalling that moment when Aiden's wife tumbled off the cliff edge, long after her fancy man took off. The sea was rough and foamy the day that she fell in. I half expected her body to be washed up on the shore the next day. But the storm that night was relentless. Nature did Aiden a favour and swept his unfaithful wife away.

I turn back to my car, exhausted by the chaos I have brought into my eventful life. I can't keep Finn in the cottage forever. But if I let her go, she'll call the gardaí. I can't risk it all coming out about Aiden's floozy of a wife. As for the rest of it . . . the residents of Doolin would have a field day with that.

My limbs feel heavy as I give one last regretful glance out to the sea. Tears sting the corners of my eyes and I get back into my car. Hunched over the steering wheel, I allow myself to cry. I've always known that this day would come. There are no happy endings for people like me. My family has a history of dying early. Even Daisy, who seemed so blessed by life, has gone to meet her maker. One small thought comforts me as I prepare to go home and drug myself into a permanent sleep: at least this time I won't be alone. Wherever I go in the next life, Finn and the babby will be coming too.

CHAPTER 52

THEN

MAURA

When I saw Daisy's swanky car on the drive outside my cottage, I almost collapsed with surprise. My knees became weak as I got out of my father's old car. I had to take a stiff breath to force myself to go on. The screams of the seagulls overhead echoed the warning bells in my mind. I pushed my damp hair from my face before taking my shopping out of the boot. I needed to be brave.

My first thought was of the baby I had claimed from the car crash. Had Daisy found her and called the gardaí? This would surely mean the end. Anxiety overwhelmed me. I almost threw my groceries on the ground. If it hadn't cost me so much money, I may well have. The heavy bags swung from my arms as I trotted towards the cottage.

I found Daisy in the living room, shushing and calming the crying baby. I'll never forget the look on her face as I dropped the shopping bags to the floor. It was the same expression of shock Jimmy had when I confessed to killing Granny Maura.

'Oh, Maura.' Daisy stared at me in disbelief. 'What have you done?'

But I was more interested in what she had done first. 'Have you called the gardaí? Have you told anyone?'

But Daisy didn't seem to register my words. She was dressed like my mother, in a slim-fitting blue dress that pinched at the waist. Her hair had been styled, and she was wearing a pair of ridiculous high-heeled shoes. She didn't belong on Misery Hill. Who was she to tell me what to do?

She looked at me like I hadn't said a word. 'Whose baby is this? Why would you leave her alone?'

I was sweating by now, my throat dry. I ground my back teeth and my left eyelid went into a jerky spasm. 'I only went out to get some shopping. I had trouble starting the car on the way back.' Dad's old Toyota Corolla was on its last legs.

I raked my nails down my arm. Why did Daisy always make me feel so bad? Anger closed in, thick and unyielding. I wished I could make her disappear.

'For God's sake, Maura,' she insisted, her voice tight and high pitched. 'Stop scratching and tell me. Where has this baby come from?' She rubbed the babby's back in circular motions as she rested her against her shoulder. Finn looked like a dolly in the pink onesie and cardigan that I'd found in her changing bag. The car crash had made local headlines but seemed to go no further than that. A mass was held for the loss of both mother and child. A quiet hush seemed to settle over the village as they accepted yet another tragic loss. But life went on for the baby, and now Daisy knew.

I picked up the shopping and my sister followed me into the kitchen, the little one in her arms. There was no avoiding her questions. She was like a hen pecking at my head.

'I'm looking after her for a friend,' I said eventually.

But Daisy was bound to see through my lies. She was my twin after all. Despite everything that had happened, we had an unbreakable bond.

'Well, you're not doing a very good job,' she retorted, 'leaving her on her own like that.'

I bowed my head, finding a home for a ridiculously expensive tub of Aptamil powdered baby milk. 'I told ya. I had no choice. I had to get some shopping in.'

'Well, I hope you got fresh baby food, because the jars in your kitchen are out of date. Where did you get them from?'

I rolled my eyes, because it sounded like she'd had a good rummage around in my home. I'd collected a lot of things from cars over the years. Baby food made for a nice dessert of an evening. Date or no date, I could hardly throw them away. What doesn't kill, fattens, as Granny Maura used to say.

'What are you doing here, anyway?' I made room in the cupboard and unpacked the rest of my groceries. The little one was calming down. She was quiet most of the time. 'This is my home now,' I continued. 'You can't just walk in here any more. I should get the locks changed . . . I . . .' My words stilled while I took in the expression of hurt creasing Daisy's face. I regretted my outburst as she approached.

'Are you . . . Are you saying I'm not welcome here any more?'

I dug my fingernails into the palms of my hands. 'No, of course not. All I'm asking for is a little bit of respect. Give me some warning the next time you come for a visit, so I can be ready.'

'Ready for what?' Daisy said, as I took the sleeping baby from her arms. She lowered her voice so as not to wake her. 'Because we both know that you don't have any friends, much less someone who would trust their baby with you.' She tilted her chin upwards, the way she always did before she gave me a telling-off. 'I'm not leaving until you tell the truth.'

Silence fell heavy as she rested her hands on her waist. My twin had my blue eyes, my nose, my height and facial features but that was where the likeness ended. She would never understand.

'I need to put her down to sleep.' I made to move out of the kitchen but Daisy blocked the doorway. *Fine*, I thought, and rested her in the old navy pram that I'd rescued from the loft.

'Did you take her from the hospital?'

'No!' I frowned, tucking the infant in. 'I'm no babby snatcher!'

But that was exactly what I was.

A wave of maternal instinct washed over me as the babby began to suck her thumb. I had to get Daisy on side because I couldn't give Finn up. I would do better. There would be no mistakes this time around.

'There was a car crash.' I locked eyes with Daisy so she'd know I was telling the truth. 'They were speeding and flew over the guard-rails.' Reluctantly, I relived that night, altering the details to suit. 'I ran down to help, but it was too late for her mother. She was dead.'

Cupping her mouth, my sister spoke behind her hand. 'Another death? How many people have to die before they do something about that road?' I watched her eyes widen as she put the pieces together. First, she looked at the baby and then back to me. 'Oh my God, Maura, you didn't?'

'I saved her life,' I blurted. 'Grabbed her from the car before it went over the edge.'

'Did it go over? Or was it pushed?' Her tone darkened. 'Because I know what you're capable of.'

I tried to look indignant but my cheeks flamed from the lie. I gently rocked the pram. I needed to plead my case.

'She was a single mother, it said so in the paper. There's no father involved. The child would've ended up in care.' I stared at my sister with conviction. 'I'm calling her Fionnuala.' But Daisy was shaking her head.

'Jesus. That's . . . that's not right. Not after . . . You can't.'

'I already have. Now would you like to see me in prison? Because that's what will happen if they find out what I've done.'

'You can't just take a baby and make it a replica of what you had. People will ask questions. They'll wonder where she's come from.'

'I'll say she's mine. I'll make it work.'

'How? You need paperwork. A birth certificate.'

'There's ways around these things,' I muttered. But Daisy did not look convinced. 'You have your life in Limerick. You got the college fund. I had to look after Granny Maura and you know that woman was cruel. All the years I humped bags of shopping up and down that hill, watching the pennies and skivvying for them all.' My voice was rising but I couldn't help myself as specks of spittle flew from my mouth. 'Please,' I cried. 'If you go to the authorities, I'll kill myself. I mean it. And you'll have to live with that.'

She knew I was telling the truth. She saw it in my eyes. My sister nodded, unspeaking.

I got Finn settled. Daisy sat next to me beside the fire. I told her how hard life had been. We cried together. We laughed. We talked about our childhood. She told me things about Limerick, how her life wasn't as perfect as it seemed. She hated her job. She'd been seeing some consultant and her colleagues had turned against her because he was a married man. We talked long into the evening. I listened with interest, offering advice when I could. For the first time in years, it felt like we were sisters again.

When we had talked ourselves out, my sister finally stood.

'Well.' She cleared her throat, dabbing away the mascara stains that shadowed her eyes. 'If we're doing this, then I'm moving back in. And we'll have to come up with something watertight.'

CHAPTER 53

FINN

The cold air in the dimly lit bedroom seems to crawl over every surface, the shadows clinging to the corners of the room. I shiver, exposed and vulnerable as my wrist burns from the tight tie that binds me to the bed.

Kathryn stands in front of me, her eyes darting between me and baby Saoirse who she holds close to her chest. It's obvious that she is torn; part of her wants to believe that the baby she holds in her arms is her own, while another part protests that it's my blood running through the baby's veins.

'Please, Kathryn,' I beg, my voice cracking with desperation, 'don't take my baby.' I push myself to the edge of the bed, but the tie holds my wrist in place.

Kathryn hesitates, her grip on baby Saoirse tightening.

'Maura will be back soon,' I warn. 'She's not stable. You don't know what she's capable of.'

'But it's Kiera . . .' Her eyes shine with tears as she takes in my little girl's face. 'Her tuft of dark hair . . . the shape of her face . . . those little ears.'

But my baby breaks the spell as she grizzles and turns to reach for me.

Desperation claws at my insides when Kathryn looks at the door. She bows her head towards my baby, closing her eyes as she takes in her scent.

'It's her . . .' she says wistfully. 'I'm sorry. I can't give her up.'

'And what if you're wrong?' My hand trembles as I reach for my little girl. 'How are you going to explain to my daughter that you're responsible for killing her mum? Because that's what Maura will do, Kathryn. She's killed before. We can sort this out. But let's do it right, eh?'

I try to read Kathryn's expression. The revelation about Maura's violent streak doesn't seem to surprise her.

'I knew she was a crazy bitch.' She exhales a strange laugh. 'Will you really do a DNA test? Swear down. Because I won't let this go.'

'I swear. Hurry!'

Frustration mounts as the storm rises outside. Was that the sound of a car or a sudden gust of wind? I could cry with relief when Kathryn places my daughter next to me on the bed.

'Jeez, this is tight.' Kathryn grimaces as she tries to loosen the tie around my wrist. But her movements come to a halt when the bedroom door is almost pushed off its hinges. It reverberates against the wall with a thud as Maura storms into the room.

Saoirse's chin trembles and she begins to cry.

'It's okay, babe,' I murmur, but it's not okay: Maura's face is thunderous and I'm still bound to the bed.

'You! What are you doing in my house?' she screams at Kathryn, her eyes wild and unpredictable.

'Maura, calm down. She's only trying to help!' I shout, trying to protect my baby from her obvious fury.

'You cheeky bitch!' Maura screams. Kathryn is no match for her strength as Maura pushes her back on to the bed. 'Dublin floozy! Whore!'

'Maura, please!' I try to reason as I pull my baby close. She clings to me, holding on tight. The sound of her anxious sobs are breaking my heart.

'You've no idea who you're dealing with!' Kathryn retorts, finding her feet.

I try to wriggle free from my restraint, the tie digging into my wrist and tearing my skin. There is a small bit of give from where Kathryn has loosened it, but not enough. My priority is keeping my baby safe.

Kathryn stands her ground, her face pale but determined. Though thinner and smaller than Maura, there is an aura of toughness about her.

'I mean it. You don't want to mess with me,' she warns, her voice steady. 'I'm a Toíbín. My father will bury you.'

Maura laughs – a chilling, off-kilter sound. 'That doesn't matter a damn.' She steps closer to Kathryn. 'We'll all be leaving Misery Hill in a box.'

The glint of madness in Maura's eyes confirms that there is no reaching her now. I clutch Saoirse tighter, my thoughts racing like a freight train. I try to kick out at Maura, but she is focused on Kathryn.

The fight between them erupts suddenly – a whirlwind of flailing limbs and harsh grunts. Kathryn manages to land some solid blows. Kathryn exhales an 'oof' when Maura punches her in the stomach. Kathryn crumples to the floor like a rag doll. I watch in horror as Maura straddles Kathryn and wraps her fleshy hands around her throat.

'Stop!' My voice rises over Saoirse's wails. 'Maura, you're killing her!' But there's no reasoning with the woman as she screams at Kathryn in a rage. Finally, Kathryn's limbs fall limp.

Grunting from exertion, Maura gets up. Her nostrils are flaring, her forehead coated in sweat.

'Whist now,' she says to Saoirse, her voice growing eerily calm. 'It'll all be over soon.'

'Please, Maura, don't hurt my baby,' I beg, tears streaming down my face. 'None of this is her fault.'

'Stop that crying now.' Maura grabs the pillow from the bed. 'Once the wee one is gone, it'll be easier for you to follow her.'

CHAPTER 54

KATHRYN

I'm no stranger to violence. In the old days, when I was young, Daddy would bring me on jobs with him. Sometimes I'd sit in his city office and play with my Barbie dolls; other times, he entertained people who he believed had done him wrong. He used to tell me that respect was the currency of power, and every handshake was a power play. But there were no handshakes when it came to Maura, who had more strength than brains.

As I lay on my back beneath her bulk, the safest thing to do was to play dead. I didn't care about Finn and what became of her. If anything, it would be better for me if she was out of the way. But I did care about my baby. When I held her in my arms, my instincts cried out that it was Kiera. But what if I was wrong? I know the pain of grief. When Finn said I would have to explain her death to that little girl one day, I couldn't walk out that door.

But I hadn't expected Maura back so soon. She launched herself at me, spitting swear words as she grabbed for my throat. Punching her was like hitting a brick wall. I tried to get my flick knife from the inside pocket of my jacket. Toíbíns always go equipped. I was just about to use it to cut Finn's ties, but Maura was too quick as she launched herself upon me.

Now that crazy bitch is going for my daughter with a pillow. I ease my knife from my inside jacket pocket. Like hell, she is. I'm putting an end to this. Silently, I rise, pressing my lips together as I suppress a gasp. Everything hurts and I need to cough but now is not the time.

Finn doesn't see me because she's too busy reasoning with Maura. But there's no getting through to her. I'm finishing this now.

'Get back!' Finn screams and kicks out at Maura as she raises the pillow over the crying baby.

'Whist now,' Maura snaps. She doesn't see me creep up behind. The baby has fallen quiet as Maura presses her weight upon the pillow, forcing the baby down on the bed.

The knife extends with a flick. I'm about to slice her throat from behind when she turns around, mouth gaping. I exhale in satisfaction as I plunge it above her collar bone. Specks of blood slap my face. I retreat when Maura slumps on to the bed and then falls to the floor. Finn screams as she pulls the pillow from the baby's face. The seconds that pass feel like an eternity before my little girl exhales a shaky cry.

It takes seconds to slice the tie from Finn's wrist. I lift my baby from the bed and rub her back as I try to soothe her once more. Finn delivers a pained look and she rubs her reddened wrist. Kiera is mine now. Back where she belongs.

Finn stumbles off the bed, her movements uncoordinated, like an old drunk. She stares at Maura bleeding out on the carpet but I pull her away.

'Come on, we need to get out of here,' I urge, grabbing her arm and pulling her towards the door. My baby is inconsolable, but the sounds of life coming from her body bring me joy. Kiera isn't dead. She lives on.

As we stumble out of the cottage, the cold night air hits me like a slap in the face. I inhale a few deep breaths. They couldn't have been more welcome.

'My phone,' I tell Finn, who is barely managing to stand upright. I notice for the first time that she's not wearing shoes. 'It's in my pocket. Call the police.'

I can't bear to let go of my baby for long enough to make the call.

'Hey now, Kiera,' I say, wiping away her tears as we walk away from the cottage on Misery Hill. 'Mammy's here. I've found you. We're going home.'

CHAPTER 55

FINN

I exit the lift and glance around nervously, my fingers gripping the handle of Saoirse's pushchair. The lobby of the plush Dublin hotel is decorated for Christmas Day already. Any other year, I would have enjoyed the carols softly playing on the speakers in the background. But this Christmas will be a lonely one. Not only have I lost the mother who raised me, but I almost lost my baby too. Hell, I almost lost my life. It seems crazy now, when I think of it, and it's not over yet. I have one more person to meet before I go back to Lincoln next week.

I make my way to the coffee shop, which charges extortionate prices, but thanks to Layla Toíbín, her husband is footing the bill. I haven't met Danny Toíbín, but it was an eye-opening evening's entertainment reading about him online. It's why I'm nervous now. His wife is pretty formidable too. The hotel offers a babysitting service, but there was no way I was leaving Saoirse alone after everything she'd been through.

I glance up at the ceiling. Crystal chandeliers cast a soft glow on the marble floors, while the scent of cinnamon and pinecones fills the air. The Christmas trees gracing either side of the lobby doors are real, and easily over seven feet tall. I glance at my watch. I'm five minutes early for my meeting with Mrs Toíbín.

The first time I saw Layla, it was in the police station in Doolin after Maura was stabbed. Who rocks up to a police station with their very own solicitor in tow? Layla Toíbín did. I watched as she leaped into action in defence of her daughter. I was happy to provide a statement to the police that Maura intended on killing us all. I also told them about Aiden's wife, Chantana, and the purse I'd found.

They say that when your last moments come, your life flashes before your eyes. But all I could see was Saoirse's life and what Maura was taking away. The loss of my little girl's first day at school, the pictures she would never draw, the Christmas plays and sports days she would never attend. How poor the world would be without her in it. I screamed, I fought, but my senses were dulled and my limbs no match for Maura and her unfailing rage. But Kathryn . . . I owe that woman everything. I just wish our story hadn't ended like this.

I'm glad she has her mother's support. Layla seemed to hold power over her daughter, persuading her to hand Saoirse over to social services at the police station. Kathryn knew she had no right to hang on to her. After being interviewed by social services, I was allowed to take my daughter back. Following an exhausting day in the police station, we were finally cleared to leave. I didn't ask about Maura. I will never accept her as my mother, not after what she did. Layla's offer to put me up in this five-star hotel was an act of generosity that I was happy to accept, but she was quite transparent about it as she explained that it suited Mr Toíbín to know where we were, particularly as we awaited the results of the DNA test. Kathryn told me at the police station that every member of the Toíbín clan had to report to their father and their every move was monitored. I couldn't imagine my daughter growing up in a family like that.

The wait for the DNA test results has been agonising. But now, finally, it's time. I imagine Saoirse having two lives – one with me in England, and one in Dublin with Kathryn as her mum. The Toíbín family may be millionaires, but they don't seem all that happy to me.

I take a seat at the booth in the hotel coffee shop and order my usual. Saoirse seems no worse for her experiences as she sits in her pushchair and happily plays with her teether, but I haven't let her out of my sight since that day. My hands are shaking as I accept the café latte. I'm so scared by what awaits me that I almost didn't show. These are powerful people. Who's to say that they wouldn't fake the DNA results for their own gain? But I tell myself that such a family would not want an outsider's child.

Layla wastes no time as she arrives, politely rejecting my offer to buy her a coffee. She doesn't give a second glance to Saoirse. How could she ignore such a sunny smile? It's as if she's not there at all. Layla's jawline is hard. Perhaps her iron-clad exterior is her defence against a harsh world. I can hardly catch my breath as Layla pulls an envelope from her designer bag.

'It's negative,' she states, thrusting it into my outstretched hand without ceremony.

But negative for who? Hands still shaking, I read the results which relay that Saoirse is not Kathryn's daughter. She is mine. 'Oh, thank God!' I exclaim, because I'm not like Layla. I can't hold in feelings as strong as these.

Layla seems alarmed that I cry so openly. She pats my back twice, then frowns. 'Pull yourself together, Finn. It's over.' The woman is an ice queen. In these moments as I sniffle and gulp back my sobs, I see a snapshot of Kathryn's upbringing and feel sorry for her. At least now we can move on with our lives.

I thank Layla for my hotel stay. She'd told me to stay as long as I wanted, while I tied up any loose ends in Ireland. I haven't been able to return to Misery Hill. I never want to see that place again.

Layla got an employee to drive there and bring me my things. She's really looked after me. I sense a fierce protectiveness for her daughter, but severity too. Kathryn hasn't spoken to me since. It's better that way. Layla gently retrieves the paperwork from my hands and tells me to stay where I am as she rises to leave. She seems uncomfortable in my presence. Perhaps such an outward display of emotion has unsettled her. Then she's gone, her heels clacking against the shiny tiled floor. I stay to finish my coffee, my limbs feel like jelly, such is the extent of my relief.

I chat to my daughter, who babbles and thumps her giraffe teething toy against the soft material of the pushchair.

'Do you want your dummy?' A chill runs up my spine as the words leave my mouth. Then I'm back to when it all happened, rooting around for my baby's dummy as she wailed in the back of my car. She used to cry a lot, back then.

She had a funny little rash between her eyebrows that used to bloom when she cried. That disappeared after the accident too. Her hair is darker than I remember. Her wide, innocent eyes gaze up at me, and her chubby fingers wrap around mine.

Family.

The thought slips in, spoken from the ghost of Maura's voice. I shudder. It feels like someone's walked over my grave.

Something tells me I'll be hearing Maura's voice for a long time to come. It's a miracle that she survived the knife attack. Once in custody, she held nothing back, telling police about her plans to finish us off before killing herself, and even confessing to pushing Aiden's wife over the cliff edge.

I wonder how Aiden is doing, but I can't bring myself to ask. I want to leave Doolin behind me. I'm putting Saoirse first. It's time for a new start.

CHAPTER 56

THEN

MAURA

I never forgave my sister for her biggest betrayal. Perhaps in her heart she knew that, and it's why she never got in touch again. The day that she left me is forever branded in the back of my mind. It wasn't raining that day, nor was it sunny. There was nothing but a blanket of mist cloaking the cottage, so thick on the frozen hillside that you could barely see your hand.

I awoke with a start that morning. Fionnuala's cot was empty, and I knew instinctively that something was wrong. Goosebumps rose on my skin as I swung my legs from the bed and pulled my dressing gown on. There was a chill in the air, despite me having banked the range with turf the night before.

I winced at the thump of a headache behind my temples, most likely from the whiskey that Daisy had laced my tea with the night before. According to the clock on the wall, it was just gone 6 a.m. I crept to my bedroom door and listened for movement. Then I heard my sister's voice, shushing the babby as she slowly opened the front door and made her way outside. My little stolen child.

It was the sight of Daisy's suitcase on the living room floor that made me gasp in despair. Finn's pushchair was gone, most likely in the boot of Daisy's car. And now my sister was out there, securing my little girl for the journey ahead. The changing bag was on the table, with newly made bottles sticking out. She wasn't just popping out. She was taking my daughter away. I stood to the side of the front door, waiting as Daisy returned.

'Where are you off to?'

Daisy shrieked as she jumped. 'Jesus, Maura!'

'Don't "Jesus, Maura" me. Where are you taking her?' I pulled my dressing gown tightly together, giving Daisy a moment to catch her breath.

She tilted her chin upwards, a small act of defiance. 'I'm taking her away for a while. It's for the best.' Even now, at that early hour, Daisy's blonde hair was perfectly styled, her plum lipstick bright against the paleness of her skin.

I stared in disbelief, my heart sinking in my chest. I risked everything for this baby, and now my bitch of a sister thought she could waltz in and claim her as her own. They'd grown close over the last few weeks, much to my dismay. Only last night, Daisy said Fionnuala had filled a gap in her life that she didn't know she'd had. Except she didn't call her Fionnuala, claiming it was disrespectful to my firstborn. She'd shortened her name to Finn.

The bond wasn't one sided, either. Daisy was able to calm the child, whereas she always squirmed uneasily in my arms. Daisy had the patience of a saint, but the grating sound of a baby's cry went through me like nails on a chalkboard. But I couldn't allow this to happen. I didn't want to be alone. I stood in the doorway, blocking my sister's path. My long white nightdress billowed as a cool breeze curled around my bare ankles. I glanced at the car, but it was nothing but a ghostly shape beneath thick mist, ready to take my Fionnuala away. Anger rose within as frustration built inside me.

'She's my . . . family.' I spoke in stops and starts. I pressed a hand to my left eyelid which twitched and jumped.

'It's for the best.' Daisy's voice softened. 'But we both know how this could end. I can't stay in Doolin forever, and you can't be trusted with her on your own.' She clutched the strap of the changing bag as if it were a life raft in a storm. 'It's for the best. I'll give her a good life . . . I'll . . .'

'YOU!' I roared. 'It's always about you!' I poked myself in the chest. 'What about ME?!'

I didn't expect Daisy to turn. I'd never seen my sister lose her temper in my life. 'You don't know how to nurture a child!' she shouted in a tone that matched my own. 'She's not a doll, Maura! You can't just pick her up and play with her when you feel like it. You must be there for the messy bits too! For the crying and the vomiting and the projectile poo!'

She had a point. I hated the pooey nappies, but I managed by dunking her in a warm bath when things got bad. My sister wasn't finished yet, as she rested the changing bag on top of the suitcase. 'But I wouldn't have minded any of that, if I wasn't scared of you putting a pillow over her head!'

I bit my bottom lip. I should never have told her how my firstborn died. Daisy had also witnessed my short tempers on the nights when Fionnuala had cried. I was getting worse. I could feel another one of my episodes coming on. My intuitive twin felt it too. I couldn't defend myself. There was no denying it. And God knows, there were times when I'd wondered if I'd made a mistake bringing the baby back.

'Your tempers are dangerous,' Daisy continued. 'And they're getting worse. You need professional help.'

I looked around the room. The cracked chair in the corner was testament to that. Fionnuala had been crying for ages. It wasn't my fault.

'Don't go,' I whimpered, looking at her with the eyes of a dog that has been kicked one too many times.

'I'll come back soon.' She grabbed her bags and approached the door. I placed a hand on my sister's arm.

'No, you won't. Please. Don't go. I'll be better. I'll try harder. Don't take her away.'

Standing in the open doorway, Daisy glanced towards the car. 'She's getting cold. I need to go.'

'But you'll come back?' I fought back the tears as I pleaded for her return.

Her eyes glistened as she patted my hand. 'Sure. We're just having a little break. And Maura . . . take care of yourself, yeah?'

I stood at that window for hours, waiting for Daisy to realise her mistake and turn the car around. She'd come back. Of course she would. She wouldn't leave me alone like this. I'd presumed that she went to Limerick. She wasn't *that* far away. I didn't think for a moment that I'd never see my sister again.

CHAPTER 57

MAURA

So Finn has left Doolin for good. I shouldn't be surprised. One way or another, everyone leaves me. I thought she would at least come and say goodbye. I won't be in a secure unit forever. I could still have a future in the outside world. I just have to get my sentencing out of the way.

What happened with Finn was out of desperation, and as for the bold Chantana . . . well, her death was down to me. My confession was an act of sacrifice, born from motherly love. I've been told my cooperation will gain me a lighter sentence. I could have said it wasn't my fault, but there's evidence. Chantana's purse was found under my bed. I just hope they don't go digging in my garden. The roots of the old oak tree should protect the body of my firstborn.

I thought I could overcome the fact that Finn wasn't my flesh and blood, but she's just like Daisy. There's no loyalty there. From the second I saved Finn from the wreckage, I believed I'd been given a second chance. But my sister Daisy felt otherwise and took her away.

I couldn't call the police at the time, because Finn's birth certificate was fake. I couldn't risk attention being drawn to the fact I'd stolen another woman's baby.

It seemed like the most wonderful blessing when Finn returned to me, a grown woman with a wee one of her own. Her interest in meeting me was a balm to the raw pain of losing my sister so suddenly. I wondered if Finn's car crash was karma for what I'd done. My life was a series of cycles, and death followed me each time. I was so excited to see Finn, but as I watched from my window another blow was dealt.

Life can be cruel. But you get what you give. It's the first thought that entered my head when I clambered down to the scene of Finn's crash and found her little baby dead. I couldn't have Finn go through the grief of losing her newborn. That's when I heard an infant crying in the other wrecked car. So I swapped the babies. It wasn't that hard to do. If Finn still had her baby she'd need help to look after it. Another reason for her to stick around and keep me company. Maybe one day Finn will find out where she originated from, but it won't be from me. Had she been a little nicer, I might have considered telling her the truth, but not now.

I was so committed to getting Finn to stay. When things got on top of me, I was ready to give up my life rather than be without her. I thought we could all go together, and put an end to this misery.

At least here in the institution, I'm not alone. I have my routine. The other inpatients know not to mess with me. I'm on proper medication now. I don't want to die any more. I'm thinking about my future.

Family.

Family is why I've taken the blame for Chantana's demise. People seem quick to believe my confession. But it wasn't me who pushed her off the cliff. I'll never forget that stormy evening, when I caught her at it with that lad from town. I sent him off with a flea in his ear, sure enough. But I wasn't the last person to see Chantana alive. Poor Aiden, her husband, was there too.

I was heading home when the hairs prickled on the back of my neck. If only I'd kept going that day. Call it a sixth sense, a sudden knowing, or the fact a peregrine falcon was circling overhead. The presence of such a rare bird felt like a bad omen as it watched the movement below. That's when I saw Aiden appear. He must have been hiding there all along, waiting for me to leave. He was so filled with rage at his wife's infidelities that he didn't see me double back on myself. But by the time I reached them both, I was too late. Perhaps I could have run, or called out to stop him. I did neither. Everything seemed to happen in slow motion as he pulled her out of the car. I slowly negotiated the pathway, a silent watcher as they argued by the cliff edge. When he began to push her, I didn't think he'd take it so far. I cupped my hands over my mouth when she went, arms flailing, over the edge. He screamed her name as she went. He didn't mean to do it. It wasn't his fault. I said as much when I found him at the cliff edge on his knees, head in hands.

I wiped away his tears. Told him to go home to his daughter, and that everything would be alright. It was the least I could do, given he's my son.

I take some small satisfaction knowing that I got to mother him, just once. I didn't just have one babby, you see. On the night I gave birth to Jimmy's offspring, I had twins. Jimmy took the boy because his new wife Maria was barren. She was more understanding than I would have been. They didn't know about the little girl. But Daisy did. She agreed that I could keep her. It was a decision she would come to regret.

Jimmy never told our son Aiden about me. After what I did to his twin sister, it was best to have no contact. I didn't trust myself.

Regardless, Jimmy never wanted me to be involved. I think he never stopped hating me for what I did. He said it made him feel dirty, being taken advantage of like that. The nearest he came to forgiving me was after Aiden's first day at school. I stood in the distance, watching my little boy, as I often did. As Maria got into the car, Jimmy crossed the road to greet me. His eyes were glistening with tears as he stopped to ask me how I was. This in itself was unusual. I told him I was grand. He thanked me for keeping my distance and for allowing him and Maria to bring up the child. Then he said that Aiden was a godsend and we left it at that. Then Maria gave me a small smile of gratitude as she sat in the passenger seat of the car. I knew I'd done the right thing. I could never have coped with two babbies on my own. I couldn't manage one.

But it seems Aiden, God bless him, has inherited my quick temper. I couldn't have him going to prison when his wife deserved what she got and more. So when I found the little red purse that fell out of her coat pocket, I brought it home. It was an insurance of sorts. I kept all the newspaper clipping reports about her disappearance too. My possession of the purse was my way of taking the blame. It was the least I could do, given I'd never been a mother to him.

Perhaps his father will sit Aiden down and explain who I really am. He must be wondering why I've taken the blame.

Now I think of my granddaughter Joy, the darling little girl who doesn't know who I really am. Perhaps when I leave this place, we can be acquainted properly. Maybe I can start again.

Family.

It's everything.

CHAPTER 58

FINN

Meeting with Layla Toíbín has filled me with trepidation. She's asked if we could move somewhere a little more private. She seems worried about how I'm going to react to the news she's about to impart. That in itself, is a concern. Now Layla and I are settled into plush armchairs in a secluded corner of the hotel lounge. Almost a week has passed since our last meeting and I'm ready to go home.

In her black and white suit, Layla looks like she's dressed for London Fashion Week rather than the lounge in an upmarket hotel. She rests her coffee on the table between us but doesn't touch it yet.

'I wasn't going to come,' she says, and as I check my watch, I notice that she's ten minutes late. Something seems to have irked this usually unflappable woman, and it sets my nerves on edge. As usual, she doesn't look at Saoirse, but fixes her gaze on me. 'There's something I need to ask you.'

I gently bounce Saoirse on my lap while maintaining eye contact with Layla. My baby is wearing the cutest stripy yellow and black tights with an adorable bumble bee dress. Her shoes are yellow to match. The outfit wasn't cheap, but I've thoroughly enjoyed spoiling her. A mix of apprehension and curiosity washes over me as I wonder what Layla wants.

Layla's gaze briefly flickers to Saoirse before returning to me.

'Is everything alright?' I try to keep my voice steady.

Layla's visit is more than just a courtesy call – there is something she needs to ask me, something important. But I can't imagine what it could be.

Layla glances around, checking there is nobody in earshot. 'Firstly, thank you for your cooperation during all of this . . . nasty business.' Her nose wrinkles in disdain. 'Kathryn is in recovery. She sends you her best.'

'Oh, right. I . . .' I don't know what to say. The stress of the situation has made my mind go blank. What *do* you say in these situations? *I hope she gets well soon?* But she can't get well, not when the cause of her problems is losing her child. 'I'm glad she's getting the help she needs.' I settle on that platitude, hating the nervousness in my voice.

I don't like this situation. I don't want to be in Ireland any more. I stroke my daughter's hair. I want to take her back to Lincoln. To go home. I've been making plans. My friend Taylor has asked me to manage his Lincoln hairdressing salon. But now I'm brought back down to earth, because Layla looks like she's about to impart bad news.

'Don't need to look so worried, I'm not taking her from you.' The slightest of smiles raises on Layla's lips. 'That's the last thing I . . . *we* want.'

I nod, but her reassurances have done little to ease the tightness in my chest. The last few weeks have taken their toll. As we sit in the quiet alcove, I wish that Layla would get on with things. But she seems thoughtful as she approaches what she's about to say. She keeps looking at Saoirse, who is playing with a crinkly toy. It's the first time I've seen her express an ounce of interest in my little girl.

'Before you leave, Finn, there's something important I need to tell you.' Layla leans back in her chair and assesses us both. My breath hitches as I sense the gravity of what is to come.

'Go on,' I urge, my voice barely a whisper.

'Your daughter . . . Do you love her unconditionally? You wouldn't want to give her up . . .'

What the hell? I think, looking at Layla in horror.

'Of course I love her. I wouldn't give her up for the world!'

'Even if she wasn't . . . biologically yours? You'd still want to keep her, right?' She arches an eyebrow.

I don't like where this is going but my response is immediate. 'Of course. She's mine. She'll always be mine. I couldn't give her up now—' I'm about to continue when she interrupts.

'The DNA test results you received were manipulated. The baby . . .' Layla pauses for a moment, her eyes searching my face. '. . . Saoirse died on the day of the accident. The baby you're holding is Kathryn's. She doesn't know, and we need to keep it that way.'

My mouth drops open. I feel like I've been punched as I take the full force of her words. I stare, unable to process the revelation.

'But you showed me the results. You said that she was mine. I saw it . . . in black and white.' And yet . . . that gnawing doubt refused to go away. I kiss the top of my baby's head as she plays with my fingers. My quiet little dark-haired child . . . who looks nothing like me.

Tears form in the corners of my eyes. 'How could this happen? Why?' I don't want to believe it. But why would Layla lie, when all I have to do is check her DNA for myself?

'My husband is a powerful man,' Layla explains. 'Power brings enemies and unfortunately Kathryn was taken advantage of. She thought she was in love. But then she found out she was pregnant.' She fixes her eyes on Saoirse, but they are stone cold. 'This baby – the product of her relationship . . . she cannot exist. Not in our world.

Do you understand what I'm saying? My husband . . . he won't allow it. Everybody has moved on, including Kiera's father, before you ask. She's better off with you.'

'How do I know you won't change your mind?' I swipe away my tears as I clear my throat.

Layla exhales a bitter laugh. 'My God, you don't need to worry about that.' Her tone is bitter and detached. 'Kathryn will never know.'

I nod, because I want to believe that it's true. My thoughts are a torrent of confusion and disbelief.

I brush a finger against my daughter's soft cheek. She is happy in my arms, blissfully unaware of the turmoil surrounding her.

I watch as Layla slips a thick, padded envelope from her bag. 'You should move away . . . There's enough money here for you to start again. There's medical histories in there too, everything you need to know for her future wellbeing. If you need more money . . . Well, if you need anything, call me on my mobile. I've saved your contact under a different name. Don't text. I don't want a trail.'

And then I realise that she's paying me off. She tells me about her husband, and how he said that it was a blessing that Kiera had died. But then the DNA test results came in, and it strengthened his resolve: that bastard child of David Kenny's would never be part of the Toíbín clan. I'm in shock as she explains that Kathryn needs her family. They never want to let her go. If she took back her baby, she would have been out in the cold. Coupled with her alcohol addiction . . . it would not end well. I shake my head in disbelief. No wonder Kathryn had problems if this was how their world worked.

Oh God, I think, bile rising as I cup my hand over my mouth. Shock registers and I cannot think. I remind myself to breathe while time stands still. My emotions have never felt so at odds. I lost my beautiful baby, but yet I feel comfort in Saoirse's warmth as I hold her close. My heart melts when she looks up at me and smiles. What sort of a life would she have growing up as Kiera Toíbín? I can't contemplate calling her that name. We've both been given a second chance. I cannot deal with any more pain. My baby is alive. I won't accept anything less. My entire world has shifted on its axis, leaving me unsteady but resolute. Saoirse blinks, her innocent blue eyes filling me with a fierce surge of protectiveness. Because she'll always be Saoirse to me.

'Sometimes lies are necessary,' Layla continues, her expression impassive. 'Kathryn's . . . well, she's fragile. She must never know. A painful truth can do more harm than a well-intentioned deception.'

'I promise,' I say quietly, my eyes locked on Layla's. 'I promise to do what's best for Saoirse, for all of us.'

Layla holds my gaze, a flicker of satisfaction crossing her features. 'Good. I know you will.'

'Why are you telling me all this now?' I ask, because I need to know.

Layla sighs. 'I haven't slept a wink all week, worrying that you'd find out the truth. I don't want this hanging over us. Kathryn needs a clean break.'

So this baby is nothing more to her than a business arrangement – a problem that needs sorting out. Yet . . . guilt closes in on every side. I'm being unfaithful to the memory of my baby. And as for Kathryn . . . can I really do this to her?

'Will she be okay? Kathryn . . . Will she come to terms with it?'

'She already has. Right now, she's focusing on herself. Her father has made her a shareholder in the company business. She's getting her life on track.' She blinks, composing herself. 'I don't know why I'm telling you this. You've got what you wanted. It's best for everyone if you forget about Kathryn now.'

I take a deep breath, pushing back thoughts of the baby that I have lost. I really can't cope with such grief today. One day, when

I'm stronger, I'll visit her grave. For now, I will do whatever it takes to protect the baby in my arms and give her the life she deserves. And in doing so, perhaps we can all find some semblance of happiness.

After all, what's more important than family?

CHAPTER 59

KATHRYN

I check myself in the mirror. The cost of this trouser suit is outrageous, but it makes me look amazing, now that I've regained the weight I'd lost. A little bit of Botox has helped smooth out the wrinkles that I've gained from the stress of the last few months. Mother's recommendations have been a godsend. We're closer than ever before. I'm even building fences with Dad. My brothers were none too pleased when he made me a director in the furniture business, but having something to focus on has helped me quit booze. I'm never going back to rehab again. I slip my feet inside my soft leather high-heeled shoes, then spritz myself with perfume before I leave to meet my date.

Mam has loaned me her driver. He's not exactly cheerful, but can be relied upon. It feels good to be back in control. But meeting David again has the power to bring everything tumbling down. I afford myself a small smile. If I can bring crazy Maura Claffey to the ground, then I can manage reconnecting with an old flame.

David has contacted me numerous times. After discarding countless unopened letters, I've finally given in. A quick call was all that was needed to arrange a place to meet up. But not in Dublin.

I'm meeting him in Tullamore, in the Midlands, far away from home. Apparently he's moved out of Dublin and bought a property there.

I turn a few heads as I enter the Bridge House Hotel. The air is warm, the plush carpet soft beneath my feet. Hues of red and gold decorate the space, but as my pulse speeds up, I'm barely taking the decor in. David and I are over, I just need to tell him face to face. But the thought of seeing him in a wheelchair is turning my insides to jelly because it will bring me face to face with the devastation that my father caused. I'm no good for him. But as much as I try to convince myself otherwise, David still has the power to win me round.

I am guided to a secluded table and my heart jolts as I see him sitting there. *Be strong,* I tell myself. Because I can't risk losing my family, not when they've accepted me back into the fold. I almost lost everything. I almost lost my mind.

I had convinced myself without a doubt that the baby who survived the crash was mine. Now I've come to the point where I realise that I don't want children. Babies aren't possessions. They have wants and needs of their own. I don't have the bandwidth to cater for that. I'm more like Mother than I imagined. I'll concentrate my efforts on business from now on.

But as my gaze meets David's, I melt a little inside. He's wearing a white Ralph Lauren shirt that fits his form perfectly. He's lost a little muscle but looks better than I thought he would. I inhale a little gasp when he stands to shake my hand.

'You . . . you can stand.' I look left and right. There's no wheelchair, or even crutches by his side.

'The wheelchair was temporary. I told you in my letters . . .' He sits. 'You didn't read them though, did you?'

A lump forms in my throat and I give a tight shake of the head. I could cry with relief. All this time, I blamed myself for his situation when the stories about him being permanently wheelchair bound were untrue. But in my father's grim world, reputation and retribution are key. The stories were most likely spread as a warning.

I mirror David's movements as I take a seat across from him. We swiftly order drinks, tonic water and lime for me. We are gracious and polite during our meal. I'm grateful that the restaurant is quiet as David asks how I am. I tell him about rehab and how many days I've been alcohol- and drug-free. He talks about his back operation and how it's given him a new lease of life.

'I won't be bungee jumping anytime soon, but I'm working out in the gym again.'

'That's brilliant,' I smile, before patting my mouth with a napkin.

We haven't touched on Kiera. I don't want to go there. Not now. It's a painful chapter of my life that I've closed the book on. But David seems to read my thoughts as I turn quiet.

'I visit her grave when I can.' He looks at me with absolute sincerity. 'I want you to know . . . I don't blame you. Not for that, not for anything . . .' He pauses in a moment of reflection. 'I wish I'd got to meet her though.'

I wasn't strong enough to tell him about Kiera myself, which is why I asked Yvonne to get in touch. He'd already heard about the accident. He deserved to know the truth. Thankfully the waiter doesn't linger as he takes our empty plates away.

'Water under the bridge,' I find myself saying, although there's no way the existence and subsequent loss of our daughter could ever be reduced to that.

'I asked you here because I want to talk about us.'

I'm powerless as he stares at me with those deep blue eyes. 'I . . . I can't, David,' I finally say. I clasp my hands on my lap, gripping tight. This is killing me. 'It's over.'

'What?' He leans forward to check his understanding.

'Us . . . We can't.'

'I know.' He delivers a sad smile. 'That's why I asked to meet you. I wanted to tell you in person. I've been seeing someone else.'

'Oh.' I exhale a breath. The decision to get back with David has been taken out of my hands. I'm actually relieved. Only then do I realise how strong I've become.

'Things are pretty serious,' he continues. 'I didn't want you to hear it from anyone else.'

'Who's the lucky lady?' My smile is slight but genuine as I finally relax in his company.

'My physiotherapist.'

'Ah.' I nod. That makes sense. 'So this is goodbye.'

He nods a response. It's just like David, a thoughtful soul who wants to do things right.

'We've been through a lot. I didn't want any hard feelings.'

This time I reach for his hand. I wish I'd read his letters. What a fool I've been, thinking that he still has feelings for me. As I catch his gaze, I see they are reserved for someone else. I don't want to know any more.

'Thanks for dinner,' I say at last. I should impart an apology for not telling him about Kiera's birth but the words won't come. As I said, water under the bridge. We say our goodbyes, less awkward now. We won't cross paths again.

I don't look back as I leave the hotel. There's nothing here for me any more.

ACKNOWLEDGEMENTS

Before I sat down to write this, I found the old letter from my agent welcoming me on board. That was nine years ago this year. Nine! I don't know where the time has gone. But I do know how happy I am to have Madeleine Milburn and her wonderful team at the helm of my writing career. Here's to launching many more books together.

I have also loved working with my publishers, Thomas & Mercer of Amazon Publishing, over the years. Their ingenuity and professionalism is second to none. They have so many of my books now, and there is a reason why I keep signing for more. I have my highly talented editor, Kasim Mohammed, to thank for this title, *The Survivors*, which suits the story perfectly. Thank you Kasim, for all your hard work and for making me feel truly valued along the way. Thanks also to Lisa of The Brewster Project who not only listened to my suggestions for the cover of this book, but creatively supercharged them. Thanks also to the brilliant Ian Pindar who totally gets my work, as well as Melissa Hyder and other proofreaders and copy editors who have ironed out my script.

I would also like to express my gratitude to my family, friends and old police colleagues for their support. If you've enjoyed my books, then check out my fellow Thomas & Mercer authors, as well as Mel Sherratt and Angela Marsons – both lovely people and talented writers I am fortunate to know. To my readers, book reviewers and social media champions – I love you lot! I hope you enjoy my latest offering. I always write with you in mind. As you come across each twist, imagine me writing it with a smile on my face, wondering if you've guessed the plot.

ABOUT THE AUTHOR

A former police detective, Caroline Mitchell now writes full-time.

She has worked in CID and specialised in roles dealing with vulnerable victims – high-risk victims of domestic abuse and serious sexual offences. The mental strength shown by the victims of these crimes is a constant source of inspiration to her, and Mitchell combines their tenacity with her knowledge of police procedure to create tense psychological thrillers.

Originally from Ireland, she now lives in a woodland village on the outskirts of Lincoln with her husband.

You can find out more about her at www.caroline-writes. com or follow her on Twitter (@caroline_writes) or Facebook (www.facebook.com/CMitchellAuthor).

Follow the Author on Amazon

If you enjoyed this book, follow Caroline Mitchell on Amazon to be notified when the author releases a new book!

To do this, please follow these instructions:

Desktop:

1) Search for the author's name on Amazon or in the Amazon App.

2) Click on the author's name to arrive on their Amazon page.

3) Click the 'Follow' button.

Mobile and Tablet:

1) Search for the author's name on Amazon or in the Amazon App.

2) Click on one of the author's books.

3) Click on the author's name to arrive on their Amazon page.

4) Click the 'Follow' button.

Kindle eReader and Kindle App:

If you enjoyed this book on a Kindle eReader or in the Kindle App, you will find the author 'Follow' button after the last page.